UNDERWATER

Elizabeth Diamond lives in Devon. She spent many years writing poetry and working, amongst other things, as a home help, a shop assistant, a typist, and a special needs teacher, and dreaming of being a published author, until a chance place on a writers' development award, followed by an arts council grant, gave her the time to write her first novel – just to see 'if she could'. The result was her debut novel, *An Accidental Light*. This is her second novel.

Also by Elizabeth Diamond

An Accidental Light

ELIZABETH DIAMOND

underwater

PICADOR

First published 2009 by Picador

First published in paperback 2010 by Picador
an imprint of Pan Macmillan, a division of Macmillan Publishers Limited
Pan Macmillan, 20 New Wharf Road, London N1 9RR
Basingstoke and Oxford
Associated companies throughout the world
www.panmacmillan.com

ISBN 978-0-330-45370-7

1 3 5 7 9 8 6 4 2

A CIP catalogue record for this book is available from
the British Library.

Typeset by SetSystems Ltd, Saffron Walden, Essex
Printed in the UK by CPI Mackays, Chatham ME5 8TD

For Ray

Le Cœur a ses raisons, que la raison ne connaît point.
(The heart has its reasons that reason doesn't understand.)

Blaise Pascal, *Pensées*

Down in the flood of remembrance
I weep like a child for the past.

D. H. Lawrence, 'Piano'

PART ONE

I

The dreams about her brother, Paul, started during those dark, grim weeks when she was shuttered in the house, convalescing from the operation. The worst of them, the one that upset her most, she dreamt on the night of the winter solstice. The same day that her father had died. Thirty-three years ago.

She dreamt Paul was swimming in the Ouse, on the stretch not far from their home, where the river curved smoothly. She was watching him from the riverbank, under the shade of willows. He was swimming far out from the bank, his thin boy's arms spinning wreaths of white spray. He stopped suddenly. Turned to face her, treading water.

'Come and join me, Jane,' he said. 'It's lovely.'

The sunlight dappled the water, made the river look inviting. She slid down from the bank, lowered her body into the water. Her limbs were young and tanned and slim. She started swimming slowly out towards him. She was surprised she could keep afloat, surprised at the rhythm of her limbs turning in the water, how easy it was. When she got close to him he suddenly disappeared from sight. She felt herself begin to panic, felt her limbs flail, felt something wrap around her legs and pull her down. In the murky green water her brother's face nudged up close to her. He was crying, he was laughing; she couldn't tell which. His arms were wrapped tight around her, holding her down. She heard his voice, as if it were inside her, in her head, in her chest.

Stay with me, Jane. Don't go. Stay with me here.

She couldn't breathe, she was drowning. Panic sharp in her chest, like a blade. She kicked and threshed underwater, she felt his arms sliding away . . .

She was sitting bolt upright in the bed, gulping back air, the sound of her sobbing breaking in waves on her ears.

She had been plagued for several weeks by the dreams. Some seemed to come from the past, as if she was reliving real events. Things that had happened in her childhood. Things she had forgotten, or thought she had.

Usually Paul was in these dreams. The Paul that belonged to her childhood, her older brother. These dreams disturbed her, distressed her. Cast a shadow upon her thoughts all through the long mornings after waking. She felt riven with anxiety. It wasn't so much because of the illness, although of course that played a part. She didn't know what it was, where it came from. But a sense of danger, lurking continually beneath her thoughts, haunting her days.

The night after the dream about drowning, she phoned the Samaritans. She had never done anything like this before, never thought she ever would, didn't know why she was doing it now. The voice on the phone was male, in his thirties, perhaps. He told her his name was Simon. They talked for a while as if it wasn't some unearthly hour of the night, as if they were just two people getting to know each other, making small talk. She had a sense of the irony of it. *This wasn't real.* They didn't talk about Christmas, only days away. They avoided that.

At some point in the conversation he asked what she did for a living. She thought, briefly, about not telling the truth. Art therapists, after all, weren't supposed to be doing this in the small hours of the night. They were supposed to be the sane ones, the ones who helped others. The ones who never felt this kind of despair. But she thought it would be immoral to lie to someone like this, who could have been at home, perhaps, with his wife who missed him. Instead of sitting up through the night, listening to desperate people who couldn't sleep.

'I'm an art therapist,' she said. 'I work in a psychiatric hospital.'

He didn't flinch.

What did they talk about? Inconsequential talk, really. If she had any hobbies, where she liked going for her holidays, even her favourite food. The central heating had switched itself off; the room was growing cold. Josie, her Labrador, snored comfortably at her feet.

Then: 'Are you married, Jane?' The first serious topic of their conversation.

'Yes. Well, not really. We've been separated for over two years now.'

'I'm sorry,' he said. 'Any children?'

'One,' she said. And then in a way she felt unsure again about what was the truth, because she'd lost the child she'd had and been given another.

'I've two,' he said. 'A boy and a girl. Ten and eight. What do you have?'

'A boy,' she said. 'Dominic. He's nearly eighteen.'

'Ah, coming of age then,' he said. 'I've got that to look forward to.'

She said nothing then. Because what was there to say?

'Any other family?'

'My mother, I suppose. She's in a care home. She's lost her memory. She gets confused. '

'Father?'

'He died when I was a child.'

Did she say it too quickly, did she give anything away?

'That must have been difficult,' he said.

A softening in his voice now. The silence of his listening was tangible, a different kind of silence to the one that had been pressing on her heart for weeks, making it difficult to breathe, to eat, to sleep.

'Brothers or sisters?'

'I've a brother. Paul. But I haven't seen him for years and years. He went missing when I was fourteen.'

And as she said it she felt strange. Like she was falling from a great height. She had never told anyone about Paul before.

'Tell me about your brother, Jane. What was he like?'

So she talked about Paul, for the first time ever. To a stranger; someone who'd never known him, never known her. And it was as if her words were bringing him back again. He could almost have been there with her, sitting across the room in the dim light, listening.

He was tall. Nearly six foot. He had red hair. Not ginger, never ginger. Auburn. Eyes, not quite green, not quite brown. Sometimes a little more one colour than the other, depending on the light. He liked birds and fishing and dogs. He was in the Sea Scouts. He liked the sea, he loved it. He was a good swimmer. The best in his class. He could swim for miles.

'Are you a good swimmer too?'

'Not really. No, not at all. Like a stone,' she said. And he laughed, and she laughed too.

His voice dipped, softened again.

'Why do you think your brother left home, Jane?'

'I don't know.' She was telling the truth, she wasn't telling it. She suddenly felt a wave of tiredness. As if the words dragged up from some morass inside her had worn her out.

But because of the way he listened, in spite of her tiredness, she told him about the day her brother left.

It had been a day in early March. A mild day, quite warm and sunny. She'd just got in from school. Her aunt and uncle – 'We'd lived with them . . . since our father died . . .' – hadn't got back from work yet, didn't get back till after five. She went upstairs to her room, she was going to start her homework. Paul was home. She could hear him playing music in his room.

'He had weird taste. He didn't like the usual stuff that

teenagers liked back then – Adam Faith, Cliff and the Shadows, things like that. He liked Jacques Brel, this German songwriter, Kurt something . . .'

'Kurt Weill.'

'Yes, that's it. I'm not sure how he got into that sort of music. Perhaps my mother introduced him to it – I think she liked it too.'

She didn't like it. She always thought it sounded depressing. She heard clattering noises coming from his room as well, and opened the door. Stuff scattered on his bed. Small piles of clothing. A torch, a pile of coins, a penknife, binoculars All sorts of things. A rucksack on the floor.

'Aren't you ever going to learn to knock first?' He looked a bit odd. Flushed, guilty, as if she'd caught him doing something he shouldn't.

'What's all that stuff for? Are you going somewhere?'

'I'm just sorting it out.'

She shut the door and left him to it, went to her own room. An hour later he opened her bedroom door. She was sitting at her desk, doing her homework. Trying to learn the past historic for the French for 'to forget' and 'to remember'. They were having a test on it the next day. He stood looking at her, like he'd forgotten what he'd come for. This light from the window in his eyes, making him squint.

'What are you doing?'

'Homework, of course.'

'What homework?'

'French. I've a test tomorrow.'

'Good,' he said.

She waited, wondering what was good about it, wonder-

ing what else he was going to say. He looked like he wanted
to say something else.

'I might be late. I'm going round Stuart's. Tell them not
to worry.'

'Okay.' She turned back to her verbs.

'Goodbye, Jane.'

Something about the way he said it. But she thought
nothing of it at the time, was lost in her head with the past
historic. Just a short while after she heard the front door
close she had this urge to get up and go to the window. He
was walking away down the road. He walked like someone who wasn't in a hurry, who had plenty of time to get to
where he was going. He had his green khaki rucksack on
his back, the one he used for his scouting trips. It looked
full, all the little pocket compartments bulging. *Why has he
packed his rucksack to go to Stuart's?* She thought of opening
the window and calling out, to ask him, but didn't bother.
She turned back to her homework . . .

She paused. The past was stealing into her heart, was taking
over. She was fourteen. She was looking out of her bedroom
window, her hand on the catch. Then changing her mind
and turning away.

'Funny, I can't remember them at all now. The French
verbs. I used to be good at French. I used to know all the past
tenses. The imperfect, the pluperfect. I can't even remember the French for the verbs "to forget" and "to remember"
now.'

Oublier, se souvenir. Simon's voice, so soft it was like the
imprint of a voice on her ear.

9

'The thing is,' she said, 'this stuff's been coming back to me. These memories.'

'Do you mean flashbacks, that sort of thing?'

'Yes, I suppose so. But in dreams, mainly. I haven't thought of him for years, or dreamt of him. And now suddenly I dream of him often.'

'When did it begin?' he said.

She told him they'd only recently started. They just seemed to happen, to come out of nowhere.

'I never used to be the sort that dwelt on things. I was always one just for getting on with things before.'

'Maybe that's part of the problem,' he said. 'Maybe you need to take the time now, to think about the past.'

'I don't know.' This tiredness again, overwhelming her. Like something heavy on top of her, like the weight of water.

'The thing is, it doesn't help that I'm on my own a lot. I'm not working at the moment. I've been ill, you see, I've had an operation. I'm still convalescing.'

He didn't ask what kind of operation, what was wrong with her, but she told him anyway. About the breast cancer and the consultations with Mr Fazil. The lumpectomy, and the radiotherapy she was due to start in a fortnight.

'I could go back to work then, if I want. They don't mind you working during the radiotherapy, providing you feel well enough to.'

'Do you think you're well enough?'

'I'm not sure. Perhaps not. I'm not sleeping well. And these dreams, sometimes they bother me. Sometimes I feel rather desperate. But then you know that. I wouldn't have phoned you if I didn't.'

'Have you talked to your doctor about the way you feel? It might be a good idea to do that.'

'Yes, perhaps. I'll think about it.' But she knew she wouldn't. She couldn't talk to her doctor the way she'd talked to him. Her doctor knew her. She'd have to see him again, whenever she went to the surgery. Sit across the desk from him knowing he knew those things about her, had written them down in her notes.

'It sounds like you've been through a great deal these last few years. It would be surprising if you weren't feeling depressed, Jane. Anyone would, going through what you've been through.'

'Yes, I suppose you're right.'

'Do you ever think of suicide?'

It was said quickly, carelessly, like words thrown away, but it took her by surprise. She wondered if she had mis-heard him.

'I'm sorry, what did you say . . . ?'

Maybe it was a ploy. Maybe she was buying time.

'I said, do you ever think of harming yourself?'

But he had changed it now. Softened it. Made it sound more probable, more commonplace. *Aren't there a thousand ways to harm oneself?* she thought. *Don't we all choose at least one way?*

But she knew that wasn't what he meant. He meant the first word. The one she'd heard but pretended she hadn't. The one that sounded medical, like *sarcoma*. Dry, tearless.

Conjuring the smell of antiseptic, the white coats of doctors, pills that stuck in the throat.

'No, not really.'

'Not really?' he echoed back. As if he didn't believe her.

'No, I haven't. Not seriously, anyway. I would never actually *do* anything. I mean, I may have thought about it, but only in a vague way. There's a world of difference between having a thought and carrying out an action, isn't there?'

'If there wasn't my wife would have sued me for adultery a long time ago,' he said. And they laughed, uneasily.

'So you'll be okay? When we finish talking?'

'Yes, of course.'

'What will you do?'

'Go to bed, I expect.'

'You must be tired.'

'Yes. Yes, I am.'

She was. This weariness filling her head, like water.

'Well, if you feel like ringing again. Any time. Don't hesitate.'

She sat alone in the darkness for another hour. She was tossing the word over in her head. As if it was something she had suddenly found. An artefact. A stone with an interesting patina. She had heard the word so often. In the mouths of psychiatrists and nurses at case reviews. She had read it in patients' files, had written it there herself. *This patient has suicidal thoughts. This patient is currently on suicide watch.* She had seen the morbid fantasies in their paintings and sketches. In the hospital, on the ward, in the claustro-phobic confines of the art therapy room where anything can happen in a painting, in a shape wrought from a lump of clay, it was just another word. Removed from the world out-side, the normal world. Like *psychosis, schizophrenic, mania*. But now it was stripped of that context and given another. Handed to her by a stranger on the phone.

Have you ever thought of suicide?

Had she?

She wasn't sure. She didn't know.

No, not really.

Ambiguous, deceptive. The only kind of answer she could give.

She felt she was putting the word away now, as if in a corner of the room. On a shelf perhaps, hidden behind books. Tucking it away in a corner of her mind. Still there, but out of sight.

But that night she had a different dream. This time it didn't seem to come from the past. She didn't know where it came from. It felt like the future was spinning itself backwards into the present.

She dreamt she was in a room crowded with people. A stranger was sitting in the shadows in the corner. She couldn't see his face. A blonde woman with an open smiling face came up to her.

'Let me introduce you to someone. He thinks you may have met somewhere before.'

The woman had a slight American accent. She led Jane towards the stranger. Her heart was racing. As the man saw her approaching he stood up, moved out of the shadows, and then she could see that it was Paul. His hair that had been auburn, russet like autumn leaves, was faded now, greying at the temples. He was older, a man in his middle years, not the boy of eighteen he had once been. But she knew without any doubt that it was him.

When she finally woke it was late. Long past the time she would normally wake, weary from a night of broken sleep. She got out of bed and drew back the curtains and she knew she was past the worst now. There was a hard, bright, January light. The grass sparkled with frost. The winter solstice was behind her.

She had always hated the depths of winter. The darkness would feel to her as if it were something physical, that had the power to still her blood, take her breath from her. Her aunt had died just after Christmas and her father just before. In all the years she'd lived with Adam, when Dominic was little, she had to force herself to celebrate Christmas. Put up the tree, the decorations, buy the presents and wrap them. Whilst all the time, this feeling of suffocation. This dread that ached in her bones.

But now, waking from this dream that seemed to come from some future place, a Paul she didn't know and hadn't met, she knew she'd passed the nadir; the light was coming back, bit by bit.

He wants me to find him, she thought, a small bubble of excitement rising within her. *That's what he wants. He wants me to find him.*

2

All day the feeling stayed with her. She busied herself tidying the house, which had been neglected for weeks until now. She cooked herself a proper lunch, which she hadn't done for a while. A jacket potato, with grated cheese and a salad. She sat down at the kitchen table and ate the food slowly, as if every morsel was important. Josie sat in her basket by the wall, watching her. She had learnt not to beg for scraps at the table long ago, when she was just a puppy.

We never forget the things we're taught when we're young. What did we learn, Paul? When do our memories start?

She wasn't sure. She had trained herself not to look back, not ever to remember her childhood. And now it was an effort to.

The first memory she could find belonged to a summer's afternoon when she was small. Three, perhaps even younger. She is running around in the garden, wearing only bikini bottoms, pink ones, with tiny white rosebuds. She is running in and out of a paddling pool, limp and shallow, holding tepid water. Paul is splashing her and she is pretending to run from him, and all the time, despite their play and their laughter, they are aware of him, this man, their father, down the garden painting at his easel, as he often did. Watching him, even when they were forgetting to watch him, as though they had eyes in the back of their heads.

He takes no notice of them. He acts as though they are not there. But if Paul is too rough, grabbing her, splashing her with water, making her shriek.

'*Behave yourselves! Stop that bloody racket.*'

His voice is tense, threatening, like a storm cloud. Their bodies stiffen, subdued. Paul doesn't answer back. He never does. Neither does she.

Is that what we learnt, Paul? To be afraid?

And yet at the same time remembering her father, like a giant stepping loudly into her world. Holding her wrists in his two big hands and spinning her around, so that her feet are lifting from the ground. The blur of his body at the pivot of her spinning, his broken smiles. Her shrieks of desperate pleasure shattering the hot summer air. Beyond the excitement, something like fear, like the edge of a knife in her chest. *How fast would he spin her? Would he know when to stop?*

Sometimes an uneasy attachment, an uneasy love. Or as close to love as she ever felt, in those days when she was small. Her father bouncing her on his rough lap. Walking her around the living room, her small feet stuck to the tops of his giant ones, her knees locked like a marionette's against his hard shins. When she was older – five or six – sticking her on a chair in the corner of the summerhouse he used as a studio, and painting her portrait. They were well enough executed, those paintings. A pretty child in summer frocks, holding a rag doll to her chest, with black button eyes and a blue stitched mouth, like a down-turned slash. *Keep still*, her father would say. *Don't twitch like that.* She kept still, to please him. She enjoyed the attention. These quiet hours alone with her father, his eyes upon her. Although he didn't really see her. His gaze flicking back and forth from the surface of her face to the white paper, the brush loaded with paint.

She didn't remember what happened to those pictures. Her mother didn't seem to like them. They were never framed, put on the walls. There was a likeness there, he'd captured a likeness. But a quality of stiffness about them. A brittle smile on her face, as if she too was a doll, rather than a child.

They'd grown up, she and Paul, in a hunched, brown-roofed house among the flat fields of the Fens. Fields of wheat and potatoes, yellow rape in the spring so vivid it hurt their eyes. There was a large garden. An allotment that extended beyond the stretch of lawn. Fruit trees: plum, apple and pear. In the spring and autumn, her mother digging in the sticky, black soil. She would plant carrots, onions, swedes. Green beans that sprang high on stakes. Rows of cabbages, lettuce, leeks. Paul would sometimes help her. She would show him how to drill out rows for the seed, how to sow it. How to thin out the pale young plants. She could remember watching them, their backs bent and turned from her, as she bounced a ball against the side of the house, gyrated a hula hoop on her thin hips.

Beyond the allotment and the fruit trees, at the far end of the garden, sprawling bushes of soft fruits. They would nudge their hands through the brambles in late summer, shake away the wasps. Eat the half-ripened fruit until their stomachs ached, until they made themselves sick, the red juice staining their hands and faces.

Memories coming back of the house and the fields, the lanes that they would lose themselves in when they were older. Returning on long summer evenings only when their bellies were hungry. When they were small they had friends down the lanes. She could remember few of their names now, or their faces. And if she was honest, they were more Paul's friends than hers. Because there was always that quality of stiffness about her, an inward shrinking. Much more so then, of course, when she was small. An extreme of shyness then. As if she often felt more like a doll, too. Not knowing what look to wear on her face. When to move and how, what to say or feel.

But with Paul it was easier. He had a more spontaneous way about him, as if the energy that came from within him flowed easily out into the world, and back again. She trailed in his shadow, joined in the games with the rough-faced children that lived down the lane. Took her cues from him, benefited from the shield of his protection. If the children sometimes teased her, as they did – for children always seek out the weakness in others, have an instinct for it – Paul would instantly come to her defence. *Leave her alone, she's all right.* And they did; it wasn't so much his authority they respected as his likeability. They wouldn't fall out with him.

This realization slipping back to her now, clearly, that these friends, these other children, never came round to their house to play. As if somehow everyone knew, without needing to be told, that this wouldn't be approved of, wouldn't be allowed. She remembered this sensation that she often had, standing in the garden. As if there was always someone there watching. Her father? As if at any moment she might turn around and see his dark figure at the window. At the bedroom window, the kitchen window, the French doors that led out into the garden. Light flashing from the glass in his hand.

Their father drank. He wasn't exactly a drunkard; she doubted whether he could be called an alcoholic. There were plenty of times when he was sober, long, dry droughts in between the black spells, when he didn't drink. He held down a job as a teacher and wouldn't have been able to do that, she thought, if he had been a perpetual drunk. But then, every so often, he would go on benders. Red wine, whisky, brandy. She remembered dark clouds of sullenness, his body slumped at the kitchen table, the bottle in front of him, the slurping of the liquid into the glass, and his mood souring and darkening, turning against everyone and everything. They kept out of his way. Just the sight of them, when he was in these black moods of drinking, could bring on his rage. The sight of their mother too. She felt a sickening dread in her stomach, just remembering. *Why* was she remembering? She didn't want to.

Is that what we learnt, Paul, most of all? To be afraid?

She had shut out these memories for years. Told herself, *It wasn't so bad.* Perhaps it wasn't. They had the garden and the fields, sometimes children down the lanes to play with. They had each other. But now this longing to see her brother again, to see Paul again, so intense it felt almost painful. If he was here, she thought, if she could talk to him about the past, about that house, their father . . . if she could remember *with* him, it would be all right then, it would be safe.

After lunch she jostled Josie into the back of the car. She would take her out for a walk to Dunstable Downs. She'd moved away from the flat fields of her Fenland home many years ago, another life ago. She lived, still, in the home she'd once shared with Adam. A neat semi in a Hertfordshire red-bricked village, with a small high street of mock-tra-ditional shops, a village pub on the Green, four-wheel drives going to and fro on the school run. A long way from the childhood house that crouched under big Fenland skies.

Bob Evans, her neighbour, was up now. He had sleep in his eyes, as he stood inside the glazed porch and stooped to pick up his post. She raised her hand to wave to him. He waved back.

Out on the Downs, under the washed-blue sky, she felt freer, lighter. Josie ambled amongst the bracken and ferns, rooted out the scents of birds and rabbits, broke into brief, clumsy trots, as if she was remembering her youth when she could run like the wind, when she wasn't plagued by arth-ritis in her hips.

underwater

She walked for an hour. Paused now and then, to watch the paragliders in the new, blue sky. A strange restlessness, a strange excitement. As if the scar knitting under her skin was stretching and tearing. Memories seeping.

3

When did it begin? Simon the Samaritan had asked on the phone.

She wondered if it hadn't really begun way back on that Sunday morning last October. The day she'd discovered the lump. She'd been doing stretching exercises in front of the mirror in her room. Naked, almost, stripped down to her knickers. Muslin curtains shielding her from the outside world.

She always felt disturbed looking at her body in the mirror. Not because it was unsightly. She was slim, supple, still carried the essence of youth about her. It was more as if her body didn't belong to her. When she saw her own reflection in the mirror, she would sometimes feel as if she had slipped outside the barriers of her skin. Was watching herself from somewhere in the room.

Who is this woman standing here? Moving. Stretching up, stretching down.

Then she noticed it. She didn't *see* it. It was much too small to be seen. It was more that she sensed it. Something under the skin, sitting near the nipple of her left breast. She moved in closer to the mirror. The sun filtering through the muslin curtains haloed her head in a fuzz of light, as if she was already consigned to the afterlife, angelic.

A slight abnormality perhaps. The skin slightly stretched, shiny. The slightest pulling down of the nipple. She moved her hand instinctively over the lump. Hardly a lump. The size of a pea. It felt hard and resistant. As if it had a life of its own.

A few days later, stripped to the waist before the new young doctor at the surgery. He prodded her breasts with harsh fingers.

'Why did you cancel your last breast scan?' he'd asked. He was Dutch, spoke in that measured way the Dutch sometimes speak in. She'd mumbled some excuse.

'You could have remade it. Why didn't you?'

His voice was stern, and despite his youth, parental. She felt judged. As if this was a punishment. God getting back.

The lump had pressed endlessly on her mind during those early weeks.

'What do you see?' she asked Tara, in the art therapy room. Tara was in her thirties, although looked older, marks of suffering etched in deep lines on her face. She had been in and out of the hospital several times before, caught in the revolving-door cycle of the mentally ill. She was manic depressive, would slide down from mania into almost catatonic states of depression, that normally resolved themselves in botched attempts at suicide. Once, on an upward swing into something resembling normalcy, she had relayed to Jane, in a black-humoured manner, all the many ways in which she had sought to end her life. Plastic bags over her head with breaks in the seam to foil her. A noose on a rope tied to the banisters that had broken. Pills that had just left her with sledge-hammer headaches and a thickly furred tongue. This time, perhaps she had planned it better, had meant it for real. She'd slit her wrists and lain in a bath of warm water, to be dragged out soon after by her flatmate, who had returned earlier than predicted.

Tara, in her upward swings, would paint hearts and flowers in vivid primary colours, childlike pictures of girls ringed with skipping ropes outside crooked tenements. Now, she drew charcoal pictures of huddled figures crouching under towering black hands.

What do you see?

Tara gazed mutely at her drawing.

'Nothing,' she said.

The lump that wasn't a lump, that was still only the size of a pea, as dry and hard as a stone, pressed endlessly under the soft cloth of her T-shirt. What pictures would she herself create, she'd wonder, if she picked up a stump of charcoal and drew alongside Tara? Another cowering figure. A dark cloud, like a lump, hovering over her head.

These memories of her childhood, these dreams of Paul, hadn't started until weeks afterwards. During convalescence, confined to the house. But she would wonder if the past hadn't first stirred in her then, like something that had been sleeping for a long time beginning to awake. She'd evoke her brother, conjure him up beside her like a ghost returning. Imagine his voice in her head: *What do you remember, Jane? How much do you remember?*

Twins were supposed to be close. So close they can feel each other's distress across separations of time and space. They weren't twins. But hadn't they once shared that kind of closeness? Back then, in that tumultuous house, under those vast revealing skies, in that place where the soil was as black as ash.

Mr Fazil, the oncologist, had prodded and squeezed the small beaded lump that sat stubbornly next to her nipple. He tried to aspirate it with a fine needle, but it stayed intact. Hard and dry as a stone. She knew that was not a good sign.

'We need to take a sample of tissue to send away for tests. To see if it's cancerous or not,' he'd said.

The clipped, even way he spoke, his blunt honesty, reassured her. No need for drama or fuss. As if his down-to-earth manner would in itself shrink the tumour, send it on its way.

She had taken Wendy with her to hear the results of the biopsy. Wendy, her OT friend from work, who had found her earlier sobbing in the toilets, wiped her tearstained face on a rough paper towel, slipped an arm around her shoulders and led her away to a small room the psychiatrists used for their consultations. A bland, almost empty room. Only two chairs in it, a small table in the corner for their client-profile files. Soundproofed walls, and a lock on the door to keep out the world. Jane had sobbed her heart out, like the patients sometimes do. When the sobs subsided, when she was able to speak.

'It's not just that I'm scared of dying.'

'What is it, then?' Wendy said softly.

'I've made such a mess. Of everything. Dominic. Adam. Now I'm running out of time.'

Wendy had gone with her to hear the results. A nurse trained in breast cancer counselling stayed in the room with them. Jane sat there as cold as ice, waiting for Mr Fazil to speak.

'I'm afraid the tumour is malignant. Cancerous. However, your prognosis is good . . .'

Like the bad news followed by the good. As if the good softens the bad, cancels it out. Perhaps it does. The cancer she had, Mr Fazil told her, was one of the most treatable forms. They had identified it early. She was still young, healthy. An operation would remove all cancerous tissue. Then a course of radiation. No need not to expect a full recovery . . .

Wendy had taken her hand. But she'd hardly noticed. And she hadn't needed the nurse's counselling. She sat there quite calmly, listening to Mr Fazil's clipped Iranian accent telling her what modern medicine would do. How it would cut out the offending tissue, feed radium into her body to try to ensure it didn't return.

She had slipped outside her skin again.

Who is this woman sitting dry-eyed and still on the chair, while cancer cells divide and multiply like a dark secret in her flesh?

*

underwater

They went to a pub close by the hospital afterwards, and Wendy bought her a brandy. She thought she needed it.

'You mustn't worry. I know it's hard, but you mustn't. Thousands of women go through this every day and live to tell the tale. You heard what he said. You've every chance of recovery.'

'I know. I'm not worried. I was, but I'm not any more.'

'You must tell Adam, Jane. You need his support.'

'I don't think it would be right to go crying to him now. He's got his own life to get on with.'

'He won't care about that, you know he won't. He'll want to be there for you.'

The brandy, in the middle of the day, going to her head. She felt light, almost carefree. If Adam had been there, she wondered, what would he have said? What look would he have worn on his face? Pity, mixed with resentment perhaps, as if somehow she had brought it on herself. She was glad he wasn't there.

'No, Wendy. I can't tell him. Not yet. I need to go through this on my own.'

4

In the end she didn't go to the doctor to talk about depression. She didn't want his questions, his notes in her records. His suggestions that she thought about counselling, went on a course of antidepressants for a while. And anyway, she felt strangely better now, despite the weeks of radiation treatment she was facing. The fact that January was bringing, bit by bit, the longer, lengthening light, and the fact that she had talked about it. These feelings of being underwater. She'd been given that word to look at, to consider. The word that so many of her patients knew so well. The word that Tara had known, lying in her warm, rose-coloured water. She could pick it up, look at it, put it down again.

She started back at work again. And it was fine, it was okay. It did her good. Seeing familiar faces, getting back into a routine. Catching up with the gossip, with the occupational therapists and physios and psychiatric nurses. Having a role again, a purpose to her day. *Jane, the art therapist.* And anyway, it was only three days a week. She had arranged to reduce her hours before the lumpectomy, to give herself the best chance of recovery. She could manage financially, at least for a while.

Tara was there still, coming into the art therapy room every day. But a different Tara to the one before. She was wearing make-up these days, her hair in a shorter, more becoming style. She had exchanged her black clothes for brighter colours. A pink jumper that put a bloom in her cheeks. She had moved on from the obsession with charcoal. She was using paint now. Bright colours. Blue, yellow and red. She painted a blue figure sitting by a window. Yellow light spilled on to her back.

'Do you think the woman might turn around to face the window?' Jane asked.

'Perhaps.' Tara gave her a quick, bright smile. She was sitting next to Ken Richards. He gazed down over her shoulder at the painting.

'I like that, Tara. That's good, that is.'

Ken was another revolving-door patient. He had been an inmate of the hospital for years, on and off. Long spells of admission broken only by short skirmishes into the world outside that normally set his psychosis spiralling out of control, not able to cope, so that he would do anything – break a shop window, attack a policeman, run down the streets shouting obscene words back at his voices – anything, to have himself sent back again.

Tara giggled, blushed, turned the radiance of her sudden smile upon him too, her shoulder nudging up against his. They were sitting next to each other, almost on top of each other, in spite of there being plenty of empty seats around the table.

There's something between them, Jane thought. *Something has happened since I've been away.* She felt a quick stab of concern for them. As if they were her children. Fledging teenagers stumbling into puppy love, tender-hearted and exposed.

Five times a week, for six weeks, she went to the oncology department, to lie on a metal bed to be fed radiation to kill off any surviving cancer cells. It didn't hurt; she'd expected it to. She could have been lying on a solarium bed, for all the discomfort it gave her. How easily we trust when the chips are down, she thought. 'The perfection of hopelessness,' Wendy would say. When there is no choice, no option, we let go of caring, surrender easily to hands wearing surgical gloves, to masked faces.

Sometimes it was the same nurse, sometimes a different one. Usually it was Brenda.

'And how are we feeling today, Jane?'

The royal 'We'. As if illness now made her immediately subservient, despite her seniority of years.

'Fine. A little sore, but okay.'

The scar tissue, where they had taken the lumpectomy, was still red and angry. It would weep a little. Thin yellow tears.

'Just shift a little to the left. Raise your arm. A little higher. Hold it there. Good girl.'

Sometimes she'd come home feeling more or less fine, but later in the evening a wave of nausea would overwhelm her. She'd hang her head over the toilet bowl, waiting. Sometimes an empty retch would shudder through her body, making her eyes water. But nothing ever came.

underwater

Most of the time, though, she was all right, she was coping. Even beginning to enjoy the small routines of life again. Her time at the hospital, that took her out of herself, that gave her something else to focus on, a comforting feeling of being needed by others. She was eating better now, between the spells of nausea. Would enjoy preparing herself small, careful meals. Enjoy listening to music, reading a book. Enjoy her walks with Josie. Particularly on bright days, dry days, when the sun was out and it was possible to believe, in the light, mild air, that spring was coming, that spring was on its way. They would walk slowly, the two of them. The old dog, who needed to stop and rest every so often, whose back legs would stumble and falter, and the woman who was not old yet, but no longer young, more conscious now of her own mortality.

The dreams continued. Not every night, not constantly. But now and then, the past slipping through her dreamland like flowing water. Like the dream she had one night of the time her father nearly drowned her.

He used to take Jane and Paul swimming through the long, hot summer holidays, sometimes as often as two or three times a week. He was an art teacher at the local comprehensive, and so of course shared with them the same long holidays. For much of the time he would be holed up in the summerhouse-studio that he had built for himself at the bottom of the garden. He would spend long hours there, turning photos of beach scenes into paintings that sold in the galleries along the north Norfolk coast to the tourists that flocked in the summer. Jane always felt that

31

her mother slightly mocked these paintings. Maybe not openly to his face, but behind his back to her and Paul. They were too facile, too easy. Not true, perhaps, to his artist's soul.

When she thought of her father her head clouded with confusion. She remembered the bulked figure at the French windows, the glint of glass in his hand, the sense of foreboding she always had – *Like we had eyes in the back of our heads.* She feared him, she didn't fear him. She hated him, she loved him. She wasn't sure which.

But the dream of the past returning made something harden in her, crystallize. As if the feelings deep inside her were swimming up to the surface, taking shape. *She feared him; most of all, she feared him.*

Her father loved the sea. Loved painting it, walking by it. Loved swimming in it, too. He was a strong swimmer. Would wade out quickly, well beyond the breakers into the deep, until all she could see of him was the dark bob of his head out in the blue-grey water, the strong striking of his arms. When the sea was too far away, any water would do for a compromise. A lake, a river, a canal. They lived in the Fens, where water was never far away. This was land that had largely been reclaimed from the sea. Jane always had a sense that the sea would return one day and claim it back. She would be playing in the garden, down the lanes, or on those summer holidays walking on the marsh pathways at Cley or Blakeney Point, hear a roaring, a rush of blood flow to her head, and imagine a giant tidal wave rising from far out to sea and moving vengefully towards the land, the wrath of God behind it urging it on. She would stand still wherever this feeling found her, close her eyes tight, and wait for the water to reach her, to surge over her head and suck her down into violent eddies. Moments later she would open her eyes, click her limbs into action again, reason returning. She would tell herself, *Don't be stupid, it'll never happen, God never works like that.*

There was a stretch on the Ouse they would go to often, where the river was fed by a tributary, near a cool riverbank shaded by willows. Their mother would sometimes come with them, would sit reading on the bank while their father took them in the water. Paul took to swimming like a fish. Right from the beginning, throwing himself off the river-bank, plunging under the water, coming up shaking his head and laughing. He more or less taught himself to swim, hadn't waited for his father to teach him. That had been characteristic of him, that independence. Never going to his father for anything.

In the dream that brought back the memory, as clear and vivid as the day it happened, Paul had jumped straight in, swum up the river until he was almost out of sight.

'Come back, Paul. Come back now. That's far enough!' Their mother, standing on the bank, waving frantically. Paul's small head emerging like a seal, his red hair darkened with water, flattened to the sides of his head.

Jane hated the water. Stood shivering in the shallows, hugging her body with thin, goose-pimpled arms, her lip quivering with tears. Her fear triggered something in her father.

33

'Put your head under the water. Don't be so stupid, girl. Go under. There's nothing to it.'

The tears spilling. 'I can't. I don't want to.'

Her father angered by her tears, impatient. She was letting him down, disappointing him. Her father's hand, weighing hard on her head, pushing her down. The water filling her eyes and her nose, her open screaming mouth. The weight on her head suddenly released. She shot up, as if she had a spring in her, gulping on the air, the high pitch of her wailing slapping suddenly on her ears.

Shaking the water from her eyes and wailing, she saw that her mother was staring at her, a smile flicking up the corners of her mouth. *That couldn't be real. That couldn't have happened.* That surely must be where the dream had parted with reality.

She picked over the memory, like a dog picking on a bone. Which parts were real, had really happened, which parts only dreamt? What *had* her mother done? Moved to comfort her? *Or stood there, smiling?* She couldn't remember.

He had left her alone after that. Perhaps he thought he'd gone too far. She would sit on the bank with her mother, watching her father's sulky back turned from her in the river. Wait for his head to plunge down under the water. To disappear.

For weeks afterwards, throughout that long, hot summer, Paul took her to that riverbank. They had a lot of freedom back then, especially if their father was preoccupied, intent on his painting down in his garden studio. They disappeared together for hours on their bikes, cheese sandwiches wrapped in polythene stuffed into the saddlebags.

Back at the shaded bend in the river Paul coaxed her gently down into the water, holding her hands. They swayed together like slow dancers in the shallows of the river, watched by river birds, shrouded by reeds.

'It's all right, Jane,' he said. 'I won't let you go.'

And after days and days of doing this, she gradually let the fear drift from her, allowed Paul to ease her down, down ... until she opened her eyes to murky greenness and his face close up to hers, creased into blurred and rippled smiles.

Towards the end of the period of radiotherapy treatment, she dreamt that she was standing on that same riverbank, watching Paul swimming. He was swimming upstream again, striking out confidently. He stopped suddenly, and trod water. Turned to face her, and waved.

It's all right, Jane. It's safe. Come and join me.

The sun dappled his face with light and shade.

The water's warm, Jane. Come and join me.

She wasn't afraid now. She wasn't afraid that he would hold on to her, if she swam out towards him. Wasn't afraid of being dragged underwater. But before she knew what she would do, she woke up to find the sun was streaming through a gap in the curtains on to her face. It was the end of February now. The worst was definitely over. And she had a feeling in her chest, in her stomach, that she wasn't used to, that she hadn't felt for a long time. She lay there beneath the blankets, trying to shape a name to the feeling. A buzz inside her, like a loosening of energy. Like something tightly coiled was stretching and unravelling. She felt alive again, she decided. It was as if she had been dead for a while and now was coming back to life.

She imagined the flesh under the small scar on her breast, knitting and healing, becoming perfect again.

I need to tell someone, she was thinking. *I need to tell somebody else about Paul.*

5

She made the appointment the following day. Found the number in the yellow pages. There were quite a few of them, just in her area, which surprised her. That there should be such a need for them.

Which should she choose? In the end she'd just picked the one whose name she liked. Mr David Mansfield. He sounded capable, dependable, with a name like that.

The woman who answered the phone had an engaging voice.

'Next week, Mrs Reynolds? How would Monday suit?'

She didn't work Mondays. 'Monday is fine.'

'Two o'clock in the afternoon? Or would you prefer a morning time?'

'No, two o'clock is okay.' She was thinking, I'll take Josie out for her walk in the morning. I might not feel like it later. What *would* she feel like? But the fact that she was even asking herself these questions, was feeling anything at all, after the long, dull sleep she had been in during the worst of those winter months, that was enough for now.

*

On Sunday Bob came with her to the Downs with Josie. They stood on a high point of the hill, watching the paragliders in their brightly coloured harnesses launching themselves off the hill into the wind.

'Ever fancied having a go?' Bob said.

She laughed, slightly nervously.

'I don't think I'm brave enough for that!'

She was shivering slightly despite her thick anorak. It was a cold day. A bite in the wind.

'Come on, I'll take you to lunch. Time you had a proper Sunday dinner,' Bob said.

But thinking really, she knew, *She's looking better these days, she's putting on weight again . . .*

They found an inn outside Ivinghoe that did a carvery. They piled up their plates, but she had little appetite. Pushed the food around her plate, gazed out of the window. As if she was looking for those paragliders still, high up in the sky. Her thoughts wouldn't settle.

'You should eat more,' Bob said.

She smiled.

'You sound like my dad.'

'He used to say that?'

'He was always saying something, telling people what to do.'

She was thinking, he could be her dad; he was almost old enough. She wouldn't mind if he was.

'How's the treatment going?'

She hadn't told him for weeks, not until after the

operation. She thought it would disturb him. Talking to her, having a coffee with her, imagining foreign cells building in the soft tissue of her breasts under her jumper.

She had told him later, after Wendy had brought her home from the hospital. He'd called round for coffee one Saturday, as he often did, and she had said, 'I might need your help for a few weeks, Bob, taking Josie for walks, if that's okay. I might be out of sorts for a while.'

She had sat there on the stool in the kitchen, hugging her arms around her body as if she was shielding her breasts. She knew she looked awful: thin, her face blanched with tiredness, dark circles ringing her eyes.

'Of course, Jane. What's been wrong?'

And that's when she'd told him. When she used the word 'cancer'. He'd looked at her, speechless with shock. She knew he wanted to comfort her, but didn't know how to. For a long time he couldn't let his eyes look anywhere near her chest.

All through the weeks of her convalescence he would come round, usually about three in the afternoon, when he woke from sleeping after working the night shift, put Josie in the back of his van and take her out. Usually he took her to the local park. On winter weekdays it was almost empty. Maybe a couple of other dog owners and their dogs. Mainly older people with time on their hands. It made him feel useful, Jane knew, it made him feel good. He looked almost sorry when she'd said later, 'It's all right, Bob. I feel better, stronger. I think I can walk Josie myself now.'

'Anything else you need, you know you've only to ask,' he'd said.

She knew he had meant it. He always did.

She told him now, sitting in the carvery at Ivinghoe, 'I've finished with the radiotherapy. I will need to have a test in three months, just to make sure that it's clear, that the cancer cells haven't returned. But I'm feeling good. New lease of life really.'

He looked relieved. He gave her hand a squeeze.

'It'll be clear. It'll be all right. I'm so happy for you, Jane.'

Then she said it, what had really been on her mind.

'Bob, that time when Margaret first went missing . . . did you ever think of going to see a private investigator?'

Bob's wife, Margaret, had left him suddenly. He'd known nothing about it, until one night when he'd come home from a darts match and found the note. *Bob, I'm leaving you. I won't be back.* He had come knocking on her door that evening – years ago now, when she'd still been with Adam – his face distraught, mumbling incoherently, thinking she might know something. Margaret had worked as a secretary at the same school where she'd been a teacher. Another life ago. Funny, she was thinking now, that was when their friendship had started. From that time, when he had needed her. The tables were turned now. *She* needed him. Or perhaps the truth was they needed each other. Were both stranded at the edge of their lives with no one else really to turn to.

'That's a funny question.'

'Just wondering.'

'Maybe I did. Maybe I thought about it for a while. But then I got a letter from her anyway. So I didn't have to.'

'Yes. Yes, of course.'

'Why do you ask?'

'No reason. Just curious.'

She was on the edge, just on the very edge, of telling him about Paul. Something stopped her.

It doesn't feel safe, she thought. *Not yet.*

She had started to visit her mother again. Before being ill she used to go regularly, every fortnight if she could. Then, over the course of her illness, the visits had fallen away. Of course, she had phoned the care home to explain. Mrs Clements had been warm and kind on the phone.

'You mustn't worry, Mrs Reynolds. Your mother is fine, she's in safe hands here with us. You just concentrate on getting well.'

But now here she was, all patched up and mended. Slipping out of the house into the ashy, pre-dawn light, driving through still sleeping streets, Josie snuffling drowsily on her rug on the back seat.

Saturday morning. The A1 was quiet, no rush hour building today. In little more than an hour, the big skies of the Fens opened up, and this feeling coming back to her, as it always did, returning to the landscape of her childhood. A disquieting familiarity. Both a comfort, and unease.

I'm earlier than I used to be, she thought, pulling up on the gravel forecourt. Some of them will still be in bed; the elderly are never in a hurry to start their day. She got out of the car, walked over to the imposing front door of the Orchard Park Care Home. Rang the bell.

Cheryl, her mother's carer, answered the door.

'Jane! How lovely to see you again!' Stepping towards her, kissing her warmly on the cheek. 'You look fine, you do. You look really well.'

'Thank you, Cheryl. How's my mother? Have you told her I'm coming?'

'Aye. She fair leapt out of bed this morning. She'll be as happy as Larry now, seeing you again.'

'That's good to hear,' she said, but thinking, that's not true; she says it to spare her feelings.

'You know where you'll find her. She's up already. Always an early bird, your mam! Usual place, by the French window. She'll be over the moon to see you, so she will.'

The thick carpet swallowed her footsteps. She walked past the dining room where a few other early birds sat hunched over cornflakes, past the door to the kitchen, and the one that led to the bedroom wing, towards the sun lounge at the back of the house. That smell again, beneath the disinfectant and bleach. The smell of ageing flesh.

Her mother was sitting in her usual chair by the French windows, reading the *Daily Mail*, or pretending to.

'Hello, Mum. How are you?'

'Very well, dear.'

Her mother always called her 'dear', never by her name. With 'dear' she couldn't go wrong. Old Mrs Fields, sitting at the other side of the room, with her elephantine leg propped up on the footstool, was 'dear'. As was Mr Collins, who moved slowly across the room, knotted hands gripped tightly on his walking frame. And Cheryl, who breezed gaily in with the hot drinks trolley.

'Cup of coffee, Jane? Milk, one sugar, isn't it?'

Cheryl put two steaming cups on the low table near the chair. Scattered some biscuits on to a saucer.

'Nice oatmeal ones today. A little bit of what you fancy does you good, I always say.'

They talked for a short while about the weather. The weather was inconstant, unpredictable. Today was fine, but tomorrow there could be a squall of hailstones. Or even a gale that could sweep a life away.

'All the daffodils will be out early, if this fine spell continues,' Jane said. 'I've a few through already.'

'That's global warming, for you. Well now, no peace for the wicked. I'll leave you two to natter then. You must have lots to catch up on.'

Cheryl left them, clattering the trolley away over to Mrs Fields in the corner. Jane pulled her chair up closer to her mother. But felt as if she could be miles away.

'What have you been doing with yourself then?'

Her mother groped for words to say.

'Tuesday, isn't it, dear? That's nice.'

Jane leant closer.

'I said, What have you been doing with yourself?'

'Nothing much, dear. Same old thing.'

'Been out anywhere special?'

'I think so, dear.'

'Where have you been?'

On the minibus, wrapped up against the cold wind. Coffee and cake somewhere, where people jostled for tables and space.

'I'm not sure, dear. Somewhere nice, I expect.'

Jane sipped her tea and looked at her mother's crumpled face. But her mother was already turning her head away, tired perhaps with having to think, remember. She was looking through the French windows, down the smooth sweep of lawn where a few birds pecked on a bird table strewn with seeds and scraps of bread.

She wasn't going to say it. But now she did.

'I'm going to see Paul again. Someone's going to help me find him.'

Was there a sudden chill? Did her mother shiver suddenly? A shadow pass across her faded eyes?

She remembered you, Paul, I didn't imagine it. For an instant she remembered you, and then she chose to forget.

6

That evening, sitting alone in the house, staring at the walls.

She was thinking back to the time when she had received the phone call from the Social Services in Peterborough. From a Mrs Stevens, who worked in Elderly Services. She'd spoken politely, carefully, but Jane had felt that underneath the careful words she was being judged. *The absent daughter, the ungrateful daughter.*

'I've hardly seen my mother for years and years. We've never got on,' Jane had told her.

They had had no choice but to phone her, Mrs Stevens said; she was registered at the doctor's as 'the next of kin'. That had surprised her, that her mother had done that. But then she had thought, who else is there now? It didn't really mean anything. No special bond. No particular affection.

There was reason to be worried about her mother's welfare. A number of reports had been received from neighbours expressing concern. Her mother frequently went out for walks leaving her front door wide open. Sometimes going out in her carpet slippers even when it was raining, or not wearing a coat when it was cold. Once she left the iron on, face down, burning a black brand on the back of a blouse.

Somebody passing by had eventually noticed the smoke coming through a window and called the fire brigade. It was fortunate, on that occasion, that the house hadn't burnt down, Mrs Stevens said. Another time she'd been picked up by the police, wandering around Wisbech in the dark, looking lost and distraught. She didn't seem to know who she was, where she lived.

'We really don't feel your mother is safe any more, living alone. Especially in a house like that, a large house in a fairly isolated position. She has been taken into care at the moment, for her own safety. But it's a temporary measure. An assessment unit. Not a place where she can stay indefinitely.'

'It's difficult for me,' Jane said. 'We haven't had anything to do with each other, you see. Not since I was a child, actually. When I went to live with my aunt in Stafford.'

'Yes, I understand from your mother's records that there is a personal history here of a very sad nature, but you are the next of kin. We haven't got the authority to dispose of your mother's assets to pay for her care without your involvement.'

What did she mean? A personal history? But she knew, really, what was meant. She knew that if they were talking face-to-face this Mrs Stevens would have that look in her eyes; she would see her as different. As everyone did, who knew.

'Well yes, I understand. I realize there's no one else.'

Mrs Stevens gave her the details for the assessment unit, so she could ring them and arrange a visit. Then, just before hanging up – 'By the way, who's Paul? Your mother calls for him sometimes.'

You see, always you, Paul. Never me. She told them she only had a son. He was lost, she needed to find him . . .

It had been in the depths of winter when Mrs Stevens had phoned her. The dark time, the time she hated. It was only months after she and Adam had separated, and in a way, it was welcome. It created a diversion, gave her something else to think about. Winter always the worst of times for her, and especially now she was on her own.

The time of the solstice, Christmas, the New Year, had been unbearable. Adam had somewhat begrudgingly invited her down to Cornwall to spend it with him and Dominic – but his voice terse, as if he knew she wouldn't come, wouldn't want to. And she didn't. She *couldn't* go; she wasn't ready for that. Bob asked her round to share Christmas dinner with him, and she'd taken him up on it. They'd sat at his kitchen table together, eating a roast chicken, because a turkey was much too big for two. Bob made her pull crackers with him; he'd put his paper hat on his head and grinned at her inanely. She wouldn't wear hers, she couldn't. It would have been more pitiful somehow, if she had. It would have shouted out to the world – if the world had been there to hear – that the two of them, she and Bob, had shunted up on some forgotten track, like disused railway carriages, and were likely now to stay that way. She'd left Bob's just after the Queen's speech. Made some excuse to him. Taken to her bed for the rest of the day, with a bottle of sherry to dull the pain.

The separation was supposed to have been what she and Adam had both wanted, but she'd been the one who had asked for it, in the end. Adam had said, 'Yeah, fine. That's what I want too. That'll be for the best.' But he said it sourly, edgily; they both knew she'd given him little choice. In the last few weeks ticking down to the day he would leave they had orbited around each other in silence, neither of them willing, or able, to say the truth. To try to stop this thing from happening, the inevitable conclusion. *Please don't go. Don't leave me.* She had wanted to. One part of herself had cried out to ask him not to go. But she knew that to do so would require a kind of emotional honesty she hadn't allowed herself before. A follow-through, too. She couldn't just say it and then go on being the same. She would have to change. She wasn't capable of that.

Adam was waiting for the half-term break, so as not to disrupt Dominic's schooling too much. Dominic was scheduled to start at his new school in Cornwall after the holiday. Finally, Adam had cracked; he'd been the one to say those words. She remembered, only days before the date he would leave, how he had stood there in the kitchen and pleaded with her.

'Jane, let's give it one last try. Let's get some help. Relate. Let's go to Relate. Don't we owe it to Dominic at least to try?'

She shook her head at him. 'What's the use?' she said. 'What can they do?'

underwater

The truth was, of course, she was scared, she was terrified, of what they might unearth. What she might be forced to reveal.

What she hadn't bargained for in the months that followed was the loneliness, the intensity of it. It had pressed upon her heart like a stone.

In those first few months she'd come home from work – she was working full time back then – and put all the lights on. She'd turn the television up loud, so the noise would drown out the thoughts in her head. She'd bring home bottles of wine, buying them every night in discreet brown-paper bags from the off-licence, thinking, *Didn't it work for others? Won't it work for me?*

And it did, up to a point. But beyond that point, after the first few glasses, she would feel worse. The walls slipping, the tears coming. She would look at her face in the mirror, tearstained and bleary.

I'm becoming like my father, she would think, staring back at her own unsteady reflection. *I'm turning into him.*

Bob had come round regularly, and in a sense he had saved her. Although, who knows, she may in the end have saved herself. He would call round on the evenings when he wasn't working nightshifts, bringing his cheerfulness, his anecdotes about work, his guileless jokes. He would distract her from drinking too much and getting morose, by playing Scrabble. They would sit up together, until late if it was the weekend, poring over letter tiles. Jane became fixated for a while on the letter 'L'. Would spell out 'love' and 'loss'. And then she had a phase of getting all the letters on her rack to make the name 'Adam'. But she couldn't use them of course. Proper names weren't allowed.

'You know, you can have him back, Jane. Anytime you want. He'd come back to you, in a flash,' Bob said one night. He'd been watching her face in the soft light. He'd seen the sadness. She had just laid the word 'miss' on the board.

And then, in the weeks after Christmas, in that deadly time just after the New Year when nothing much happens at all and spring is still too far away, she got that phone call from Mrs Stevens about her mother. She did her duty; she did what needed to be done. It took her out of herself, out of the lonely house, the silent evenings when Bob was working. When she'd sit alone and stew in too much thinking, and the danger of too much red wine.

She put the house in the Fens up for sale. The house of her childhood, with the dark, fertile soil, which her mother would dig in the spring and autumn. The large living room with the open fire, where she and Paul would warm their backs and listen to their mother playing the piano when they were small. The French doors that led out on to the garden, where her father would stand sometimes, watching them as they played. The summerhouse he used as a studio, down the bottom of the garden, near the fruit bushes that swarmed with wasps in late summer. The house that contained all the memories. The good and the bad.

She did it all on her own. Built a big fire in the garden. Dragged out packing chests and boxes of things. Files and

folders, papers and books. Even albums of family photographs.

There were no photographs of her and Paul. That had
surprised her, at first. And then she had remembered that
they had been sifted out, taken away by her aunt and uncle,
after they'd gone to live with them. There were none of her
father, either, when he was young. But that didn't surprise
her. He always seemed as if he had come from nowhere, a
man with no past. Or one he had never wanted to share.

She remembered, when she was small, how she used to
wonder sometimes how they'd met, her mother and her
father, how they'd ever got together. What did she know of
love, then – what did she know of it now? – but all the
same, even as young as seven or eight, she knew it wasn't
right. That there was something missing. That her parents
were bound together by something closer to hate than love.

She asked her mother once. She didn't remember how
old she was, but young enough perhaps not to realize when
she was straying into danger. She was in the kitchen, watching her mother spoon spoonfuls of batter on to a baking tray.
She had been thinking of weddings and marriage. Sharon
Baker – *you remember her, don't you, Paul?* – who lived in
the big house down the lane, the only friend she had who
belonged more to her than to Paul – had been to some
wedding, one of her cousins'. Sharon's mother had been
showing her the photos. Sharon in a frothy bridesmaid's
dress, the bride beautiful in ivory satin.

'Did you and Daddy have a white wedding in a church?'
she'd asked.

'We weren't going to waste money on that.'

Her mother's voice was tight, like it was a day she didn't want to remember, and she had thought that was strange, even then, at that age. She thought that when she grew up a Prince Charming would stride into her life, and she would know straight away he was the one. Hadn't that been true for her mother, too?

'How did you meet Daddy?'

'At teacher-training college.'

Her mother was a teacher too, a music teacher. But had never worked as one. Paul had come along almost as soon as she had graduated, and in her mother's day, women who had children rarely ever worked. Although Jane had some vague memories of several pupils – children in their early teens who could travel out on the bus from neighbouring villages on their own – entering the house with shy, nervous smiles and practising scales on her mother's piano when she was small.

'Did you love him straight away? More than anyone else?'

Her mother looked up at her then, her eyes sharp.

No pictures of him. Not one. Not even a photo of their wedding day. Maybe there had been some, once, she had thought. Maybe her mother had taken them out, destroyed them. Mostly there were photos of people she hardly knew. People from her mother's past, perhaps distant relations. Some of her mother and Aunt Jean when they were young. Wearing square-shouldered coats and stilettos, their hair in tight curls worn close to their heads. Her mother looked pretty back then. *In this one picture, especially. In her early twenties – before she married, I expect.* She had this light in her eyes Jane had never seen before. She was laughing so carelessly at whoever it was that was taking the photo. Jane had never seen her look as happy as that.

I did all that, Paul. On my own. Bob of course would have helped if I had asked him. So would've Adam. But it seemed important that I did it alone. The only person who I would have wanted to be there, helping, dragging those boxes out of the eaves, down the stairs, out into the garden, doing it with me, would have been you.

But you weren't there.

Her mother had been taken into a hospital unit for the elderly and infirm for a while, but she didn't fit in there. Wasn't as crazy as the other inmates, who would walk around naked, if they had a chance to, shout angrily back at voices that only they could hear. She had been nervous, going there the very first time to see her mother. Afraid of what her mother would think, what her mother would say. *Why are you here? Why did you never want to see me before?* Afraid, perhaps most of all, of how her mother would make her feel, had always made her feel. Those eyes with flint in them, the scathing tone of her voice, that had made her shrink inside, as a child.

But she needn't have been. Her mother just looked at her, looked *through* her, as if she was just another person. Another nurse, another social worker. Someone unconnected with her. Who wasn't her daughter, hadn't shared a past with her, back in that house where storms visited without warning. And for once she was glad of that; that she was nothing to her mother, that her mother didn't even seem to know her any more. It had made it easier for her to cast aside the resentment that she'd carried for years. Her mother was just an old woman, frail and lost, who sat silently staring out of the window at the birds. Eating only when she felt she had little choice, when food was held up to her lips by solicitous carers.

'We don't think it's the onset of Alzheimer's,' the doctor told her. 'Your mother's confusion seems to come and go. Sometimes she can say what day of the week it is, even manage to recall some astonishing facts about her life. Where she lived as a child. The name of the school she attended. Her father's occupation.

'It's more possible that a small haemorrhage in the brain has caused this. The lesion is localized, only affects certain parts of the memory. Long-term memory, childhood for instance, normally stays relatively intact.'

'Will she get better?' Jane had asked.

'It's unlikely there'll ever be much improvement, not to the extent of enabling her to live independently. An appropriate residential home should be sought for her. Her physical health is good. We're not talking about a high level of nursing care, costs shouldn't be too prohibitive . . .'

So you see, Paul, I did my duty. I sold the house. Used the proceeds to pay for her care in Orchard Park. There's enough money to keep her there comfortably for the rest of her life. It's a good place, it's suitable. She's well taken care of. I go to see her regularly. Usually once a fortnight. Except these last months when I've been ill myself, and couldn't go.

Yes. But you can't forgive her, Jane. You can't even forgive yourself.

7

It was like she had imagined it would be. Tucked down a side alley in the town, at the top of an insurance office. A narrow staircase led up to the reception. Inside, a slightly threadbare carpet. An old sofa that had seen better days. A coffee table with scattered magazines. The receptionist didn't quite match the deceptively polite, polished voice she had on the phone. She was older than her voice had suggested, with a tired face, make-up caked into the lines around her eyes and mouth.

'Take a seat, Mrs Reynolds. I'll tell Mr Mansfield you're here.'

He wasn't what she'd hoped for, going by his name. Strong, capable, a fatherly air. Someone who'd take her under his wing, put her at ease. Instead, he was portly. He wore a slightly too tight, slightly shiny, grey suit, that hunched at the back of his neck. His beer belly protruded over the belt of his trousers. Receding grey hair, jowls that swallowed his jawline and chin. There were tiny burn marks from cigarette ash scattered down the front of his grey-white shirt.

On the desk in front of him, two framed photographs,

an overflowing ashtray, an empty coffee cup. He half stood as she entered, held out his hand. She felt calluses on his palm as she shook it.

'Mrs Reynolds. Take a seat.'

She sat on the worn leather chair, feeling its upholstery dig into her flesh. She felt nervous. As if she was at the doctor's again, waiting for his probing fingers on her breast.

'Your brother, you said? You want to find him. How long ago, did you say?'

She told him. Thirty-two years.

'That's a very long time, Mrs Reynolds.'

She felt judged, when he said that.

'Why do you want to find him now, in particular?'

'I don't know. I suppose when I was younger, I was busy, getting on with my life. Getting married. Having a family.'

'Those are my two,' he said, indicating the framed photographs on his desk. Turning them slightly towards her, so she could see them better. Two teenagers. They were smiling, but there was something a little hard about their eyes.

'Megan and Keiran,' he said.

She wondered what she was supposed to say.

'The boy, Keiran, he's just graduated. Engineering, with honours.'

'That's nice,' she said. 'I've just the one. A son. Dominic.' *But he'll never graduate, not now.*

'So. Tell me everything about your brother. Paul, did you say he was called?'

'What do you want to know?' she asked.

57

'Full name. Last known address. Date of birth. Place of birth. Physical description: height, build, colour of hair and eyes. Any distinguishing marks. That sort of thing.'

She reeled off the facts. It was easy.

'Auburn hair,' he said. 'That's good. People with auburn hair don't often dye it. If they bleach it they can end up like a carrot. Of course, he'll be getting on now. Fifty? Could have faded, be turning grey.'

Anything else?

'Where he went to school. What he was good at. Hobbies – any of those? Favourite places. Places you went to on holiday, perhaps. Oh, a photograph. Did you bring one? You won't have a recent one, of course. But it might be useful.'

She fished out the photograph she had brought with her. The last one she could remember that had been taken of Paul. He would have been about seventeen. He was standing with Stuart in the back garden at her aunt and uncle's house. They were wearing their Scout uniforms. They were just about to leave for a trekking weekend in Snowdonia. He was holding in his arms the khaki rucksack that he had been carrying the last time she'd seen him.

'Good-looking lad,' Mr Mansfield said. He looked a bit wistful then. Maybe he was thinking about his son, Keiran. How he would feel if his son went missing.

'Always a bit sad, these missing persons cases.'

'Yes,' she said.

'You say you've no idea why he left?'

'Not really.'

Why don't you tell him? Tell him now. Come clean.

'Well, there had been some trouble in the family. My father died, suddenly. My mother, she took it badly. She went off on her own somewhere. I didn't see her for years. We were sent to live with my aunt and uncle in Stafford. He was sixteen when my father died. It was a difficult time for him.'

'For you both,' Mr Mansfield said.

'Yes. But Paul was very close to his mother. *Our* mother. When she ... when she left, he took it particularly badly. More than me, I expect.'

'Your father's death. How did he take that?'

'Well, that was bad too,' she said.

'Tell me about the day he left. What happened. Everything you know.'

So she told him about the day she'd come home and heard Paul clattering around in his room. When she'd opened his bedroom door and seen the stuff he was packing spread out on his bed, the rucksack on the floor.

'Did you think that was odd?'

'Not really. I don't think I really thought about it at all. I was fourteen. I had stuff on my mind. School, homework. Maybe I thought he was packing to go away for the weekend. He was in the Scouts, you see. He often did go away for weekends.'

'What happened after that? After he left?'

He made her feel nervous. He was looking at her intently, as if he was reading her body language. Noticing when she swallowed, the quick flick of her eyes when she had something to hide.

But now she was telling him the truth. *Her* truth, at least. As close to it as she could.

No one had been worried until the following morning, when he didn't come down for breakfast. Her aunt had gone up then, to his room, and noticed his bed hadn't been slept in. She'd phoned Stuart, and he'd said, no, he hadn't seen him. He hadn't been with him that previous evening. They had no plans to meet at all. Her aunt started to get alarmed. Uncle Bill had left for work; he didn't know Paul was missing yet. Her aunt had to decide what to do on her own. She called the police. She let Jane stay off school. The police might need to talk to her, and in any case, she didn't want to go. Wouldn't have been able to concentrate.

They came round several hours later. They asked her aunt questions, like the questions Mr Mansfield had asked her.

His name is Paul Christopher Saunders.

Aged seventeen. Will be eighteen in May.

Five foot ten inches tall.

Dark auburn hair. Wavy, just over his ears. Greeny-brown eyes.

Distinguishing marks. A scar. Small one. On his forehead. Just over his left eye.

'What was he wearing?'

'Not sure. His sister was the last to see him.'

They turned to her, then. She told them, *Blue jeans, a red T-shirt, denim jacket with a check lining. He was carrying a khaki rucksack on his back.*

'What time would that have been?'

'About half four. I hadn't long been home from school.'

underwater

'Did he say anything about where he was going?'

'He said he was going round to his friend Stuart's. He said he might be late.'

'Can you think of any reason why your son would have wanted to leave home?' the older policeman asked, turning to her aunt again.

'He's my nephew, constable. My sister's boy.'

He raised his eyebrows at this, seemed to be waiting for an explanation. Her aunt shifted uncomfortably in her seat.

'Jane, would you mind? It might be better if I talked to the police officers on my own now.'

She'd gone dutifully up to her room. She'd lain on her bed, staring at the ceiling, imagining what her aunt was telling them, what they were thinking...

But she doesn't tell him that. This man, in his seedy office, looking somewhat unwholesome, with his own secrets behind him, perhaps. A failed police career perhaps, something a little crooked and shady in his past.

She only tells him what she can bear for him to know.

Bob came round that evening for tea. They had a routine; he cooked for her Thursdays, her turn, Mondays. He brought a bottle of wine to go with the pasta, made a fuss of Josie, gave her a hug. Stood back and looked at her, his face dropping slightly with concern.

'You all right today, Jane? You look a little peaky.'

'I'm fine.'

'You sure? You remembering to get enough rest?'

'Don't worry, Bob. I'm fine.'

Why don't you tell him now, Jane? Tell him everything.

She wanted to. She wanted to tell him about the visit to the private investigator, her missing brother. The dreams that were coming back to her, disturbing her. About what had happened to her father, all those years ago. She wanted to, but she couldn't. She sat across the kitchen table, winding spaghetti round her fork, toying with it on her plate, her appetite poor today, and pretending to listen to him telling her some story about work, pretending to find the story amusing, because he needed her to, and thinking, *He sees me as special. What have I left, besides Josie, and Bob's friendship?*

She was feeling deflated now. The excitement – *hope* – ebbing away.

It wasn't what Mr Mansfield had said. When she left, he'd shaken her hand, told her not to worry. 'If a person can be found,' he'd said, 'I'm the man to find them. I've never failed to find a missing person yet.' He'd looked kindly at her then, almost fatherly. Less like a hard-bitten, failed ex-copper. 'Don't worry, Mrs Reynolds. I'll have some news for you soon.'

She should be feeling reassured, expectant. But instead, this heavy feeling in her stomach. A sense of something tightening, coiling up again.

That night she dreamt the dream again, about the crowded room, and the stranger watching from the shadows. The woman with the American accent was wearing too much make-up; her bright, red-lipsticked mouth trailed in a hideous grimace across her face.

'I've someone I want you to meet,' she said.

underwater

Her voice swung in a sharp upward pitch that made Jane shudder. She followed her blindly across the room. The man got up, moved forward into the light. His face was scarred and disfigured. She didn't recognize him at all.

8

For the following few days she tried to put it out of her head. *If I'm meant to find him, then I will.* She carried on at work, wearing a bright face, a bright persona. Set out crayons, charcoal, paints. Clean brushes, clean water. A selection of coloured and textured papers. She wedged boulders of sticky, dark-red clay ready for use.

She brought in music to play while patients worked. Soothing music. Mozart, Brahms, Celtic harp music. Or lively ethnic rhythms. Cajun, Salsa, Afro-Caribbean. She moved among them, using her caring therapist's voice.

And when she wasn't at work, she tried to keep busy at home. Tidying, clearing out clutter. Even getting out in the garden now and then. It was the third week of March and everything was growing. She pruned the shrubs, the lavender and lilac, the rosemary that grew so rampantly. And for a few days she began to settle. Even her nights became relatively uneventful. She would wake sometimes. Too hot. Too cold. An ache in her neck from her pillow. She would think, *Was I dreaming? What was I dreaming?* But nothing. Just a feeling of having been swimming. Sightless, soundless. Underwater.

A week later, Mr Mansfield phoned. He sounded jovial, pleased with himself.

'I have an address here. It's the last known address of your brother's I've been able to find.'

It was difficult for her to find her voice, and when she did it sounded like somebody else's.

'Are you sure it's his? No one else's?'

'I've checked out all the records. There's little doubt in my mind.'

She picked up a pen and tried to listen. But his voice seemed to be coming from another universe; she could hardly follow what he was saying. Her hand was shaking. She asked him to repeat it again. And again.

'He was registered as living there nineteen years ago. Of course, it's likely he's moved again, although I can't find another address for him. You could try writing, see if he's still there. If he's moved, there might be a forwarding address. Depending on how long ago it was.'

'Yes,' she said, 'I will. Thank you. Thank you so much.'

A phone call on an ordinary spring morning. Few words spoken. Words scribbled in a shaky hand on a scrap of paper. A woman who has gazed for months now into the possibility of dying, whose body is still healing, whose future is uncertain, sits gazing at the words on the paper. Her coffee grows cold in the cup, her toast is left uneaten on the plate.

Number 6, Harbourside Cottages. Findhorn. The Moray Firth. Scotland.

She could have been reading a foreign language. The words meant nothing. The place meant nothing. She had never been to Scotland, never that far north. She sat there. For how long? An hour, maybe longer. Until gradually her heart seemed to shrink and settle back again, and the room around her became real again. The chair she sat on, the table she leant on, hard and solid once more. Josie watched her, soft eyes pulling her back into the present.

She took out the atlas of the British Isles from the bottom drawer of the bureau and turned to the map of Scotland. She found Inverness, crouched in the far north, at the tip of the long inlet leading to the Moray Firth. She moved her finger right, following the coast, up past Nairn. There, in tiny italics, *Findhorn*. A word. Nothing more. A touch of the Norse about it, a breath of Scandinavia. She rubbed the word lightly with her fingertip, hoping to trace the shape, the feel of the place, some idea of its mystery. A fishing village no doubt, situated on the long mouth of the Findhorn river that opened into the Moray Firth and the cold North Sea.

That's where I've been, Jane. That's where I still might be. Waiting for you to find me.

That evening, sitting up late again, a buzz of excitement returning. She picked up the pad of writing paper. Smooth, fine sheets of pale blue, with a watermark in the corner. She picked up the marbled green fountain pen. She had kept it since her childhood in its velvet-lined case in the bureau. Her aunt had given it to her for her sixteenth birthday; she had hardly used it till now. She started to write. Writing slowly, carefully, in her best hand. Her address at the top, her telephone number.

Dear Paul,

If this letter finds you, then please get in touch with me. I am desperate to find you. I miss you. I would love to see you again. Please write to me at the above address, or phone me.

Your loving sister,
Jane

She took another sheet of writing paper. Then she wrote:

To Whom It May Concern:

I am trying to trace a Paul Christopher Saunders, who used to live at this address. Please give the enclosed to him, if you are able to. If he no longer lives at this address then I would be grateful if you would return the enclosed envelope.

Yours sincerely,
Mrs J. Reynolds

She sat there for a long time. She felt strangely light and free, as if she was letting go of something. She was floating through water towards a sun-drenched surface. Through the gap in the curtains, out in the night sky, she could see the thin slice of a new moon.

Then she picked up the phone and dialled Adam's number. She listened to the clicks on the line, and waited. She was remembering how she had felt on the day he'd left.

It had been a cold day in October. She'd stood out on the street, hugging her body with her arms. Watched him lift Dominic into the car, collapse the wheelchair, throw it into the boot. Slide Dominic on to the front seat of the car.

'You'd better go in,' Adam had said. 'You'll catch your death.'

She was shivering. They had stood there, two feet yet a world apart.

'Well, you know where we are. Cornwall's not a million miles away.'

But it was, Adam, she was thinking now. *For me it was.*

She listened patiently to the ring-tone.

He won't be in bed yet, he never goes early. He'll be sitting at home, in that cottage he has created from the happier memories in our past. He'll be working in the room he uses as a studio. Making those large, misshapen pots, perhaps, that I've never really liked. Dominic will be tucked up in bed. His big callused feet sticking out of the bottom of the bed. A man's feet on a man that's still only a boy.

'Hello?'

underwater

He sounded tired. Perhaps a little suspicious. *Who's phoning so late?*

'Adam. It's me. It's Jane. I was thinking, I'd like to come down next week, for Dominic's birthday. Is that all right?'

9

She had been thinking of Dominic's birthday for weeks. Every now and then, the thought dropping into her head. At the hospital sometimes, working with a patient not far off Dominic's age. In town on a Saturday, shopping. Squeezing past a wheelchair in a crowded supermarkets the handles digging into her hips. Walking down the street, passing groups of disabled people out with their carers. Talking too loudly, grinning widely at everyone they see. *My son is like that*, she'd think. *My son who is nearly eighteen.*

Memories would come unbidden into her head. *Dominic's birthday, Dominic's day of birth.* It hadn't been an easy birth, as first births seldom are. Adam had taken her to hospital in the small hours of the morning after her waters had broken. He'd driven her there in his beaten-up old car; they hadn't much money back then. She remembered how she'd felt anxious in case it broke down on the way. The car stalled at traffic lights, spluttered and protested as he tried to restart it. But it got them there in the end.

The birth went on for the rest of that night, and into the following morning. Adam stayed with her most of the time, but left now and then, slightly bored, disappointed that it was taking so long, preferring the grand gestures, the drama, to this long protracted affair. And then when the birth had properly started, the pushing and the heaving, his wife's legs shoving against the shoulders of the young nurses and cursing and babbling incoherently between the screams because of the gas and air, and then the baby's heart monitor showing distress, that had been drama enough for Adam then, she remembered. There had been talk of forceps, and the chief obstetrician was called, her legs straddled and stir-rupped, ready, but then released again.

'Baby's coming now. Push!' the midwife shouted, and Jane had tucked her chin down on her chest and pushed, her face darkening, clouding, swelling bluish-red with the effort, and then, 'It's coming, I can see the head crowning!' from the midwife, and along with the head all the blood and mess that comes with it, that made Adam blanch and threaten to faint, until she bit his hand with the pain of it all, and revived him.

It's strange, she thought, remembering all this. *It's strange, how quickly I forgot.* The pain that made her feel ripped apart, on the rack. And the mess and the gore and the sheer indignity of it all, the world gaping at the wound between her legs. How quickly she forgot all this, although at the time, while she was in it, living it, she'd sworn to herself, *Never again!* – she'd never put herself through that again. Then that waxy, bloodstained, mewling newborn thing was put in her arms. The crooked puckering of its face, and the dark-blue eyes that contained volumes of space, and its head turning immediately, nudging into her breasts. It was as though there was some potent chemical, something secreted in the glands, that dripped a slow elixir of forgetting, so that all that, the bad stuff, the pain and the horror, was erased, replaced almost directly by this heady intoxication, this slavish love.

She remembered how blotchy and crumpled the baby's face was, how she feared it would always stay that way. But of course, it didn't. Within days, his skin clearing, plumping out, growing smooth and luminous, as if he had a light lit inside him. And his eyes that couldn't track, as no newborn babies eyes can. She'd thought: *There's something wrong with him, his eyes will always be wonky like this.* But of course they weren't.

'You're neurotic, Jane! He's perfect, he's gorgeous,' Adam had said, laughing. And of course he was, he was perfect. Adam was right. But that hadn't stopped her worrying about every tiny thing. If he was the slightest bit late getting to a milestone: First loss of a milk tooth. First time he'd sucked puréed food from a spoon. First time he crawled, took his first step, made a sound that mirrored a recognizable word.

But he was never really late. He was bright and lively and oh so normal. The word 'normal' being the most desired word for her now. And so, over time, she'd begun to relax, to take it for granted. He was all right, he'll be all right, everything would be okay.

'You need to let him go,' Adam had said to her once. Dominic was about five or six at the time. He wanted a skateboard, like all the other kids had. Wanted her to take him to the park, where they had smooth, shallow slopes for the smaller boys to try out their skills. Their turns, their flips, their sudden brakes.

'Don't wrap him in cotton wool, don't make him a mummy's boy,' Adam had said, and so she tried to let go. Made herself stop worrying, stop watching, relaxed her control. Then God had punished her, God had paid her back.

She had walked round the shops last week, looking for a present for her son. What to buy now, for a son who'll be eighteen next week? Eighteen years now from that day, where so much promise and perfection had been wrapped up and placed in her arms. What to buy for a boy who should be on the edge of being a man, but was still just a small boy inside? The last time she'd seen him, which was only two and half years ago – *he can't have changed that much*, she thought – he had still liked being read to, still had a nightlight beside his bed, still hugged that awful yellow hippo to his chest. Funny, she was thinking, she'd no idea what Dominic liked, what he was in to these days. Computer games, that sort of thing, perhaps? He wasn't when she'd seen him last; but now? She should have asked Adam.

In the end she decided to buy him a watch. It wouldn't be too expensive, wouldn't be too much a waste of money if she'd got it wrong. She bought it from the sports shop. It was waterproof, had a sealed red and black rubber casing, a red and black rubber strap.

'It's got extras,' the assistant pointed out to her, showing her how they worked. 'A stopwatch, a calendar. You can set an alarm. Press a button and make the face light up so you can tell the time in the dark.'

Before it was wrapped for her, she held it up to her ear, listening for the sound of *tick tock*.

'I can't hear it ticking. Does it need winding up?'

'It's battery operated. You're behind the times.'

He'll be disappointed about that, she thought, remembering the watch Adam used to give Dominic when he was little. An old-fashioned watch, with its tiny, precision-set wheels and cogs, its delicate mechanism, that by some miracle of skill and invention had kept perfect timing for years. Dominic had been fascinated by the noise it made. He would make Adam slip it off his wrist after reading him his bedtime story. He would settle down under the covers holding the cool face of the watch to his ear. Listen to the steady metronome of the *tick tock*, smiling, his eyes closing, slipping into sleep.

Jane would go up later and see his face guileless and angelic, as all children's faces are in sleep. Slip the watch out gently from the small fingers and return it to Adam downstairs.

Paying for it, taking the carefully wrapped up present from the assistant. *He'll think it's broken.*

Cheryl answered the phone. The burr of her Glaswegian accent warmed Jane's ear.

'I thought I'd take her out this Saturday. For a change. The weather forecast is good. Dry, at least.'

'That sounds lovely. Anywhere special?'

'There's a place on the coast she used to love. We used to go there for holidays when I was a child.'

'I could do you a packed lunch, if you'd like . . .'

'No need. There's a little tearoom I remember. I'll take her there.'

Cley next the Sea. Only it's not true, it's not next to the sea. It's near it. Then again, it used to be. At some time, in its infancy. Back in the Middle Ages, when there was a small port there. Boats from the Low Countries bringing in grains, coal, cloth. The presence of the Flemish traders and weavers, still there in the fluted gables on the roofs. When did the name first shape itself in their mind? Cley. No one seems to know now what it meant. The locals say it to rhyme with 'lie'. But written down it looks like 'clay'. Clay, meaning earth, land. Land juxtaposed to the sea.

Only it isn't, any more. A hinterland of marshes between the two. A wide, flat landscape which is not quite land, not quite sea. But both. Broken by a network of creeks, reed beds, fresh-water pools and saline lagoons. Places where all manner of strange creatures can be found. Creatures that can't live on the land, can't live in the sea. Prefer this in-between state.

We loved these marshes, didn't we, Paul? We loved the way they would be dry in one season, waterlogged in another, yielding to the imprint of our boots. We loved the hidden chattering of the birds in the reeds. The bittern's dark voice.

The sun had come out by the time they reached the village, a brief interlude between the cloud. They left the car in the car park near the village hall. Walked down the narrow, winding main street. Past the smokehouse, where fish hung like dried leather in the window. Past the old windmill – the windmill that was not a windmill, was now a small hotel. Through the turnstile that led to a rough pathway that extended as straight as an arrow across the marshes towards the sea. They stood and gazed into the distance, towards the high shingle ridge that hid the sea from view.

'Do you remember coming here, Mum, when Paul and I were small?'

There, she thought. *I've used his name again. Broken the taboo. Brought him back to us. He is standing on the marshes with us. The breeze is lifting the auburn curls of his hair.*

Her mother didn't answer. She was gazing fixedly into the distance. Jane looked towards the sky. A few drops of rain, cool on her face, a shower threatening to fall. Her mother turned towards her, a question in her eyes.

underwater

Why have you brought me here? she seemed to say.

'Can we go back now, dear?' she said, instead.

They'd come here over a span of years when Jane was a child, for their summer holidays, despite it being so close to home. They used to rent a flint cottage on the Green, a stone's throw from the old church. The same one, every year. What was it called? *Fisherman's Rest.* Another untruth. Any fisherman living there would have a long trek across the marshes before he could catch his fish. Their father would take them out walking, looking for birds and wildlife, binoculars strung like trophies around his neck. They would walk for hours. Taking the path that led over to Blakeney Point. All around them, the tawny marshes. A chattering of birds in the reed beds, hidden from view.

Sometimes, if the summer that year had been long and hot, and the marshes firmer and drier underfoot, edging back from water to land, they would leave the footpath and plunder the reed beds and long marsh grasses. Their father would point out teal and lapwings. The occasional spoonbill, redshank or avocet. Once, only once, a bittern. They had heard them before, a distant booming in the reeds, like a warning.

'That's the male. Establishing his territory,' their father told them.

That time, the only time she ever saw a bittern, Paul hadn't been with them. She had been out walking alone with her father. It was the last summer they ever went to Cley for their holiday in the summer.

They came upon it, wading through the reeds. Her father put his hand on her shoulder to make her freeze. It made her feel strange when her father touched her. He so rarely did. A mixture of surprise and shock. *Shush.* He handed her his binoculars. Something like a heron, but smaller. A mottled golden-brown, still, crouched shape. Its long beak pointing sharply to the sky.

In the café it felt as if they had invaded somebody's house, were sitting in somebody's cosy, oak-beamed living room. A fireplace cluttered with knick-knacks. Oil paintings of Norfolk scenes on the walls. Some clumsily executed, as if they were painted by an amateur, a favourite aunt. The girl who served them looked barely sixteen. A Saturday job, for her, Jane thought. She'll spend the money on make-up, cheap clothes from Top Shop. She stood, looking bored, while they made up their minds. The lunchtime menu had impossible things on it, things they couldn't stomach at this time of day. Crab salad. Smoked mackerel.

'I'd like a cream tea, dear,' her mother said. 'Is that all right?'

She always liked her cream teas back then, Jane thought. Wouldn't have them at home, only one and a half hours' drive away. But would have them here on holiday, maybe two or three times in the week, as if this was a place where the rules could be bent. Where you could pretend the rules weren't there at all, that you were free.

'Of course. You have what you want. My treat.'

The girl scribbled down their order. Soup of the day for Jane, a cream tea for her mother.

'One scone or two?' the girl asked morosely.

'One, dear. Can't manage two.'

The girl scuttled off with the order. Jane looked across the table at her mother. But her mother was looking away. Pretending to be interested in an oil painting hanging on the wall. The beach at Holkham.

'Dad painted scenes of that beach many times, didn't he?' Jane said suddenly. That she was able to evoke her father too, bring him back to them here, surprised her. Was she annoyed, she thought, that her mother wasn't paying her attention? Looking away again.

'Did he, dear?'

'Don't you remember? They did quite well, those pictures. People liked them. They were better than that one.'

'If you say so.'

Jane felt a sudden flash of anger. *She's pretending she doesn't know who my father was.*

The girl brought the order. Spinach and potato soup, a brown crusty roll. The scone, with its small pots of jam and cream. Earl Grey tea, served in an elegant white teapot.

Her mother now gazing absentmindedly out of the window. Outside on a cobbled patio, earthenware pots displayed straggled brown leaves and stems. Too early yet for flowers.

She won't look at me. She won't look at my face.

'Tea, Mum? Milk, no sugar, isn't it?'

'That's right, dear.'

Her mother picked up the knife, scraped it in the butter.

Don't say anything else. Don't be cruel.

'I'm thinking of going to Scotland soon. I'm going to see Paul.'

The knife held in her mother's bony hand paused in mid-air. She glanced quickly towards Jane's face, then looked away again.

'Are you, dear? That's nice.'

Why did you say that? She's old, it's too late. Let it go . . .

In the car going back, her mother was silent. She sat in the passenger seat, staring out of the car window at the still, leafless trees, the flat fields of dark earth, dykes and waterways stretching like ribbons of silver and pewter in the early spring sun.

Jane was remembering those holidays they used to have back then. There was something she couldn't grasp, something not clear. Like an overexposed negative, shapes blurred in a white haze. In the place that is not quite on the sea, not quite on the land. Where rules could be bent a little, where she and her brother could pretend for a short while that they were free.

Her father had always been in a better mood here than at home, or at least so it seemed. He would bring out cards in the evening, to while away empty hours. Teach them games like poker and gin rummy, show them tricks that made her speechless with wonder. She remembered a feeling of ease sometimes that they rarely felt at home. She couldn't remember him drinking that much there, in that poky cottage. Couldn't remember the flash of whisky in his hand, the soured odour of wine on his breath and clothes.

underwater

What did she remember?

There had been an old upright piano in the cottage. Not as grand as the one in the house in the Fens, but it was serviceable, a little out of tune, but okay. Their mother would sometimes play snatches of melodies on it in the evenings, while their father taught them card games, showed them tricks.

Her mother played well, she played by ear. She had taken piano lessons once; someone had taught her, back in that distant youth that she kept to herself, that she never shared with her daughter. Jane remembered, from an early age sitting at home with Paul in front of the fire, the comfort of her mother's music slipping over her ears. English folk songs, mainly. *The lark in the clear air. Lavender's blue. Greensleeves.* She would sing too, as she played, but softly, as if she was singing for herself alone, the words muted, under her breath, but in a voice that was fine and perfectly pitched. Jane remembered how it made her thrill to hear her mother singing. A sensation touching her neck, like the hairs quivering.

She had rarely allowed herself to think back to those holidays in Cley. This was only the second time she had been here since she was a child. She had brought Adam once, soon after they had met; for some reason she couldn't account for it had felt important that she had. Now, thinking back to those holidays, the poky cottage opposite the church, the walks on the marshes with her father, she was remembering something. Something she didn't want to remember.

*

The summer before her father's death. The last holiday they'd had in Cley. Only months before her father had died, that terrible time that had changed her life for good. Paul had just turned sixteen, and was moody, difficult at times, as all teenagers are. She was losing him, he was drifting away from her. Discovering girls and sex, shutting himself away in the dark train of his thoughts where she couldn't follow. He nearly didn't come with them that summer; it had been almost agreed that he could stay behind, spend the week at Stuart's house. But then her mother had said something to him. She never knew what it was, but suddenly he'd changed his mind. Now he was eager to come.

That summer had been particularly hot, the marshes dry and sucked of water. Her father took her out walking most days on their own. Paul had given up going with them for some years by now. The resentment between him and his father had evolved into something as impenetrable as a wall. They rarely spoke. *It was different for you, Paul, maybe easier. Your hatred for him, so cold and unswerving.*

He'd stayed back every day with his mother. They would go out together, to find a beach they could sit on, one with real sand like at Cromer or Holkham, to relax, read a book, work on their tans. Sometimes into King's Lynn, for the shops, the museum.

Her father had scoffed at Paul for wanting to spend time with his mother.

'Big nancy boy,' he'd called him.

That day, the last day, the one that was returning clear and vivid now into her mind, she had walked with her father over to Blakeney Point and back. He'd been in a good mood that day. A good mood, that is, for her father. She remembered he had chatted to her about school. How she was getting on, if she'd thought about what she might do when she was grown up. She was thirteen; being 'grown up' was a state she couldn't imagine. It was enough to live from day to day, contained by the small swings of her moods, her changing body.

'I don't know,' she'd said.

'You could go to university, you could. You've got a good brain on you. You could go whichever way you chose to. What subjects do you prefer?'

'I like art best.'

'No money in art. You'll end up like me, teaching it to kids who have no talent.'

But it pleased him, she knew, that she had said that. There was this link between them. She took after him; she was good at art, like he was. Not like Paul, who preferred music like his mother. She felt a pale glow of pleasure, warmed by his approval. They fell into silence then, tired by the walking. She walked behind him, placing her feet on the marks his boots made on the track.

On the way back, they stopped off at Wells harbour for a rest.

'Fancy fish and chips?'

Walking back along the jetty from the fish and chip shop, holding the warm, greasy newspaper parcels in their hands. The smell of grease and fish filling her nostrils, making her stomach groan with hunger. Her father stopping suddenly in front of her, and she shunting up against the weight of his back.

Across the road a car had pulled up. A sleek, dark, expensive-looking car. Her mother and Paul were climbing out. Her mother was smiling, laughing, perhaps at something the driver was saying. Her mother's head turning, and seeing them, the smile fading to a pale, shocked blur. The car pulled away. She didn't notice who was driving. She was staring at her father. A wire of fear tightening inside her, at the sight of his darkened face.

What happened later, Jane? Do you remember?

Memories, slipping back now, with the ease of water. As if a resistance had given way, a dam crumbling...

Her father said nothing at first about the car, or who had been driving it. No interrogation, no accusation; nothing. He asked her mother and Paul if they fancied fish and chips as well. A weak smile visiting her mother's face, as if she was allowing herself for a while to fall for the foil.

He went back to the shop, returned with two more parcels. They sat on the quay, picking at their food, watching the boats. There was silence and space between their bodies. Her mother peeled the batter off the fish, discarded it. Most of the chips as well.

'Aren't you going to finish them?' An edge in her father's voice he couldn't conceal.

'You finish them for me.'

But he didn't. Her mother screwed the unfinished food up in the newspaper and dropped it in a bin.

They caught the bus back to Cley. For the first hour the pretence continued. Her father sat reading the *Daily Express* and smoking his pipe. An aura of silence around him, a tension. The easing of his mood, the relaxation of the day, gone now, vanished, as if it had never been there. She felt – they all felt – as if they had to pick their way around him, walk on eggshells. But at least he said nothing. No accusations, no ugly words that tore at the air. At least his silence was preferable to that. Perhaps he had forgotten the incident, perhaps they had got away with it, perhaps nothing would be said.

Then he started drinking. Getting up every so often to pour out another glass of whisky from the bottle he had picked up from the off-licence on the way home. The sound of the liquid hitting the glass, a sickening thud in her stomach. Paul had disappeared straight away up to his room. He said he was going to pack – they were leaving the next day – but she knew he wanted to keep out of the way. He couldn't stand the sight of his father drinking. It wasn't fear so much with Paul, Jane knew; it was hate. Purer than hers, less clouded. *He couldn't stand it.*

She was sitting in the armchair across the room from her father. She was reading *Jane Eyre*, which she had found in the school library and had chosen because she shared the heroine's name. She was curled up in the chair, her body slightly averted from her father opposite. She was reading, or pretending to read, because all the time out of the corner of her eyes she was watching him, as if waiting for something. What was she waiting for? He put down the paper. Picked it up, put it down again. His face had reddened and coarsened with drink. He glared at the open kitchen door, where beyond in the kitchen her mother was making sounds of tidying up. Cupboard doors opening, closing.

Coming in now, carrying things in her arms she intended to pack into the box on the living-room floor. And the question came. As she knew it would.

'Who was he?'

He said it with a sneer, as if he already knew the answer. The way he said it, already sullying what the answer might be.

'Who do you mean?'

'The fucking man in the car.'

'Must you use that language?' Her mother sounded weary. As if she knew there was no point to it. As if she was already resigned to what would happen. She had been there so many times before.

'Can't you answer a simple question, woman?'

He had raised his voice now, was almost shouting. Jane heard a door open upstairs, the sound of feet shuffling slightly over the boards on the landing. Paul was listening. She was slipping outside her skin. As if she wasn't there, she didn't really exist. *Who is this girl sitting so calmly and quietly in the chair, reading a book?*

Her mother walked across the room to the piano, placed the crockery she had been carrying, the extra pieces she had brought from home, on the polished wood. She turned to face him.

underwater

'That was Paul's piano teacher. He gave us a lift, that's all.'

'Don't lie to me. Don't treat me like a fucking idiot.'

'I'm not lying.' Her mother's voice was cool, was quiet. 'He lives in Wisbech. Paul sees him once a week.'

'Why can't you fucking teach him? You're supposed to be a music teacher, aren't you?'

'I haven't taught anyone for years, I'm out of touch. And you know it never works very well ... trying to teach your own children.'

'What's he doing here, if he lives in Wisbech?'

'There's a music shop in King's Lynn he likes.'

'Is that what you expect me to fucking believe?'

'You can believe what you want. I'm telling you the truth.'

Her mother was pretending to be tidying things away. Pretending she didn't care; his anger didn't frighten her. It was passing over her head. But her indifference, her coolness, just fanning the flame. Jane had seen it, *felt* it, so many times before ...

'Why didn't he drop you off here, then? Instead of at Wells?'

'We thought it would be nice to catch the bus the rest of the way.' But her voice faltering now, she was losing.

Her father staggered to the bottom of the stairs.

'Come down here, you little bastard! I know you're listening.'

The quick suck of her mother's breath. Paul came slowly down the narrow stairs, his face set with a cold resolve. *Show no fear. Give nothing away.*

87

'There's a fucking piano. Play it, then. I want to hear what you've been learning.'

Paul said nothing, staring back unflinchingly. *Make me. Just try and make me, if you dare.* She was thinking, where did he learn that, and when? Not to be afraid.

Her father lunged at him, grabbed his arm.

'Fucking play it, I said.'

'For God's sake, John! Leave him alone!'

She felt the sharp, rising edge of her mother's fear. She sat unmoving. Saw Paul shake his father off, step back. He glared into his father's face. Something had changed in him. She knew it. Something new had entered him, given him courage.

'Leave him alone, John. He doesn't want to.'

Her father turning, grabbing her mother's shoulders, forcing her down on to the piano stool.

'*You* play it, then. You fucking show me what the little shit's been learning.'

How long did it take her mother to decide what she would do? To swing her body around to face the keys, to open up the lid, to start to play? *Plasir d'amour.* The melody faltered under her mother's fingers. Hairs prickled on the back of Jane's neck. Then the body that she didn't belong to flinching suddenly, as the piano lid slammed down, the keys jangling violently to silence.

Fucking slag. Fucking whore. Don't fucking lie to me.

Her mother's high-pitched scream of pain. The crash of breaking crockery as the plates tumbled to the floor. Her father was holding the lid down, leaning his full weight upon it, his face contorted with fury. Jane sat there, the open book on her lap, frozen like the bittern in the reeds. *Who is this girl sitting still and calm, not moving, not reacting?*

Paul sprang forward and grabbed his father's arms, wrenched them free of the piano lid. Her mother's fingers slipped out, crushed and reddened. Her father turned, grabbed his glass from the table, pushed it hard into Paul's face. He staggered back, made no sound. Pressed his hands to the wound above his eye. Blood welled through his clenched fingers, fell in slow, dark drops to the floor.

The memories stopped there.

11

She would usually seek out Wendy to have lunch with at work. Wendy lightened her, brightened her mood. Her company at lunchtimes made the hospital canteen a little less grim. The chipped Formica tables, the food that was occasionally unpalatable, served lukewarm and greasy by women with murderous faces.

'I'm going down to Cornwall next week. Just a few days, to see Dominic. It's his birthday, his eighteenth.'

'That'll be nice. Adam will be pleased to see you.'

'Yes, I expect so.'

Will he? she thought. *Perhaps there's someone else by now. I wouldn't blame him if there was.*

'How long are you going for?'

'Only a couple of days. I'll be back at work on the Thursday.'

Outside the canteen window where they sat, Ken and Tara were sitting on a bench. They were gazing into each other's eyes, as if they were the only people in the world that mattered.

'Have you told him?'

'What?'

'About – you know – being ill.'

'No.'

'Jane!'

'I couldn't. It didn't seem fair. Hasn't he enough to worry about?'

'He'd have wanted to know. You're still married, he's a right to.'

Jane said nothing. Ken and Tara were standing up now. He was tall and skinny; she was short, dumpy, the top of her head reaching only up to his chin. He stooped to kiss her. Jane noticed how tender the kiss was. How their lips lingered, not wanting it to end too soon. Ken started to move away, to walk across the grass away from Tara. Perhaps he has to see his psychiatrist, has a group to attend, Jane thought. Tara stood looking longingly after him. Raised her hand and waved to him. A small wave, like a child makes.

Wendy had followed her gaze.

'They're being resettled soon, aren't they?'

'Yes. A half-way house. Not the same one. I don't know how they'll cope, not being together all the time.'

They were both still attending her Tuesday art therapy group. Tara had moved on, far away from crouching figures under threatening hands, away too, from women sitting with their backs to the light. A naive surrender to hope again. Hearts and flowers, small dogs, little girls skipping in pastel dresses.

Ken's pictures were more persistent, more relentless in theme. He painted hospitals. The psychiatric institutions he had spent most of his adult life in and out of. Grim, dark

Victorian edifices, with rows and rows of windows. Some of the windows were empty. At others, faces gazed out, shaped like teardrops, mouthing distress.

Ken had known for months that his days in the hospital were numbered. Knew talks were going on almost daily now, trying to match residents to places on the outside. *Resettlement, community care.* He knew it wouldn't be like it had been before, when an act of desperation could bring about his return to safety. He'd done a painting recently in the confines of the art therapy room. The grim facade of the hospital again, but this time the walls ripping open, splitting like an egg, the roof collapsing. Bodies of inmates spewing out from those myriad windows, arms flailing in terror.

Jane had looked at it in glum distress.

'They don't care about us,' he said. 'Nobody cares. "Care in the community". Care, my arse! D'ya know where we'll all end up, Jane, people like me? On the streets, with our cardboard boxes. Or in the nick.'

Jane had said nothing; there was nothing she could say. But his words had disturbed her, brought back memories of Paul again. She wondered if that was how Paul was living now. Sleeping in doorways, in cardboard boxes, only thin blankets between his body and the indifferent cold.

'How long do you give them? Do you think their relationship will have a hope when they've been moved out?' Wendy said.

'I don't know. But I hope it lasts. Good luck to them.'

Wendy had noticed the wistfulness in her voice. It had surprised her.

'You're getting to be quite a romantic in your old age!'

'Perhaps!'

Wendy looked at her watch.

'Better go. I've a group at two. The elderly and senile. I get them to throw balls to one other, try to remember one another's names. Shouldn't mock. We may all get there in the end – if we live long enough.'

That night she sorted out the clothes that she would be taking to Cornwall. She wouldn't need to pack much; she was only staying a couple of days. A winter coat, some warm jumpers. Some walking boots, perhaps. The weather was always changeable down there, she remembered. One day, warm and sunny. The next, gales could buffet the cottage, bring rain down in buckets.

She used to spend those holidays in Cornwall watching the sky. Even in the summer, watching it for sudden changes. She'd developed a sixth sense. Would smell a storm coming in the air . . .

They'd seen a tornado once. They'd been walking up on Bodmin Moor and all afternoon the cloud building, thickening, until only a band of light was left in the sky. The wind was whipping up, making walking difficult, as if they were walking uphill, leaning into a weight.

Dominic was high, excitable, as kids are in the wind. He was running ahead, over the rough, hillocky grass. He'd seen something fly up suddenly from a straggle of bushes.

'It's a chough, I'm sure it is!' he called back to them.

The chough. A rare bird; sightings were precious. It had returned to its homeland after long years away.

'Probably not, son,' Adam said. But kindly, not wanting to douse Dominic's excitement. 'You don't get them up here on the moors. Maybe a jackdaw, a rook instead.'

His voice was torn away in the wind. The sky in the west had darkened now, almost to black.

'Look, Dad! Over there!' Dominic yelled. He'd seen something now that was more exciting than choughs. A dark tail, whipping downwards from the black wedge of cloud.

It began to rain then. They ran for cover and found a tree to huddle under. There were few trees on the moor. What trees there were had crooked, leeward-leaning branches, as if they'd spent their lives twisting away from the wind. They clung together, under the tree's thin cover, and laughed like maniacs. Jane had seen patients at the hospital run into high winds and laugh like the three of them laughed that day. But her laughter was laced with fear. Fear that the tree would be torn from the ground and they'd end up crushed underneath it.

The wind died suddenly. Like rage dies, after it's vented. When they got back to the whitewashed cottage they rented every year for their holiday, the guttering had been ripped from the roof, tiles blown away. The pots in the garden lay on their side, some smashed and broken, soil and plants spilling out.

I developed a sixth sense, I could smell it in the air. We went back the following year. Why did I let us do that?

They always had their holidays in Cornwall. They would go to the north coast, preferring its wildness to the tourist

underwater

traps in the west. They would rent that same small, white-washed cottage in the hamlet of Advent. The one that Adam was now re-creating, or trying to, in the cottage he'd bought with his inheritance when his mother died. The same rough whitewashed walls, oak beams, uneven flagstone floors.

A year after seeing that storm, the tornado, disaster had struck.

I'd taken my eyes off the sky, Jane thought. I'd stopped watching . . .

They nearly didn't go back that next year.

'What about somewhere different for a change?' she'd said to Adam. 'What about Spain? Dominic would like that; all his mates go to Spain, he says.'

Had she felt something, some vague premonition? She couldn't be sure.

'What's Spain got that Cornwall hasn't?' Adam had said. 'Except sun and sangria. No, not even the sun. The weather's usually been good for us in August down there.'

'Yes, in between the storms,' she said.

But they had gone. Adam got his way, and the truth was, she didn't put up any real resistance. She knew how much he liked Cornwall, how much he felt at home there. His parents used to have a second home in Padstow. He'd been going to Cornwall for summer holidays long before they'd ever met, since he was a boy himself. *His spiritual home*, he used to call it. Probably still does, she thought.

And Dominic wanted to go, so of course she couldn't argue with that. That sense of premonition hadn't really been there, she was making it up. Easy to read omens and warnings after the event, easy to imagine they'd meant more than they had. For the last few years Dominic had made friends with a boy of the same age, Daniel. His parents had a holiday chalet near Tintagel. They were in love with Cornwall, like Adam was. Would return there every August for their holiday, year after year.

Adam and Jane had become friends with Daniel's parents. Cards were exchanged at Christmas, the odd phone call. They had fallen into a pattern of contriving to have the same weeks in August on holiday together, so the boys could meet up.

And so they had gone to Cornwall, as they usually did. The summer that year had been particularly long and hot. They would join up with Chris and Barbara, Daniel's parents, and spend long days baking on the beach, roasting in the sun, watching the boys riding in the breakers on body boards. They would meet up again in the evening, fresh and showered, the sand and salt washed out of their skin, and drive somewhere. Padstow sometimes, to sit by the harbour with a cool glass of lager and admire the yachts anchored up that were getting bigger, more expensive, each year.

Two days before the end of the holiday. Dominic wanted to go on a coastal walk with Daniel and his family. Chris was a Scout leader. He was used to taking boys hiking up mountains, white-water rafting. He had an ambition he'd been working on for the last few years, to take his family trekking on the south-west coastal path, completing a section at a time each year they came for their holiday. This year it was the stretch from Padstow to Portquin.

'Please let me go,' Dominic begged them. 'There's nothing to it, Daniel does it all the time.'

Jane hadn't been too sure. 'Perhaps when you're a little older, perhaps next year.'

But Adam persuaded her. 'He's growing up, Jane. You need to loosen your apron strings. Chris is a good bloke, he'll take care of the lads. He does this thing all the time.'

She had prepared a packed lunch for Dominic that morning. Ham sandwiches wrapped in foil, a cup cake, a Twix, an apple. She placed the food, along with a bottle of fizzy drink, carefully in the rucksack his dad had bought him for his birthday. It was khaki-coloured, not unlike the one Paul had been carrying on the day he'd left. Along with his new binoculars, his Olympus Trip camera, a sketch-pad.

She stood outside the cottage and watched him clamber excitedly into Chris's car.

'Don't worry, Jane, they'll be fine. He'll sleep well tonight, I promise you,' Chris said.

She smiled weakly, and waved as the car started to pull away down the narrow lane. Suddenly she had the strangest feeling that she should run after it, yank the rear door open, pull her son out again. Standing there, watching them disappear, the boys with their faces pressed up against the rear window, waving, she felt for a moment as if she was back in the past. She was getting up from her desk, where her French textbook from school was open on the verbs *oublier* and *se souvenir*. She was at the window, watching Paul walking away in a false spring sunshine. She hadn't said it then, she wasn't saying it now:

Come back! Please come back again!

*

The boys had been playing chicken. Chris had told Adam that later, several nights afterwards. She hadn't been with him. She would have been at the hospital, waiting for Dominic to come round from the coma he'd been in after the first of what was a succession of operations. They had a bed there that she slept on, or didn't sleep on. She ate her meals there, or didn't eat. She paced long waxed corridors in the long evenings. She gazed through the glass partition at her son, or sat by his bedside, appalled at the tubes that fed in and out of him, that monitored his heart rate, his blood pressure, his hydration. Feeding him oxygen, fluid, nourishment. For weeks her son had slept in that unknown land. She had sat by his bedside and had longed to join him there. She thought, that if she could, she would find him whole and happy, running around on two strong legs.

'They had been playing chicken.' Chris was slumped on a chair, ashamed, couldn't meet Adam's eyes. Adam was angry at first, but his anger died quickly, seeing the state of the man. *What's the use?* he'd thought.

'Daniel told me. I made him tell me.'

'Playing chicken! On a bloody cliff edge!'

'Barbara and I were just ahead. We were looking for a good spot to stop for lunch. They were only out of sight for a minute, not even that. There was a bend, they were dawdling. I told them to hurry up. Barbara said something about there being a good patch of grass up ahead. Only for a minute did I lose sight of them. Not even that.'

Adam told her all this later, weeks later. When Dominic had returned from his long deep sleep in that unknown land. When she knew without doubt that she would not be getting the old Dominic back, but a new one, whom she would have to learn to love all over again. *Playing chicken.* Seeing who could stand close enough to the edge, who was brave enough. A seagull had flown up suddenly from the ledge below. It had startled him. She would close her eyes and picture her son tipping off the ledge, falling like a wingless bird. Why was it *our* son? she'd think. Was Daniel the one who was 'chicken' then, in the end, not brave enough to stand that close to the edge?

She took her purse out of her handbag. Opened it up and slid out the photo from the soft folds at the back. A photo of Dominic when he was just a baby. His head a mass of soft curls, glinting gold in the sun. He was sitting on a rug, amidst a sea of bluebells, laughing. All that hope and future smiling from his face.

She slid it away again into the purse. Her eyes were blurry with tears. That surprised her. It had been a long time since she had allowed herself to feel any sadness about her son.

PART TWO

PART TWO

12

Adam had been asking himself ever since Jane's phone call, *Why now? Why now after all this time?* Getting Dominic ready for school, waiting for him to come home again, keeping himself busy in his studio or the garden, making Dominic his tea when he came back, getting him ready for bed. The thought forming in his mind again, making him feel uneasy. A bubble of hope building in him too, under the surface. He squashed it down.

In the early months during the first year of their separation, he'd phoned her now and then. Kept her informed of Dominic's welfare, told her what his new school was like, what friends he was making, what his end of term reports were saying: *He's getting stronger, he's using his standing frame every day, can even walk a few steps with his specially adapted walking frame. His speech is better, clearer than before. He can hold a pen properly now, write words out on his own.* He would make himself tell her these things, as if she cared, but thinking really, resentment building, she doesn't care. Nothing had changed. Absence hasn't made her heart grow fonder.

He would say, in those early months, 'Come down. The

weather down here is lovely. Dominic misses you.' And hoping she'd hear what he hadn't been able to say: *So do I*. But she hadn't come. She always had an excuse.

I'm busy, I've lots on at work, the house needs decorating, the garden needs tidying. *I can't spare the time*.

Eventually he'd got the message, and the phone calls stopped. She never came. He'd taken Dominic on one occasion to visit her. In the home that used to be *their* home, but was now just hers. It hadn't worked out. She had found every excuse to keep herself busy, would hardly look at him, would hardly look at their son. Then that night, he'd wanted to go out to catch up with an old mate, Dave, a teacher he'd known at work, and had popped in to say goodbye to Dominic before going out. The boy had messed himself, his pad needed changing; it was leaking out from the seams, was staining the sheets.

'Christ, mate! You've picked the right time for this!' He already had his coat on, he'd been just about to go out of the door. *Dave will be waiting, I'll be late*, he'd thought.

Jane was in the living room watching the television.

'Sorry. He needs changing. Do you mind?' he'd said. Knowing she would mind, but thinking he'd risk it anyway. Like it was a test. And realizing as soon as he'd said it that he shouldn't have, he shouldn't have bothered. Her face turning to him, helpless, hopeless, her eyes full of fear.

'Never mind,' he'd said, that edge back in his voice again. 'I'll do it myself.' Like he always had done. Like he'd done for years.

*

In a way, it was easier. Once he'd accepted it was over, that she wasn't coming back, that nothing would change. He put the energy instead into his life down here. It was good, it was better. He was making new friends. Dominic liked it: the sea, the fresh air, the more clement winters. The old refrains – *Where's Mummy? Is she in the old house? When will she come?* – beginning to wear thin, to dry up.

He wasn't going to tell him yet, but then he did. One morning, after breakfast, while Dominic was waiting for the bus from school.

'Hey! Guess what, Dom! Your mum's coming to visit. She's coming for your birthday. How about that?'

Why did he ever imagine that Dominic had forgotten? His face split into a wide beam of delight.

'Mummy! When she coming, Daddy? Today? Tomorrow?'

He'd asked again that evening, two or three times. And again, over the weekend.

'Mummy come, Daddy? Mummy coming today?'

'Not today, Dom. On Monday. Three more, two more sleeps away.'

But now Monday had come. And the question *Why now?* was hovering again in his mind, getting his son up, getting him washed, dressed, making his breakfast. But Dominic was quiet on the subject now, as if the record had run out, time being only so elastic for him, only stretching from one periphery of time to another. A span of a day, a weekend. After that, disappearing into something too vague to keep hold of.

A knock on the door. Adam's first thought, *It's her! It's Jane!* Then Dominic, shuffling the last spoonful of Weetabix into his mouth, seeing the look on his father's face, the thought springing back into his head on its piece of elastic.

'Mummy!' he cried, waving his spoon in the air. 'Mummy at the door!'

'Sorry, mate. Can't be her yet. Too early.'

And it wasn't. Anna stood there, in a spell of bright sunshine, a bunch of daffodils in her hand.

'How you doing? Need any help?'

'That'll be great,' he said. 'Would you mind watching Dom while I go and shave?'

'Not at all.'

She thrust the daffodils towards him.

'Thought we could find a vase for these. Brighten the place up a bit. What do you think?'

'Lovely. I think there's one under the sink.'

Anna walked past him into the kitchen, and just for an instant Dominic's face registered, perhaps like his had, a flash of disappointment, then broke again into a wide grin, because who could resist Anna, looking like an angel, bringing the spring sunshine in her face, in her gleaming blonde hair.

'Hi, Dom. Nearly birthday boy. How are you?'

She stooped to kiss Dominic's Weetabixed cheek. His eyes brushing up against her chest, and the smile broadening now, because Dominic was at that age when women's breasts held a new magic for him.

'Hi, Anna. I'm fine. You pretty today!'

*

underwater

Adam went upstairs to shave, leaving them to it, and when he came down again, the daffodils, their trumpets of yellow still folded, not quite open yet, stood in a glass vase on the centre of the table, which was wiped clean now, as was Dominic's face. Anna was at the sink, washing the breakfast things.

'You shouldn't be doing that.'

'Why not? I don't mind.'

The bus would be here soon, to take Dominic to school. He struggled with Dominic's jacket. Anna came over to help, and Dominic's eyes swinging around to her chest again, the smile pasted back on his face. She never minds, Adam thought.

'Come on, Dom. Straighten your arm.'

He could hear the bus draw up outside the gate. Dominic's arm suddenly locking into place, the arm shooting up the sleeve.

'Well done, mate!'

His son, nearly eighteen, coming of age. Laughing like a drain.

Jim and Trudie were coming up the path, bringing their smiles and gossip into the kitchen, taking Dominic in his wheelchair with them out through the door.

They sat together in the sudden peace of the kitchen. She looked at him silently, taking him in.

'You're tense today, Adam. This is because of the visit from your wife, I think.'

'I'm fine.'

She raised an eyebrow.

'Well, maybe a little,' he said, smiling.

He thought, she always picked it up. When he was tense, sad. When he had a headache. When a cold was coming on. He never had to say anything. She always seemed to know.

'I could give you a quick session now. It might help.'

'Maybe later. I'll be even more tense when she's gone.' She smiled with him, an ironic smile, at the joke.

There was something between them now: a knowing, a secret they had shared.

Anna was Danish, but lived permanently in Cornwall now. 'It suits me, the energy here is better,' she would tell him. She was into energy, all sorts of energies. Ley-lines, auras and angels, chi and yin and yang. She was studying shiatsu, was in her last year of a three-year diploma course, and sometimes she used him as a guinea pig to try her skills out on. But not really as a guinea pig these days, because she was nearly qualified now, she was quite an expert.

She'd come round one evening, a month or so ago, and he'd put on a baggy T-shirt, a loose pair of jogging bottoms, and stretched out on a rug on the floor. She knelt down beside him. He suddenly grew self-conscious. She wasn't the same Anna, who dropped round at weekends to help with Dominic, who chatted to him about gardening – how to repel slugs without using chemical fertilizers, what vegetables grow best in the sandy, salty soil. She was someone else. A new Anna. Professional, practised. Her fingers were strong, moved fluently down his body, seeking out the reflex points.

'Your heart energy is strong,' she said.

'What does that mean?'

But she just smiled. Her hands were kneading his abdomen, working the soft muscle of his belly. 'In shiatsu,' she'd told him once, 'we call the abdomen the *hara*. It is considered in many ways the most important part of the body. *Hara* also means a kind of consciousness, a knowing, a sixth sense. The mind and body acting as one . . .'

Sometimes she'd used her elbow, her knee, her shoulder, her whole body. Pressing and leaning into him with her weight. Sometimes pummelling. *This disperses the chi.* Sometimes stretching him, this way and that. *This opens up the chakras.* There was one movement she'd made, with one hand placed on the top of his thigh, near his groin, the other on the opposite side of his abdomen, pressing down and pressing away from each other, so that the place in between, his genitals, felt opened up, released. Something had stirred then, something had a life of its own. She'd noticed, and they had both laughed. He was embarrassed for a moment. And then he wasn't embarrassed, he was kneeling up, holding her, kissing her.

'This isn't very professional,' she'd said. But laughing, her mouth opening as she laughed so that his tongue found her neat white teeth. But then that part of him that had a life of its own, that registered like a barometer each nuance of desire and non-desire even before it was conscious in his mind, losing energy now. But he'd tried to deny it, carried on, his hands on her body, on her breasts.

She sat up then, eased him away.

'No, Adam. Not now. You're not ready for this.'

Jane had been between them then. As she was always.

As she still is, he was thinking. Anna was getting up to go.

'I hope all goes well for you, Adam. Wish Dominic a happy birthday from me, won't you.'

'Can't you wish him it yourself? How can you miss the chance to see him sinking his chops into birthday cake!'

She looked at him, an expression on her face he couldn't quite read. Or didn't want to.

'Perhaps I should wait until after your wife has left. Perhaps you need some time together.'

That made him flinch. Hearing her call Jane 'his wife'. But she's right, he thought. *She is still my wife.*

Before she left, Adam took Anna into his studio, which was really only a lean-to at the back of the kitchen, and showed her the designs he was working on for Nick Pierce for the vicarage window. She studied them carefully. In one, a white lighthouse, perched high on rocks, flashing a yellow beacon. Around it, the sea a turbulent blue. Blocks of cobalt, ultramarine, white-foamed waves. Pitched at the top of a wave, a small fishing boat, heading towards the lighthouse. In the other, a dark-haired, bearded man, holding a small child in his arms. He was dressed simply: blue jeans, a red T-shirt. Behind the man and the child, yellow cornfields sloped to a cliff edge, and beyond that in the distance, the blue of the sea meeting the blue of the sky.

'Where's the mother?' Anna said.

'Thought I'd give fathers a look-in for a change. Instead of Madonna and Child a modern uptake on Joseph.'

'I don't think this man is called Joseph. I think his name is Adam instead.'

Now, tidying up, whizzing the hoover around, washing the mud brought in by the wheels of Dominic's wheelchair from the flagstone floor, he was thinking of Anna, and her strange, singsong Danish accent, her clear skin and those perfect white teeth he had known with his tongue. Thinking, *She could be mine; what stops me?* Thinking of Jane, the reason for her visit. Thinking of his son.

Dominic would be at school now. What was on the time-table this morning? Life skills? Counting apples into a bag in a supermarket. Cookery? Making pancakes or cheese on toast. He was thinking of these things and feeling – what was he feeling? A wave of sadness. Sorry for himself. That was something he wasn't used to feeling. That he wouldn't often allow himself to feel.

What age is Dominic coming to? he wondered. Closer to the age of being kicked out of school, a lifeline for both of us. When I get a chance to get down to some work, visit friends, get my life back for a few hours. When he gets a chance to bang a drum in music therapy, grow seedlings in greenhouses, salivate over teaching assistants in skimpy tops. What then, after nineteen, the throw-out age? Horticulture, cookery, pottery classes perhaps, on the *New Horizons* pro-gramme.

Adam knew about their courses, at the local college. The

false optimism of the tutors, the way they wove untruths into their assessments and progress reports. He taught there for two sessions a week, teaching pottery to Special Needs students, who hardly, sometimes, had the wherewithal to squeeze the clay in their hands, to manipulate the simplest of tools. *So-and-so is able to exercise his own choice about some elements of design, can work for short periods without supervision.* A distortion of the truth, that helped pay a few bills. *New Horizons! Who dreams up these names?* he thought. What new horizon will Dom have, when he's forty, wasting hours at a day centre somewhere, where girls in skimpy T-shirts won't find him cute any more?

And then, just for a moment, this feeling of dread came over him. He was on the homeward stretch to fifty, now.

Who will help me look after Dominic when I'm old?

13

He watched her walk up the garden path. Watched her pause under the elm, reach up to touch the mobile hanging there. Fish cut from slender strips of glass: flashes of turquoise and silver swinging amid the still leafless branches.

Prepared his face to greet her. Opened the door.

'Jane. It's good to see you. You're looking well.'

She looks tired, he thought. Something in her eyes he hadn't noticed before.

He moved towards her, his lips brushed her cheek.

'You look well too, Adam,' she said.

'Journey okay?'

'It was until I left the A30. I got lost a couple of times. You know what these Cornish lanes are like. A nightmare!'

She used to love them, he thought. The surprises they held, the secrets. Discovering a sudden cottage buried around a bend, a hamlet you'd hardly know was there.

She followed him in. They passed the door that led to Dominic's room, and went through to the open-plan sitting room, an archway from that leading into the long kitchen extension at the back. She stood there for a moment, looking slightly lost, confused. She thinks she's back there, he thought, wildly. Back in the cottage in Advent. Same thick oak beams overhead. Same flagstone floor. Same huge granite-stoned inglenook, wood-burning stove.

'Is your case in the car?' He felt a sudden urge to do something, to move away. 'Give me your car keys and I'll fetch it.'

Opening up the boot of the car, lifting her small case out, he was thinking, it's as if time had slipped backwards. *If the accident had never happened, where would we be? – where would Dominic be now? Going to university, leaving home?*

They talked together over a goat's cheese salad, like old friends, but not like old friends. Like acquaintances catching up.

'I've cut my time down at work. Only three days a week at the moment. I felt I needed a rest.'

He thought, should he ask her how she manages for money; was that his place still, to do that? But then he couldn't help her even if it was. He didn't have a regular wage coming in. Carer's allowance, Dom's disability benefits, the mobility allowance that paid for the lease on the car. The money from his teaching and the odd bit of cash when he sold a piece of work. A little bit of a nest egg left aside from his inheritance money when his mother died. It didn't add up to a fortune; but he managed, their needs were simple. But nothing left to spare. She must have read his mind.

'I can manage for a while. I had something put aside. Anyway, it's only temporary . . .'

They talked about ... what did they talk about? The kind of things you talk about when you are avoiding talking about what you really need to. The weather. What vegetables he was planning to plant in the garden this spring. Even her mother.

'I've started visiting my mother again. I didn't go, for a while.'

It was strange to hear her talk about her mother. The mother who hadn't been there throughout all the years of their marriage. Now here she was, back in her life. How did that happen, and when?

'How is she?'

'The same. She's always the same. She still doesn't know who I am!' She laughed, a quick and nervous laugh. 'I took her out for lunch last Saturday. To Cley next the Sea.'

'What did you do there?'

'Nothing much. We walked down a path near the windmill. Looked at the marshes.'

'The path there – it leads across the marshes to the shingle beach?'

'That's right.' She glanced at him, flushing slightly. 'Yes, of course. You've been there, haven't you?'

'You took me there soon after we met. You told me it was one of your favourite places. You used to walk on the marshes when you were a kid. You liked the open skies and the birds, you said.'

'Yes, I remember.' But she was looking away now, pretending to be interested in her food.

We had made love on that beach. It was September, the early evening. The beach was deserted. I took off my jacket and spread it down on the shingle. Your body had felt warm beneath mine, your lips had tasted of salt . . .

'We didn't stay long,' she said. 'It felt cold when the sun went in. We had a spot of lunch in the café and then I took her back.'

Afterwards, I picked up my jacket and slipped it over your shoulders. You were shivering, you were cold. We stayed the night at a guesthouse in Cromer, and I asked you to marry me in the dining room over beef casserole. You were so happy, your eyes were shiny with tears. Do you remember?

She was surprised to see the sea of glass in his studio. Panels of glass, long, dangerous strips, fragments in bowls. She picked up a piece of textured lavender, held it to the light. Flicked through the stack of designs.

'I did this workshop last year. Got hooked. Do little else these days. Although I still make my pots occasionally.'

She had never liked his gigantic, misshapen pots. Too crude for her, perhaps.

He showed her his two recent designs. The lighthouse, the bearded man with the child.

'The child in his arms. He reminds me of Dominic,' she said.

He wanted to touch her then, to hold her. But he didn't. He was too scared.

He'd promised Nick Pierce that he'd drive over that afternoon to show him the designs. Jane said she was tired, she needed a rest, she wouldn't come. He was disappointed; he'd wanted to show her off, to show her his friends.

Wanted to stay, working quietly in the studio, knowing she was upstairs, sleeping. Wanted to pretend that the past hadn't happened, that she was here to stay. Dominic, their son, was a young man who would be having a mad birthday celebration with his university mates, would get laid, get pissed. Throw up somewhere, wake up the next day feeling like shit. Wanted to stay, imagining what his wife looked like, sleeping upstairs. In the room he'd slaved on for hours, stripping tired paper off walls the night after she'd phoned.

Had she taken her clothes off? Got properly into bed, under the covers, pulled the sheet half over her face the way she used to? Was she lying on her back, on her side? She used to sleep stretched out on her stomach, one knee tucked up towards her chest, he remembered. He would complain she had dug him in the back in the night, in the kidneys. How could he have minded? When he would do anything to have what had happened, not happen. To undo the past. To have her back in his bed again.

The first time Adam had met Nick Pierce was at Dominic's school, at an end-of-term assembly. Nick had been new to Cornwall then, new to the parish. Had only weeks before exchanged the urban jungle of Liverpool for the laments of fishing folk and small hoteliers. It had been that time when the headmistress had made Adam stand up while everyone applauded him for the mural he'd done for the hall. Nick had come up to him afterwards, while he'd been helping Dominic on with his jacket

'Nick Pierce,' he'd said, holding out a firm hand for Adam to shake.

'Adam Reynolds. This is Dominic, my son.'

'Glad to meet you, Dominic.' He'd shaken his hand too.

'I like your mural very much, Adam.'

'Does the trick.'

'Why don't you come to tea sometime, at the vicarage? Bring Dominic too. He'd enjoy my wife's chocolate cake.'

He'd given Adam his card, with his name and address on it. *Reverend N. Pierce* in small gold lettering.

'I'm not much of a church-goer, Reverend,' Adam had said, stumbling over his words, feeling awkward.

'What's that got to do with the price of bread! Give us a chance, Adam. We don't bite. And the name's Nick, by the way.'

Adam had laughed then, accepted the card, slipped it into the pocket of his jeans.

'Thanks.'

'Any time. You're always welcome. Good name, Dominic, by the way. Adam's not bad either!'

'I hear he didn't fare too well in the Bible.'

Nick laughed. 'He had a lot on his plate!'

He pulled up outside the church. An ancient church, going way back to the fourteenth century. A Celtic cross, carved into the granite above the heavy oak door, grinning gargoyles to ward off sin. A church that belonged to the crossover time, when churches were built on the pagans' sacred land. If he'd been a church-goer, Adam would think, it would help if it was a church like this.

'You've got a medieval mind,' Jane had said to him once. She'd been studying something in her art-therapy course.

'What does *that* mean?'

'You believe in absolutes. Dualities. The body and soul, good and evil, heaven and hell.'

'And you?'

'Post-modernist. I don't believe in absolutes. Everything is relative.'

'That'll let you get away with murder,' he'd joked. Her eyes widened then, as if she'd seen something she hadn't wanted to see.

He pushed open the oak-barred gate and followed the path through the gravestones to the rectory at the back of the church. Raised the brass knocker, let it fall on the heavy door. Nick opened it, standing there in jogging bottoms and a sweatshirt, not quite looking like a vicar is supposed to.

'Adam. Good to see you! You didn't bring Jane, then?'

'She was tired, she needed a rest.'

He stepped into the warmth of the hallway. A smell of baking from the kitchen beyond. Jenny popped her head around the door.

'Hi, Adam. How's Dominic?'

'He's fine. We're both fine.'

'You'll stay for a cup of tea before you leave, won't you? I've got a batch of cheese scones in the oven nearly ready.'

'That'll be great, Jenny. I'd love to.'

Nick showed him into the library-cum-study. The room where he received parishioners, offered spiritual counselling.

Stitched up souls, or tried to. The room the stained-glass window would be for, to replace the one that looked out rather dismally to the back porch area.

'People need something beautiful to look at when they're hurting,' Nick had said.

He was sweeping an array of files from his desk. Adam unzipped the portfolio, took the designs out and spread them out. Nick slipped on his reading glasses to study them.

'The lighthouse is beautiful,' he said. 'The parishioners will like that one. They'll relate to that.'

Most of the congregation were connected to the sea. Generations of lifeboatmen, trawlermen and their families. Many of them, particularly the older ones, whose memories went further back, could relate a story if pressed to about some family member lost at sea.

'I thought you might think it was clichéd,' Adam said.

'That's all right. Nothing wrong with clichés. They state the obvious, but it's still the truth. But tell me about the other one – why just the father and child? Why not the mother as well?'

'I wanted to redress the balance. What about poor Joseph. He did a great job too, bringing that kid up. Especially as it wasn't his!'

Nick laughed.

'Trouble is, people here are very traditional. I may want to bring in the modern world, but they still want it in a familiar form. We need a woman, Adam.'

'Don't we all!'

'Yes, but don't tell my wife.'

Adam loved this man: his warmth, his big-heartedness,

the way he never judged. He had told Adam once that he used to run soup kitchens and homeless shelters in the back streets of Toxteth. Some of the druggies and the down-and-outs had become regular attenders at the church, in the end.

Jenny was knocking on the door, easing it open, coming in with the tray of tea and scones. Nick showed her the designs, and she agreed, Yes, the lighthouse is lovely, that'll do just fine. 'Not sure about the other one,' she'd said, and, 'Why does the man look like you?' and Nick laughed and said, 'Thought I'd seen him somewhere before! I thought you said his name was Joseph,' and they all laughed and Adam thought, *I wish Jane was here. Meeting my friends, seeing what a good life I'm making now.*

'I need to go,' he said, eventually, gathering up the designs, zipping them into his portfolio again. 'Jane's only just arrived, shouldn't leave her on her own too long.'

Nick looked at him then, they both did, in this knowing way, this concerned way. Adam had never talked much about Jane, and they'd never asked, never probed, but they both knew, as Anna knew, that there was something here that was broken and needed mending. Something that he wasn't free of yet.

14

Adam watched her. Watched the way she greeted Dominic when he came home from school, holding her hand out tentatively to shake his. Dominic had ignored it, had reached up his arms to her, so that she was forced to stoop down to his level, to let him plant a wet kiss on her cheek. Watched the way her hand had gone up afterwards, instinctively, to wipe the kiss from her cheek.

'Hello, Mummy. Missed you, Mummy.'

'I've missed you too, Dominic.'

Watched her watching Dominic eating his tea, eating from the special bowl with the curved sides, using the spoon with the moulded handle, to aid his grip. The beans dribbled messily down his chin, splattered down the front of his T-shirt.

'Making mess! Sorry, Daddy!'

'It's all right, son.'

Jane was leaving the room, she had something to do, she said.

He had bought two Dover soles fresh from the fishmonger in Padstow. The fish were expensive, more then he could normally afford. They sat down to eat together later while Dominic was in the sitting room, laughing at *The Simpsons* on the telly.

'Well, what do you think?' he said.

'What do you mean?'

'Dom. You must see the changes in him.'

Had he made it sound like an accusation?

'I'm not sure what you want me to say, Adam. I wouldn't necessarily say he's *changed*.'

'He's getting on well. They're very pleased with him at school.'

She looked at him. There was pain in her eyes. He thought, *She doesn't want to talk about him; she wants to talk about something else.*

'Small steps, Jane. That's what matters now.'

'Small steps, no steps.' She said it softly, as if she didn't want him to hear. He heard. There was a tightness in his head.

'What does that mean?'

'Nothing. It means nothing. It's just that I can't see any changes.'

'His motor skills have improved in the last two years. His hand-and-eye coordination is better. He can put pegs through holes, thread cotton reels on string, colour in shapes . . .'

'He could do that at two,' she said. Her voice was quiet. He carried on, as if he was reading from a list. He had a hot buzz of sensation in his head. He went on because she didn't want him to.

'Language skills. Knows the difference between a noun

and a verb. Understands past and present tense. Is articulating better word endings now ...'

'Stop it, Adam.'

'Written skills: Knows most consonants and vowels. Recognizes many words in context – food labels in shops, signs, that sort of thing. Can write short simple sentences. Noun, verb, object. Copies accurately under the teacher's writing ...'

She had put her hands up over her ears. She had tears in her eyes. He stopped now. He felt like a heel. *Why am I doing this?*

'Sorry, I didn't mean ...'

But she was getting up, pushing her chair back noisily from the table, leaving the room again ...

Later, when he'd cleared the table and done the washing up, he got Dominic out of his chair and into his standing frame. He did this for an hour every evening; the physio at school had said it was essential for maintaining what leg strength Dominic possessed, would stop the muscles from wasting further, the bones and ligaments from weakening.

'The human body,' she said, 'works better when it stands upright. We've got to get him out of that chair and on his feet every night.'

'Don't worry. I'll have him running the marathon soon,' Adam had joked.

Dominic was happiest on his feet. He had a better view from up there, could take more in. Adam placed some paper on his tray, gave him his specially adapted pen to hold.

'What do you want to do tonight, son? Draw something? Write?'

Dominic wrote the word 'Mummy' in a jerky, stabbing hand.

'Yeah. That's right, son, your mummy's here.' Where was she? Upstairs, lying down. Hating him.

'Where's Mummy gone?'

'She's having a rest, Dom. She'll be down soon.'

He started writing again. His own name, and *Daddy* and *Anna* and *Emily*.

'Who's Emily, mate?'

'New girl at school. She's very pretty.'

The boy was blushing, grinning, waving the pen around at the thought of Emily. He's got a crush on her, Adam thought. He was used to Dominic's crushes. They came and went. His first crush had been at the age of thirteen. Miss Bryce. She had been a new young teacher at the special school he'd been at back in the old days, the old life back in Hertfordshire. Miss Bryce had been very pretty; blonde, with a smile like an angel. If Adam had been younger he would have fancied her himself. Then there had been Jodie, a classroom assistant; Megan, a student physiotherapist; Polly, a speech therapist; Mary, another teacher ... And then, Anna, two years ago, when they'd first moved down here. His crush on Anna hadn't quite faded; it was still there. All of them blonde. All of them pretty, more than pretty. Stunning. He has good taste, Adam thought. But this was the first time he had heard Dominic hint at fancying one of his peers.

Is this a good sign? Dominic growing up? Getting a grasp of what is more probable. Finding his own level.

He suddenly felt a flood of tenderness towards his son. Standing erect now, in the standing frame, he looked the same height as his father, but Adam knew that when it came to body length he had inches on him.

Aren't sons supposed to end up a little taller than their old man? he thought. Each generation, a little taller, a little stronger, more equipped for survival. He wouldn't grow much more now, he'd never catch up. He wondered what height Dominic would have ended up if the accident had never happened, but stopped himself. That was a road he wouldn't go down. It *had* happened, and that was that. That was Dominic's lot now; that was his.

Anna called it 'karma'.

'So it's a kind of heavenly retribution, punishment. For doing bad things in a former life.'

'No, Adam, it's not like that. Don't get so attached to this idea of punishment.'

'What then?'

'It's more like addressing an imbalance. When one side of the scales is tipped further up than the other, you put something back to make them more balanced. You choose what lessons you need to learn, to put back what is missing. You make the choice yourself.'

'So Dominic chose to be a kid who would end up in a wheelchair, disabled, dependent on others?'

'Perhaps.'

'And I chose to be someone who would have a kid like

that, to be someone who would take care of a disabled child . . . ?'

'Perhaps. There is a karmic destiny between your two souls. Something is being fulfilled in your relationship, I think.'

'Not sure about all this, Anna. Sounds like a convenient panacea, a lot of mumbo-jumbo if you ask me!'

Anna had shrugged, smiled. She didn't need to convince him. She had the confidence of her own beliefs.

What about Jane? he'd wondered. *What lessons was she here to learn?*

Later Adam gave Dominic his bath, settled him into bed, read him his bedtime story. He didn't want Harry Potter tonight. Tonight he was feeling needy; his mum being here had unsettled him. The *Three Billy Goats Gruff*, he wanted. Every so often he asked for that, the same story he used to want read, over and over, when he was small. Adam did the noises for him, the *clip clop* over the bridge; Dominic put on his gruffest voice for the troll.

'Goodnight, mate,' he said, kissing his grown-man-little-boy son on his bum-fluffed cheek. Reaching over to turn the nightlight on.

'Goodnight, Daddy. Love you.'

'Love you too, mate. Lots.'

'Where's Mummy? Want to say goodnight to Mummy too.'

He found Jane in the sitting room, reading her book, or trying to.

She looked up at him. 'Sorry.'

'No, I'm sorry. I shouldn't have gone on like that . . .'

'I don't blame you.'

What's happened? he thought. *She's changed.*

He was thinking of the old Jane. The Jane who would never have apologized, no matter how much she was in the wrong.

'Is Dominic in bed?'

'Yes. He asked for you. He wants to say goodnight to you.'

She put her book down and got up, to go into Dominic's room.

Adam busied himself lighting a fire in the wood-burning stove. The evenings were still cold at this time of the year. When the fire was alight and on its way, he threw on a couple of logs from the apple tree he'd chopped down in the autumn. It had been diseased, rotten at its core. It had produced no fruit for years. The logs crackled in the flames, spat noisily. The wood not quite seasoned yet.

What's keeping her, he wondered. Was Dominic making her read the *Billy Goats* again? Was she thinking, *What progress?*

She came back. Sat again in the chair she'd been sitting in before, picked up her book again.

'You were a while.'

'I was talking to Dominic. About his school. He was telling me about his friends.'

'That's nice. Thought I'd light the fire. Nothing like a proper fire.'

'Yes,' she said. She glanced up briefly, then down at her

book again. He didn't want to say any more; he didn't want to disturb her mood, her thoughts, which he felt were sombre, private, needed space. He picked up a sketch pad from the low table near his chair, a stump of a pencil. He began to draw her. It was easy. He could place the downward curve of her mouth, the angle of her nose, the shadowed depths of her eyes. She was trying not to notice that he was drawing her, trying not to care. But after a while she looked up from her book.

'Well, show me, then.'

He held the sketch pad up towards her.

'Do I look as sad as that?'

And then he said it. He didn't know why he said it. Something made him.

'Why are you here, Jane?'

This startled look on her face again.

'You know why. Dominic's birthday.'

'You missed his last one, and the one before that . . .'

'This is his eighteenth, this one's important . . .'

'They're all important, Jane.'

He was thinking, suddenly, of the day his son was born. How hard his wife had worked, pushing him out into the world, how much it had hurt her. He was thinking of the way she had looked when they placed the baby in her arms. The baby's face screwed up, beetroot red, waxy still with sebum, stained with blood . . . he was thinking of that look of sheer joy on her face, as if the pain of the birth had been erased in an instant, as if a light had been lit inside her.

She was silent now. A coolness between them. Then:

'You're judging me, Adam. Don't judge me.'

'Do you love him? Dominic?'

He didn't know why he was saying this either. Something was making him. He wondered why he'd never asked her that before.

'For Christ's sake, Adam!'

'*Do* you?'

She had loved him then, he was thinking. From that moment, from even before that moment. When Dominic was just a thought, a promise, curled up in her belly. He was remembering how she had came rushing out of the bathroom that day to show him the pale blue line on the pregnancy testing kit. He'd had to screw up his eyes to see it, and yet it had come to mean so much. It had changed everything.

'Of course I love him. He's my son.'

'Yes, Jane. He's your son.' A coolness in his voice. Then: 'Do you still love me?'

He didn't know what was happening. It was like something had climbed inside his solar plexus. That place that Anna calls the *hara*. That was a kind of knowing, the mind and body acting as one. It was urging him on, making him say, these days, all the things he'd wanted to say before but had never dared to.

She was glaring back at him now.

'I don't know. Okay. Is that what you want to hear? Do you still love me?'

'Yes,' he said. He said it quickly, he had no doubt. He had always loved her. Even when he hated her, he had loved her.

'You can't do, Adam. You can't really love me. You've

never really known me, not the *real* me. You wouldn't love me if you really knew what I was like.'

She had this strangeness in her voice and in her eyes.

'Tell me then, Jane. Tell me what you're really like.'

There was something between them now that he felt had never been there before. Something tangible and real. A change of energy, a connection. *Anna and her energies. They're all around us*, she would tell him.

But then in an instant it was gone again. As if what had been there had been severed. He couldn't read her mood, her feeling; it was like a door had been shut in his face. She stood up.

'I can't do this Adam. I'm tired. I'm going to bed.'

15

Adam sat up for a long time, staring into the dying flames of the fire.

He was remembering the time they met. At teacher training college, during his postgraduate year. He'd seen her around a number of times, walking purposefully across the campus, textbooks tucked under her arms. But he'd never had cause to get to know her. He was training for secondary art, she was primary; they were always in different classes. He had imagined she must be like the other primary student teachers he knew. All of them women, maternal and mumsy. Up to their neck all the time in bits of paper and card and scissors, making things for the kids.

But he fancied her all the same. Some of his mates at college would joss him about her. 'Best keep off that one, Adam old son,' they'd say. 'Unapproachable. Probably frigid.' Apparently one or two of them had asked her out and she had refused them.

He'd seen her in the bar one evening. It was towards the end of the Christmas term. Everyone was in high spirits, getting in the festive mood, which meant pissed. He'd been standing with a group of cronies, pints in their hands, laughing at somebody's stupid joke, and she had eased past him to get to the bar. She was wearing a low-cut little black dress, high heels, seams at the back of her stockings. They were all the rage, back then. She didn't look mumsy at all.

'Excuse me,' she said, but he stepped back against her, pretending he hadn't noticed she was there. His beer sloshed over the top of the glass, spilled down her chest.

'I'm sorry!' he said, but laughing.

The spilt beer shone wetly up at him from her cleavage, spots of it drying on the low-cut front of her dress.

'Would you like me to wash it off for you?'

She cast him a look of disdain, but he felt that underneath the pretence she wanted to smile.

The next day he almost collided with her in one of the corridors. She was walking from the direction of the library, more books under her arms.

He was chastised now, sober.

'I'm sorry about last night. I was a bit plastered. I'm sorry I spilt that beer down your dress. I hope I haven't ruined it.'

She'd pretended to still be annoyed with him, but he could see that really she wasn't. It had washed out, she said. Don't worry.

And then he'd asked her out. At first she said no, and then the next time he saw her he asked her again, and she'd surprised him by saying yes. Within weeks they were an item. She wasn't mumsy at all, or frigid. She was a goer, she was hot. She was everything he wanted. She had this quality about her that he found alluring, mysterious. This quiet smile, this enigmatic way of looking at him. Eyes that had air and space in them, something he couldn't pin down. They would spend the weekends lying in bed for hours, catching late-night art films at the cinema, walking on the Downs. She loved it out there, she said. She loved watching the gliders, the paragliders. She always seemed to be looking up there in the sky, as if waiting for something to fall upon her head.

'You're like Chicken Licken,' he told her once.

In bed, in those early weeks of getting to know each other, doing all those late-night things that couples do when they're falling in love – the late-night all-night pillow talks after sex – he would spill out everything to her. He told her about his mother, who would interrogate him too much about his girlfriends, say embarrassing things about him when the girls came around. He told her about his father, who drank too much at parties and was once caught outside in the bushes snogging his mother's best friend.

He told her about the first girl he ever fancied, Pamela, who wore braces and had kissed him behind the bike shed and put her tongue in his mouth. He told her about the first girl he ever shagged, at somebody's party – he couldn't even remember whose, he couldn't even remember the girl's name – he felt a bit ashamed about that. She'd said it didn't matter; it was in the past, long before he'd known her. 'We all do things we feel ashamed of,' she said.

He told her, after all this, when he felt it was safe enough to tell her, about his kid sister who had died of meningitis when she was two and he was seven. She had held him then, as if he was that boy he'd been at seven; he'd been comforted by that. And then, after he'd spilt out his life to her, lying in her arms, with her head nudged up beneath his chin against his chest, he'd expected her to spill out hers. He'd expected an exchange of secrets. He'd expected to be the one who would comfort her now. There must be something, he'd thought. A fumble somewhere back in the past by some unwholesome uncle, an experiment with hallucinogenics that went wrong. An abortion, even, that she'd never told anyone else about, but now would tell him.

'Nothing very much has happened to me,' she said. 'Except when I was thirteen, my brother and my father died in a car accident. That's when I went to live with my uncle and aunt in Stafford. Since then my life's been ordinary, quite boring I expect.'

'What about your mother?' he'd asked. 'Is she still alive?'

'Yes. She lives in Cambridgeshire, where I lived when I was a child. She was very upset when my brother and my father died. She couldn't cope with it all. I didn't see her for years. I don't really see her or speak to her now.'

He'd felt her slipping away from him. Lying there in his arms and yet not being there at all. He'd thought – How traumatic that must have been for her, her father and brother dying in a car accident when she was young! He shouldn't probe. Should leave it alone, undisturbed.

She'll tell me, when she's ready.

Sitting there now, watching the embers glowing orange, then fading.

He'd been wrong about that. She'd never been ready.

Never opened up, not really; she had always kept herself apart. Lying in his arms, yet not being there at all.

But in those early months, early years even, they were in love; the intensity of his feelings filled up the cracks. They had lots of sex to cement the bond. Then when the passion started to ease off, the intensity to die down, find a more normal, everyday level, they had been busy getting their young lives together. Getting their first teaching jobs, finding a flat to rent and moving in together, surviving the stress and the pace and the pressure of coping with the kids at school and their probationary years.

Then they got married; that's what people did back then. Not so much these days, Adam thought. But back then in the seventies, that's what people did. They met when they were young, fell in love, lived together perhaps for a little while, but not too long. Then after a decent interval they got married.

There hadn't been much fuss at the wedding. He had few relatives. Just his parents, a few spare uncles and aunts, a couple of cousins. She had even fewer. Only her Aunt Jean and Uncle Bill from Stafford.

'Don't you want to ask your mother?' he'd asked. He had been thinking, *Now's the time to make up. A new beginning.* A chance to put any grievances behind her, to heal the rift.

'She won't want to come,' Jane had said.

'Of course she will,' he protested. Not understanding why her mother wouldn't, not really understanding any of this at all. His mother had suffered a tragedy too; she'd lost a baby daughter. It had only made her cling to him more.

He urged her several times: Jane, write to your mother. Tell her you're getting married. Whatever happened, it's in the past, forgive her.

Until in the end she turned on him, impatient, angry.

'Leave it, Adam. You don't understand.'

So he had left it. At the registry office, standing outside in the garden at the back having photographs taken, the only people who were connected with Jane were her aunt and uncle, and several girlfriends she had made at college. He thought it was sad; maybe deep down he thought she'd been cruel, too hard on her mother. But he never mentioned it again.

Not until Dominic was born, when the whole thing raised its ugly head briefly again.

'Shouldn't we let her know, at least? She's our son's grandmother. Isn't she entitled to know?'

'My aunt would have told her.'

'Yeah, but it'll sound much better coming from you.'

She'd turned a closed face away from him then, refused to talk about it. And by then her mother had been absent from their lives for so long it seemed more dangerous to question the status quo, to change things, to invite this woman in. He would console himself with the thought that maybe she was a bad person, would be a bad influence on his son – she must be bad, he'd thought, for Jane to feel the way she did.

He would tell everyone about his son. Friends, acquaintances. Even complete strangers too, if he had a chance.

He's six months now; he's cutting his first tooth.

He's nine months; he's starting to crawl.

He's just turned a year; he can walk, says a few words, he calls me 'Daddy'.

But sometimes he would catch himself feeling sad. *Dominic doesn't know his own granny. She doesn't know him.*

It seemed such a waste, he thought. *Can you miss people you don't know? People you've never even met?*

The room was growing cold now; the embers of the fire had dulled and cooled.

I should go to bed. Big day tomorrow, Dominic's birthday.

But he was remembering something else, something was bothering him. He was trying to sort it out in his head.

16

It was thinking about missing people that was bringing it back.

All through their marriage they had lived with missing people. Jane's mother, who was alive but in a sense, dead. Her father and brother, who had died way back in her distant past, in her teens. Of course, that was different; he couldn't blame her for that. But, yet it was as if they were all still there. Ghostly presences on the periphery of their lives, affecting them both in silent and insidious ways.

He had to learn not to mention Jane's mother. It would upset her. He had to learn never to mention the father or the brother who had died. It would drag her back to the trauma. He had to learn to collude in this alternative universe that they lived in, one where her mother, her father, her brother did not exist – had never existed. Yet all the time screening out the fact that they were there. Haunting their lives.

In his efforts to spare her feelings, to fill in the cracks, had he made himself not see that she herself hadn't been there in a sense? Created the Jane he'd wanted, made her up. What was that she'd said? *But you don't know me, Adam. Not the real me.*

Missing persons.

He was remembering when Jane had gone missing for real. Not for long, only a few days. But still, it had affected him, it had changed things.

When had that been? That winter, just weeks after her aunt had died.

Only months after Dominic had come home for good, following weeks of hospital care. 'Progress is still possible. But small steps, small steps are what matter now,' the consultant had said.

Memories of the son that had been, heavy now on his heart.

Dominic had shown a flair, a gift even, for sport, for football. Made a neat little centre forward, had a lot of speed, a lot of edge. He'd been the star of his school team at the primary school, and then later, about the age of eight, made it into a local junior side. During the season Adam would take him to the Common on Sunday mornings to watch him play. He could conjure him up like a genie into the room with him, even now. Dancing like a bird on that ball, his hair plastered close to his head in the usual fine mist of rain . . .

He shook the memories out of his head. It was the present he lived in now. *Come back . . .*

When Dominic came back to them, after the spell of rehabilitation, where they'd fitted him up with the special wheelchair, the leg braces, the standing frame, fine-tuned his remedial care programme to pass it on to his parents, Adam had given up his teaching job to care for him.

It hadn't even been something they'd discussed – who would be the one who would do this. It had been assumed, right from those early days, that these would be their new roles: Jane would carry on working; he would give up his job. Why was that? Perhaps because of the way she had shrunk from Dominic. Made excuses not to touch him, not to attend to his personal care. Always his job to do that. Sometimes he even thought she tried not to look at him, not to see him. How many times would she walk away, leave the room, find excuses about things she had to do? He'd made himself not notice too much at the time. Would tell himself he was being paranoid, imagining it. And anyway, hadn't his own pain numbed him to what was real, what was unreal? Whatever, they never talked about it. It was something they just fell into: Jane would be the main breadwinner. His role, to care for their son.

They hadn't had concerns about money; at least that had been easy for them. His mother had died the year before, having survived her husband, and as he was the only child – the baby sister long dead in her infancy from meningitis – he inherited what there was of his parents' estate. They'd paid off their mortgage with it, and there had been enough money left over for him to buy the cottage in Cornwall later, enough for Jane to take a year out of work, to do the art therapy course. He even had a small nest egg left, put aside for emergencies, although it was dwindling to little these days.

*

When her aunt died she'd taken it badly. He knew her aunt was very important to her, a surrogate mother. He tried to be there for her, but she didn't seem to want that. And perhaps he didn't try hard enough. He'd been immersed in his own loss, in his new role. Learning to love his son in a different way to the son he had loved before.

She'd gone off alone to the funeral, came back with the same shuttered face. She didn't want to talk about it, she'd said, and so he left her alone. Wasn't that what he had learnt for years – not to talk about the things that upset her? *She's grieving*, he thought. *She needs space.*

That Sunday he had taken Dominic to watch the football on the Common. It was a damp morning, threatening rain. They nearly didn't go, but Dominic had persuaded him. He loved going to watch the game, still loved football, even though he couldn't play. Adam would wonder, sometimes, if his son remembered – not in his mind so much, but in his body – how he'd once been on that football pitch. If he would be sitting there in his wheelchair, waterproofed in his plastic rain cape from head to foot, and be seeing himself as he used to be, his old self, his other self, out there with the other lads, tearing up the pitch, dancing on that ball again.

So he couldn't refuse him this. We all need the opportunity to dream, he'd thought, even if our dreams relate more to what we used to be.

When they got home Jane wasn't there. It was like coming home to the *Marie Celeste*. A shoulder of lamb for their Sunday roast was wrapped in foil on the draining board. He'd peeled back the foil; it was drizzled with olive oil, sprinkled with rosemary, cloves of garlic spiked in the joint under the fat. On the hob, a large saucepan of vegetables, peeled and chopped, sitting in water.

He changed Dominic's jeans, which were damp around the hem, and changed into some warm, dry clothes himself. He turned on the oven and slid the meat joint in on its roasting tray when it was hot enough. Twenty minutes before the roast was done he put the vegetables on to simmer. All the time, looking at the clock, keeping an eye on the clock, thinking, *Where the hell is she, where the hell has she gone?*

He sat there with Dominic eating his dinner, trying hard to quell this feeling of unease that she had gone for good, that she was never coming back. This suspicion that was taking shape in his mind, that everything had become too much for her, was piling on her head, and something had snapped. She had left him, would never come back. He would have to live his life alone now, being a single dad to a handicapped kid. He was trying to work out how much he would miss her.

'Where's Mummy? Mummy dinner gone cold.'

'Don't worry, son. She'll be back soon.'

Will she? Will she come back again?

While Dominic was having his afternoon nap he went to see Bob next door. They had a special bond, Bob and Jane. It didn't bother him, make him jealous. If anything he welcomed it, he knew it did her good. If she'd told anyone that she was leaving him, she'd have told Bob.

Bob answered the door with sleep still in his eyes. He'd been on the night shift, hadn't long been up.

'I'm sorry, mate, sorry to bother you.'

But Bob had noticed, immediately, the look on his face. 'What's wrong, Adam? Is it Jane?'

He told him about the empty house. The dinner prepared and ready. The fact that she hadn't said anything, had left no note.

'It's probably nothing. She'll probably be back in a minute, with some excuse. I was just wondering if she'd said anything to you about where she was going?'

'No, nothing. Adam, I think you should phone the police.'

'Christ, it's a bit early to involve them! I thought I'd leave it till this evening, then if she still isn't back . . .'

'No, Adam. Phone the police. Do it now.'

It was several hours before they arrived. He took them into the kitchen so Dominic wouldn't overhear. They didn't seem to feel Bob's sense of urgency. They asked questions – *Full name. Date of birth. Place of work.* As if they'd heard this all before. A wife suddenly disappearing, the worried husband. What do they think? he wondered. That she's left me? There's been some bloke flipping around on the edge of her life for months, urging her to leave. She'll turn up happily installed with him in some love-nest, appalled, outraged, that I've bothered to report her as missing.

'What state of mind was your wife in when you last saw her?' one of them asked.

State of mind? When had he last noticed Jane's state of mind? He told them that she'd been in bed when he left the house with Dominic. She liked a lie-in on Sundays – she was a teacher, a primary-school teacher; she worked hard all week. As if he was trying to excuse her. He'd brought her up a cup of tea and the Sunday papers. She'd supported herself on her elbow, puffed out a pillow, took the mug from his hand. A flecked cobalt-blue studio mug they had bought two summers ago from a pottery near St Isaac's. The year before Dominic's accident, when Cornwall was still a happy place for them. The rings of the wheel-turning were visible on its surface, like ripples in water. She'd sipped her tea and he'd looked out of the window. He said, 'It looks like it's going to rain.' She said, 'Don't let Dominic get too wet.'

'Is that all?' the older of the two policemen asked. He had grey, curly hair, pale blue eyes like a Cornishman. Adam felt a stab of guilt. As if between the words he was being accused of neglecting his wife.

'Have there been any recent events that could have had an adverse effect on your wife's state of mind?'

He told them how Jane had taken her aunt's death badly. 'Although I thought she seemed to perk up a bit, seemed more her old self, these last few days.'

'Any other relatives?'

'Her uncle. He lives up in Stafford.'

'That's all?'

'Her mother's still alive. But my wife doesn't speak to her. Has hardly seen her since her teens. She was brought up since then by the aunt who died.'

'I see.'

What did he see? There seemed to be a thread of something now, between the three of them. Words not said, not being asked. The other policeman, the younger one, broke the spell.

'Do you have any reason to fear that your wife may intend to harm herself, sir?'

'What are you implying, officer? That my wife might be *suicidal*?'

'We have to consider it as a possibility, sir.'

That had knocked him back a bit, taken the wind out of his sails. He was shocked that he hadn't even thought of it. That before the police had come round, with their questions and their notebooks, he only had visions of some other bloke. Jane in a love-nest with someone else. Having had enough of him and Dominic. Leaving them to get by on their own.

'I don't know.' He was telling the truth.

Later that evening the constable with the Cornish-blue eyes phoned.

'We've been in touch with the uncle in Stafford. He said he hasn't heard from your wife. He's no idea where she might be.'

He already knew that. He'd phoned Bill himself, to warn him. Bill had sounded alarmed, but reassuring as well.

'Don't worry, Adam. She'll come back. She just needs some space. She's upset about her aunt's death. We both are.'

There had been tears in Bill's voice, talking about it. He was missing his wife, he was lonely. At least he wasn't thinking what everyone else was: *Do you have any reason to think she might harm herself?* At least Bill hadn't said that.

'We've traced the mother too. She said she hasn't seen her daughter since her sister's funeral in January.'

That surprised him, hearing that. Jane hadn't told him she'd seen her mother there. He felt a flash of anger that she hadn't confided in him.

'We'll be in touch, Mr Reynolds, if we've any more information on your wife's whereabouts. Let us know, of course, if you hear from her.'

When he'd replaced the receiver, he had a sudden impulse to phone Bill. 'Why didn't you tell me that Jane's mother was at the funeral?' he wanted to ask. Then he thought better of it. Leave him alone. He's an old man, a widower; this is a hard time for him. *Of course* Jane's mother would have been there. She was Jean's sister, after all. Perhaps Jane avoided her. Perhaps they didn't speak . . . perhaps there was nothing there to tell.

The following day he had phoned the school where Jane worked.

'She won't be in today, she's sick,' he said. 'She's come down with a sudden bout of flu.'

They were sympathetic, of course.

'Give her our love. Tell her we hope she's feeling better soon.'

What will I tell them later? If her body's found? In a seedy bed and breakfast, from an overdose. Slumped over the wheel of a car in some woods somewhere, carbon monoxide fed from the exhaust. What will I say to Dominic?

That evening, Dominic asked repeatedly, like a record that had got stuck: 'When Mummy coming home, Daddy?'

'Soon, son. She'll be home soon. She's just having a few days' break.'

For days he went through the motions. He would drop Dominic off at school, then come home and sit slumped in an armchair. He'd think about the laundry that was piling up, the ironing that needed doing, the sheets on Dominic's bed that needed changing again because of another accident he'd had in bed. He could hardly bring himself to get out of the chair.

And then, on the Wednesday, three days later, she suddenly came back again.

He'd picked Dominic up from school that day and taken him to Safeways. It would be beans on toast for a second day running if he didn't. So he had to, he made himself, and when they got home, there was Jane's red Peugeot sitting there on the drive. He drew up alongside it and got out to unload Dominic's chair from the boot. Bob came out from his porch next door and they looked at each other in the still, dim February light, and Adam thought, *He's so relieved, he's as relieved as I am.*

'She's back, Adam,' Bob said, his voice almost a whisper. 'She's in there,' and he gestured with his head, with those relieved, grateful eyes towards the house. As if the car standing there as bold as brass wasn't proof enough.

'Okay, mate,' Adam said. His voice was cool, steely. His heart was racing, but he wasn't giving anything away. It wasn't as easy for him. He was relieved, but angry. Of course he was; wasn't he entitled to be? He was opening the car door, putting one arm around Dominic's shoulder, the other under the boy's knees, to slide him out from the car seat and into the open wheelchair.

'I'll leave you to it, then,' Bob said, understanding now that it wasn't as easy. That Adam's relief was necessarily mixed with anger. That there were things between the two of them, between a man and a wife, that were scarred and damaged by an event like this, that needed sorting out.

Dominic had seen the car too.

'Mummy's back!' he shouted. 'Mummy's home!'

Adam wheeled him up the path that led along the side of the house to the kitchen door, to avoid the step at the porch. She was there in the kitchen. She was standing at the sink, a knife in her hand.

'Mummy! You come home, Mummy!' Dominic cried out. He stretched his arm out towards her but she ignored him. She glanced quickly towards them, and then away. Adam caught the fear in her eyes.

'I'm making spaghetti bolognese for your tea, Dominic. That's still your favourite, isn't it?'

It used to be, Adam was thinking. When he could wind it up quickly around his fork and shuffle it in, like a normal kid. When he didn't have to have it chopped up finely for him so he could load it on his spoon. She didn't like to see the mess he got in with it, the red sauce dribbling constantly down his chin.

'Where have you been?'

His voice was as cold as ice. Inside he was thinking,

She's here, she's alive. I should be grateful. But he wasn't. He was more angry than he'd ever been. She didn't answer at first. She moved the blade of the knife down, tried to chop up an onion.

'Ouch!'

She put her finger up to her mouth and sucked it.

'Have you any idea how worried I've been? Have you any bloody idea? Where the fuck have you been?'

'Don't use that language in front of Dominic.'

'Don't use him as an excuse. Don't do that. Since when have you cared about *him*!' he shouted. He moved towards her. He felt like hitting her.

'Where have you fucking been, Jane?'

But he stopped then, he made himself stop. A low grating noise, building now, loud enough to cut through the wall of his anger. The sound of Dominic grinding his teeth that he'd come to dread. He looked at his son. The boy's head was moving in tight circles, the shoulders moving too, and his eyes turned upwards, so that the greeny-brown irises were lost almost in his head.

And so Dominic's fit had deflected them, had deflected his anger. Had given him something immediate to focus on. It hadn't been a bad fit; he'd had much worse ones in the past, before the new trial of drugs the doctor had put him on. When it was over, and his body had relaxed again, and he'd been put to bed, lost in that deep sleep that often followed, as if this thing that had seized him had suddenly sucked him dry of energy, it was too late to bring back the anger, to ask questions and demand righteously that they were answered. Jane was in the living room, pretending to watch some magazine programme, when he came back downstairs.

'How's Dominic?' she asked. But without looking at him. Without taking her eyes from the television.

'He's fine. He's sleeping.'

'Good.'

He sat down on the sofa. He was feet away from her, but it felt like miles. He felt at that moment that he'd never been close to her. He'd made it all up. It had all been a myth, a fantasy.

'I'm sorry,' he said at last. 'I shouldn't have lost my temper.'

'That's all right.' She said it coolly, flatly. But of course it wasn't.

'Do you realize, Jane,' he said, sounding weary, sounding as if he was talking through a fug, through treacle, 'how worried we've all been? Me, Dominic. Even Bob next door. We've been fearing the worst. We've been imagining you lying dead somewhere.'

'Well, I'm not. I'm here now. I'm all right.'

'Why did you go off without telling me? If you'd even left a note or something, that would have helped.'

She glanced at him then. As if she was testing, checking something.

'I'm sorry. I didn't mean to cause so much worry.'

She paused, and he waited. Somebody on the television was annoying him, talking too loudly, laughing with a brash shriek of a laugh that set his nerves on edge.

151

'Do you mind turning that off?'

She picked up the remote and pressed the *off* switch.

'Thank you. Where did you go? Where have you been these last three days?'

She looked at him again. Letting her eyes visit his face a moment longer than before. She seemed about to say something, but then stopped herself.

'Is there somebody else? Are you having an affair?'

She laughed. A sudden snort of laughter, as if she had been taken by surprise.

'For God's sake, Adam. What a thing to say! Of course not.'

'Then why go off like that? Where have you been?'

'Things have been getting on top of me, Adam. Since my aunt died ... it's been difficult ... I'm not even sure why I did it, I just felt I had to get away.'

'Where did you go?' his voice softening now, the anger going.

'I went to Norfolk. I stayed in a guest house. I just wanted to visit places I'd been to as a child. Don't ask me why. I just needed to.'

'I wish you could have told me, Jane. That's all.'

'I'm sorry. I should have.'

For a moment he had felt a wave of tenderness towards his wife. He wanted to get up, to walk over towards her, to put his arms around her, hold her. But he didn't, and now already that moment had passed. She was looking away, pretending to watch the television again, slipping away from him. He felt a wall going up between them, and sensed she was only telling him half-truths, what she felt was palatable.

He would never know the whole truth. He was losing her. It was as if she, as well as Dominic, had stood too near the edge of the cliff that day.

The embers of the fire had gone completely cold now. He shivered. It was cold, it was late. He was tired, he should go to bed.

17

There was a tension between them the following morning. As if they were both somehow more aware, more conscious of each other. Careful not to stand too close, careful not to touch.

Outside the sky was grey. The weather forecast had predicted occasional rain. Not the ideal day for a birthday. But Dominic didn't care. He was excited. Laughing at nothing, reaching out suddenly to grab Adam's arm, to grab Jane's.

'How old today, Daddy?' he said. Again.

'Eighteen, son.'

'That's a lot, Daddy.'

'Yeah, mate. You'll be catching up with me soon. We'll be drawing our pensions together.'

Hooting with laughter at his father's joke, even if he didn't quite understand it.

'This is for you, Dominic,' Jane said. She'd been holding the gift discreetly behind her back, but now she slipped it on to the table in front of him. It was wrapped in shiny gold foil scattered with a pattern of tiny champagne glasses. Dominic reached up and hooked his mother's head, dragged it down to kiss her cheek. Adam was watching her, still. She didn't wipe it away this time.

Dominic stabbed at the foil, trying to locate the seam to rip.

'Let me help you.'

She guided his hand to the paper's edge, tore back the sellotape. A scene flashed back into Adam's mind from birthdays, Christmases long past. When Dominic was little, when they had both thought life was perfect, that it would always stay that way. His son's small hand under Jane's, ripping back brightly coloured paper, shrieks of delight.

Now Dominic shrieking again with delight, as the slim, dark blue presentation box revealed itself from its gold wrapping. Perhaps for him, Adam thought, time had stood still; life was perfect, would always stay that way. He hoped so.

Jane's hand over his son's again. They lifted the lid of the box together.

'Watch! New birthday watch!'

Jane lifted it from its cushioned setting, slipped it on to their son's wrist. His face was a picture. He held it close to his ear.

'Not hear *tick tock*!' he said. For a moment, a sudden cloud of disappointment.

'Never mind the tick tock, Dom. That's old hat. This is trendy. Look, a stopwatch and a calendar. You can set an alarm. Look, you can tell the time in the dark.' Adam pressed the button for the back light. Dominic's smile lit up like the watch face.

'Thank you, Mummy. Lovely watch.'

Jane was standing now a little apart, watching them, an enigmatic look on her face.

'It's waterproof too,' she said.

After Dominic had left for school he spent the morning in the garden, turning the soil, which was moist and easy to work after days of light rain, staking out rows for planting seed. He grew whatever vegetables he could in the garden. It kept the cost of their food down, and gave him a satisfying feeling, knowing that as far as possible he was self-sufficient. Slugs were a problem later when things were growing, munching their way through the tender leaves. He wouldn't use chemicals to keep them away. Had been known to move stealthily along the rows of young shoots after dark, picking the slugs off by hand into a bucket, to be deposited in some undergrowth further up the lane. Anna would laugh at him, say he was soft-hearted. But he knew she liked that about him, the fact that he could scarcely bring himself even to kill a slug.

Jane was in the kitchen, baking. 'I'll make some peanut butter biscuits for Dominic,' she had said. 'He does still like them, doesn't he?'

He'd told her, Yes, he loves them. He had shown her where things were. The flour, the margarine, the peanut butter, the utensils. He had thought, That's a good sign, she's making an effort. But he had tried not to show her he was pleased. She's leaving tomorrow, he thought, forcing the spade down into the earth with his boot. Nothing had changed.

After an hour or so of working she signalled to him

through the kitchen window that she had made some tea, and he came in, kicking his feet free of his mud-caked boots at the door, to the tea brewing in the pot and the odour of peanut butter biscuits in the oven, She had always been baking something when Dominic had been small. Sponges and rock cakes, flapjacks, biscuits. She stood there, as if time had slipped backwards, with her pinny around her waist, flour smudging her cheek.

'They're about ready now. Would you like one?' She was bending at the oven door to slide out the tray.

'No, thanks. Perhaps later.'

Drinking his tea quickly, needing to get out again. Into the garden, into the fresh air, back to his work. Not wanting to stay there, being this close to her, these bittersweet memories slipping back . . .

They had arranged to pick Dominic up from school them-selves. On the way back they would stop at the café near Tintagel, where he sometimes took Dominic for a treat on Sundays. They knew him there, they made him welcome. Nobody ever minded the crumbs on the floor, the mess he sometimes made on the table. He'd mentioned it to Irene, who managed the café, the last time they were there.

'I'll get a cake in for him,' she'd said.

'Don't go to any trouble.'

'Don't be daft, it's not every day you have an eighteenth birthday. You leave it to me. He likes football, doesn't he? Blue icing, that sort of thing?'

'That'll be great,' he'd said, but thinking – a cake for a boy, not a man who's coming of age. A boy who likes cakes with footballs iced on them, chunky watches with back lights and dials.

They arrived at the school early and waited in the car park, watching it fill up with the parents who lived nearby, who had the time to pick up their kids in cars every day. The staff were coming out now to lower the ramps on the mini-buses. Bringing out the wheelchair kids, bolting them safely down. A couple of them noticed Adam sitting in the car and waved to him. I'm known here, Adam thought. Part of the community. *Dom's dad.*

He was remembering how they treated him when he'd finished the mural for the school hall. It had been the break-up of the summer term, the height of summer, everything verdant, the trees edging the playing field outside in clouds of creamy shades of green. Dominic's class had presented a theme on holidays and the seaside, and Dominic had been selected to go up on stage and show his work, a lump of pottery in an opaque, white glaze that he'd proudly announced was an ammonite. Then Pat Turner, the Head, said how grateful they all were to Mr Reynolds 'for the lovely mural he's done for us in his spare time', and he had to stand up while the whole school applauded, the teachers and class-room assistants, the kids, the other parents; he felt a bit of an idiot standing there, but loving it too. Pat got them to do *Three cheers!* and he noticed Dominic up there on the stage, punching the air with his fist and shouting, 'That's my dad!'

He had a sudden impulse now to tell Jane about that assembly, about Dominic up there on the stage, beaming, shouting with pride. He turned to her, but she had this look on her face that stopped him in his tracks. She looked appalled. She looked like she didn't want to be there. Didn't want to be like the other parents, the mother of a kid who's not normal, who'll never be normal. He saw Jim coming out of the main entrance pushing Dominic in his chair and started walking towards them, thinking, *Damn her!*

Later he would ask himself if he'd done it deliberately, to punish her, still resenting perhaps that look on her face.

He could have avoided the coastal road. Could have avoided driving down to St Isaac's, towards the harbour, with the view back over to the cliffs, towards the coastal path to Portquin. But he didn't. He turned off the B road, where it was signed for St Isaac's.

'Why are you coming this way?' An edge of panic in her voice.

'This way's more scenic. Dom likes it.'

She stared at him. 'How can you say that! How *can* he like it!'

He ignored her, his anger still burning coldly inside him.

'You *do* like it, don't you Dom?'

'Can see the sea, Daddy! Look, Mummy, look at the sea.'

But she wouldn't look. They dropped down to the harbour, swept up again on the road hugging tightly to the headland. He risked glancing at her quickly. She had her eyes closed. She wouldn't look back towards the cliffs where it had happened, wouldn't look down at the foamy water churning violently on the rocks below.

But he was telling the truth. They did go that way. Often. Dominic loved the views. It was a good mile from where it had happened. He never made the connection. To him it was just cliffs and rocks, sea tumbling in a white foam, seagulls circling. To him it was beautiful. He was a boy, Adam thought, for whom time now stood still, who lived in a constant present. How old was he? A small boy of two, who liked the Billy Goats Gruff. A boy of seven, who played football on Sundays, dancing on that ball like a pro. The age he was when he had fallen from a cliff, refusing to be the one who was chicken. He was eighteen, his hormones were raging; he loved girls with big tits and blonde hair. But in spite of the changes on the surface, there was something in him that was timeless. That was the something Adam loved in him. Would always love.

They'd sat in the café hardly speaking. Irene brought out the cake and they sang 'Happy Birthday'. Or Adam and Irene did. Jane's voice was barely audible, her lips scarcely moving. The cake had a blue and red football etched on to the white iced top, and eighteen candles. Dominic had taken a deep breath and blown them out, with help from his dad.

'Smile, Mummy!'

Adam had fished out a camera he had brought with him. Irene squinted through it, taking their picture. Jane smiled weakly. She sat silently, pushing the cake around her plate. Adam had thought she was sulking still, but when he looked at her he noticed her eyes were shiny. He felt a sudden flood of tenderness towards her. He felt like a bastard.

'I'm sorry.'

Dominic was in bed early, worn out with excitement. Adam found her sitting by the fire when he came back downstairs. She was gazing into the flames. She looked lost, she looked sad, he thought. She glanced up at him. There was something in her eyes that made him feel she was a long way away.

'I shouldn't have taken the coastal road. I forgot you haven't been back, you've never been that way. Not since . . . you know.'

'It's not your fault, Adam. It's mine. We both know that.'

He knew they weren't talking about the coastal road any more.

He sat down opposite her. He was feeling slightly stunned. This feeling came over him again. *She's changed.* It was like he didn't know her any more, but in a strange way was knowing her better, wasn't making her up.

'He doesn't remember it, Jane. He remembers nothing. We're the only ones who remember. He began his life that day, in a sense. What he was before, it doesn't matter. We need to accept him for what he is now.'

He stopped then; he felt that he was lecturing her, being patronizing. But she didn't seem to mind.

'I know that, Adam.' She sighed. She was still staring into the flames. What was she seeing there?

'I wasn't able to. I let him down. You were right to leave. That was the right thing to do.'

'Jane ... you know I didn't want to. If there had been any way of staying ...'

'I drove you away, Adam. I drove the pair of you away. We both know that.'

There was silence now between them for a while. He felt too full for words, too caught up with some unnamed emotion to risk the sound of his voice. She was the one who broke the silence.

'Did I ever tell you why I decided I didn't want to teach any more?'

He wasn't sure he wanted to hear this. He remembered what he'd said when she'd coolly announced her plans to take a year out from work and train as an art therapist. She hadn't discussed any of it with him beforehand; it hadn't in any way felt like a joint decision. More like a fait accompli. That had annoyed him, the way she'd shut him out, had been formulating her plans, filling in application forms, even going for the interview, without telling him. She had announced her intention to him on the day the letter accepting her arrived. He'd been engrossed in watching England get thrashed in the World Cup qualifier game. Later, he'd realized she'd done that deliberately, chosen a time when he'd be distracted. What had he said? 'That's a joke, Jane. Don't you think you should try and sort out your own issues before you can help anyone else to sort out theirs? *Physician, heal thyself.*'

She'd turned pale and silent with anger then, and didn't talk to him about it any more. Not even when he had asked about it with genuine interest and remorse. She had worked like a demon, staying up till the small hours of the night, finishing essays and case studies, ended up passing with distinction. He'd wanted to take her out for a congratulatory dinner, buy her flowers and chocolates, say, 'Well done! I'm proud of you!' but by then he'd felt so shut out from her world that it wasn't possible.

He didn't want to talk about it. But she wanted to, she needed to, he could see that.

'I assumed you just felt ready for a change. A new challenge.'

'It wasn't just that. Not just about a new challenge. There was this boy in my class. Josh. I was taking Year Five back then – he would have been about a year younger than Dominic. He had just moved down with his parents from Durham. There was something about him. A charisma, I suppose, like he had a light in him. Wherever he was, you always knew he was there. He reminded me of Dominic, I suppose. The way Dominic had been, before . . . he looked like him too. Same colour hair, build, this fantastic smile. He was good at sport as well, especially football. He would play centre forward, because he was the best at football; he was brilliant. I would stand there sometimes and lose sense of time . . . it was like watching Dominic again, like having him back again, just for a few moments, the way he used to be. But then I would come home, and Dominic would be slumped in his chair, or you'd have him out in his standing frame, or he'd have the physio round and be lying on his mat in the living room doing his exercises, and it was all so painful.

I couldn't bear to look at him sometimes, to see the contrast between what he had been – like that boy Josh I'd been watching at school – and what he was now. That's why I left, in the end. I didn't want to be around children any more. Running around, their lovely limbs and their laughter, all that future ahead of them. I didn't want to be around that every day, then come home to Dominic at night . . .'

She was bringing it back to him now, what he had lost too, what they both had lost. He could hardly bear to listen. These were the thoughts he had learnt to shut out of his mind. His job was to live in the present now. Where Dominic lived.

'Why didn't you tell me this, Jane?' But he knew the reason.

'I couldn't do that. It wouldn't have been fair. You were the one who was coping, doing everything for him, day in and day out. You wouldn't have wanted to hear that. You know you wouldn't have.'

She was right. He wouldn't have wanted to hear it then. It would have made him angry. What good would those feelings have been to him then?

She was gazing back towards the fire, this silence between them. He had the strangest feeling, sitting there, the only light in the room coming from the fire and a small table lamp in the corner of the room, the shadows on her face, in her eyes, that he had never been as close to his wife as he was now.

'You see, Adam,' she said at last, her voice soft, seeming to be coming to him from far away, a time long past, 'Dominic had been the one thing in my life that had been perfect. There was our marriage, but in a way that was flawed, because I'd lied to you, I'd kept so much from you about who I really was ... that was what I couldn't bear, that the one perfect thing in my life had been spoiled, like everything else had been ...'

What is she talking about? he thought. His heart was starting to beat faster. He wasn't sure he wanted to know. She turned her head to look at him directly. Her eyes were still shadowed from the fire.

'I've never told you the truth, Adam. I've never told you what really happened ...'

He felt as if he was standing on the edge of a cliff, he was falling slowly into space.

'Wh-what do you mean? What *really* happened?'

'In my past. To my father and my brother. My father didn't die in a car accident. My mother killed him.'

He thought for an instant, *She's mad, she's delusional*. But in a still, quiet place inside him, he knew she was telling the truth at last.

'This isn't a joke, is it?'

'He was violent. She snapped, I suppose. That's what happens in the end, isn't it? She stabbed him with a knife, and he died, and she went to prison. She went to prison for twelve years. The sentence was originally for fifteen, but she was released early on parole.'

He felt light-headed. He couldn't believe what she was saying. There was a clenching, a churning in his abdomen. *The hara, the body and mind acting as one ...*

'And your brother. Did *he* die in an accident, like you said? Or perhaps you never even had a brother.'

A sneer of contempt in his voice. It shocked him, that he could speak to her like this, that he was feeling like this, when a moment ago he had felt so close to her. He felt the shock of what she was telling him sitting like ice in his belly, like a cold second skin on his face.

'No, I had a brother. I never lied about that.'

Her voice was subdued.

'Where is he now, then?'

'I don't know where he is.'

'What do you mean? Why don't you?'

The contempt still in his voice. What could he believe, when she had lied about so many important things? How could he ever trust her?

'He went missing. He left home when I was fourteen. I haven't seen him since . . .'

He got up and walked briskly away. He didn't trust himself to stay. He walked into the kitchen. He stood at the kitchen window, staring out into the dark night. He couldn't deal with what he was feeling. Anger, bewilderment, fear. All those years when he had given her time, given her space, waited for her to confide in him. Tell him about her father, and her brother. The trauma she had suffered. *They died in an accident, a car crash. My mother couldn't cope with the grief.* None of it true. He gripped the edge of the sink; he was shaking. What was he supposed to make of it now? What was he supposed to do? He felt the weight of the years upon him, the waste of them. Living with someone he'd never really known, all those years. Loving her too. She had never trusted him. Had she ever loved him at all? Outside the window, through the thick darkness, he could see the familiar constellation of stars glittering in the clear night sky. He imagined, for a moment, someone else a hundred years ago, two hundred, even more, standing in this cottage and gazing up through a window at the night sky. The same night sky, the same constellation. But slight, subtle changes, perhaps. A small movement in the position of a star. One shining more brightly, perhaps. Another, more faded.

All those wasted years. And then suddenly something happens, something turns, changes, and the years falling like rubble on his head. When the dust cleared, would he be able to see things for what they are, see what really matters? He had loved her, but that was behind him now. He had to live in the present, not in the monument he had made of the past. A thing that was spent and useless now.

He walked slowly back into the sitting room. She sat as if frozen in the chair, staring at the fire. He couldn't see her face. He stood still, looking at her. She eventually glanced over towards him. There was fear in her eyes.

'I'm sorry, Adam . . . I should have told you years ago.'

'Yes, you should have . . .'

'I shouldn't have lied.'

'No, you shouldn't have . . .'

She turned from him suddenly. Her shoulders jerked, as if a tremor had ran through her, some dark force suddenly gripping her.

'Why *did* you lie to me, then? Why didn't you tell me the truth?'

Her shoulders tightened now, her body clenching as if to control the tremor. She was looking away from him again, as if she couldn't bear for him to see her face.

'I was frightened . . . I was too frightened to tell you the truth . . .'

'Why on earth should you be frightened, Jane?'

'I felt ashamed, Adam. I felt so ashamed. I've always felt ashamed.'

Her shoulders were shaking now. A strange, low sound, almost inhuman. Like an animal in pain might make. He realized she was sobbing, he realized he had never seen her cry before. Not even eight years ago, when Dominic had lain in a coma after the fall from the cliff. *He* had cried, he'd sobbed his heart out for weeks. He remembered her stiff, shrinking body sitting next to him in the hospital, her dry, shocked eyes. He had wanted wetness and ranting. Emotion and tears to match his own. She couldn't give him that. And now? The sight of her shaking shoulders, that dark moan of pain. He thought of Dominic, how his body would twitch and jerk at the start of a convulsion, the sound he would sometimes involuntarily make.

He moved towards her. He was acting impulsively, instinctively. Doing what needed to be done. He knelt down in front of her, held her in his arms. Her head moved against his shoulder and he could feel her hot tears on his cheek. He was thinking, if anyone could see them now, the way he was holding her and the way she was letting herself be held, they would think they were together again, they would think this was a reconciliation. In a way it felt like one, because he had never felt so close to her before. But at the same time something was calcifying in him, as solid and unchangeable as a stone.

It's over, he thought. *There's no going back.*

PART THREE

18

She lay in the narrow bed that was really a child's bed, too cramped for her. She could smell the newness of the sheets, and supposed Adam must have gone out and bought new linen, especially for her. She felt exhausted, drained, yet knew she couldn't sleep, perhaps wouldn't sleep for hours. Memories were buzzing in her head, as if something had been stirred up from the deep silt underwater. Something deformed, almost monstrous . . .

She stabbed him, and he died. She went to prison for twelve years.

It had been only days before Christmas. The darkest time, when the earth seemed to pause, its forward motion suspended, waiting for something to happen. Since then, she had always hated that time of the year. Hated it for the inertia that closed in upon her, the lethargy that seeped through her veins.

All through those years with Adam, when Dominic was little and Christmas had mattered, as it does to all children, she had to force herself to enter into the spirit of it. To put up the decorations, the tree. To help the child to tie the glittering baubles, arrange the lights among the loaded branches. To jostle shoulder to shoulder with strangers in crowded shops in the countdown days, fighting down the panic of claustrophobia that crowds always gave her. To prepare the silly nonsense that Christmas always brings: the evergreen wreath for the door, the table decoration, stuffing for the turkey, homemade Christmas cake and mince pies. All these things would bring back to her that stifling feeling of being underwater. Images of things she couldn't bear to remember threatening to break loose, to float towards the surface. It had required all her energy to anchor them down, keep them out of sight.

Sometimes it had been too much for her. The darkness would descend upon her, climb into her head, and she'd take to her bed, feign a bout of flu. Let Adam take over, do the Christmas things downstairs with their son until it was over and she started to come back to life again.

That year, just before her father had died, when her mother had killed him, there had been a weak, abortive attempt at getting ready for Christmas. Her father had pulled out the artificial tree from the attic, but no one had got around to decorating it. It had stood bare and barren in the living room, the box that contained the baubles and lights lying at its base, unopened. It seemed to represent to Jane, thinking back, all the Christmases she had ever known when she was a child. Something bleak and unadorned. A festive family get-together that never was.

Her father would normally use Christmas as a time to

drink more. As he drank he would grow more and more morose; his jealousies, his paranoia, would thicken and darken. He'd accuse her mother of things Jane hadn't been able to understand when she was a child, but had grown into both understanding and fearing as she'd approached her teens. If her mother had spent too long chatting with the milkman at the door. If she had been too long at the shops. If she'd been out of the house when he came home from work. Even ridiculous things like a wrong-number phone call, a man's voice on the phone asking for someone they didn't know; he would turn on her, especially if he had been drinking, his face darkening like a storm cloud. *Bitch. Slut. Whore.* The words twisted his mouth into ugliness, hurting Jane's ears. When she was small she hadn't understood the words, what they meant, where they came from: she had shrunk from them, hidden from them. Usually hiding in her room, playing make-believe Happy Families with her dolls, reading books about children who always seemed to be going on some quest, looking for parents they had lost, trying to return to places they had lived in and loved. Searching for Never-Lands.

Sometimes, if the storm broke downstairs, the words turning into her father's fist punching on flesh and bone, bodies falling against cupboards, doors, the terrible rattle of breaking crockery or glass, she would get into bed and draw the covers up over her head, screw her fingers into her ears and tell herself, it'll be all right; they weren't her real parents anyway. Her real parents had royal blood flowing in their veins. She had been stolen from them at birth, but they were searching for her and would one day find her and take her away to live with them on an island where life would be perfect. She would climb with them into their chauffeur-driven limousine and drive down the lane. Her father would be at the French window, his face mute and angry, the amber liquid flashing in the glass in his hand, and her mother would stand in the garden and watch her go, but not try to stop her. The fantasy would peter out at that point, the car never getting further than a hundred yards down the lane, because she could never quite decide what to do about Paul. She couldn't just leave him.

He was the one she loved most of all, the one she felt safe with. During those terrible storms, as she lay stiff and frozen under the covers, Paul would sometimes creep into her bed with her and hold her. She would feel his thin, slight boy's body warm and glued up tight to hers. They would stay like that until the morning. Nothing happened. Nothing that was bad. Just a sweetness, a peace. A sense of sinking slowly into green water.

She was remembering those feelings, lying in that cramped, childlike bed. Imagining Paul's arms around her again. Imagining how it would be if her letter brought him back again.

Now that she was coming clean, was telling the truth at last, she could take him to visit Adam and Dominic. 'This is my brother, Paul,' she would say. He would be tall, well-built, more solid than he had been in his youth. His skin would be ruddy with the outdoor life, his auburn hair fading. Adam would like him; he would like Adam. They would go sailing and fishing together. He would be good with Dominic. Having never known him before, the normal, perfect Dominic, it would be easy for Paul to accept him the way he was. She would sell the house and give up her job – it was giving her up anyway, when the hospital closed, as it was scheduled to do next year. She would buy a cottage down in Cornwall, a big one, where they could all live together. She and Paul, Adam and Dominic . . .

But you're lying to yourself again, you're deceiving yourself. You've told him some of the truth, but not all of it. Why can't you remember?

She groaned softly to herself, turned in the narrow bed. It creaked under her weight. She imagined Adam lying in his bed in the room next to hers. Was he sleeping, or awake as well? Watching the night-clock, peeling back the past in his thoughts, as she was? He had knelt down on the floor and held her. She had allowed herself to cry on his shoulder. Yet despite the appearance of closeness, a space opening up between them. *It was time to let go . . .*

Her memories slipping back now, to that night her father had died. Just before Christmas. She had arranged to go around Sharon Baker's house for a sleep-over. Sharon Baker, her only real friend. A friend that belonged to her more than to Paul. Sharon was a year older than she was, and knew things she didn't. She was sassy, in a way Jane wasn't. Would talk back to her mother in a way Jane couldn't imagine ever doing to hers. Sharon lived in a big, new-built house. With an attached garage, a wide, paved drive. Lights that lit up the porch and driveway at night. Her father worked as a solicitor in Wisbech. Despite Sharon's streetwise ways, they were 'posh' – not rough like some of the kids down the lanes.

That night Sharon's parents had planned an evening out at the theatre with friends and wouldn't be home till past midnight. They had agreed that Jane could come over and keep Sharon company. Daughters of fourteen, going on fifteen, too old for babysitters.

They talked that night about sex and boyfriends, still being at the age when it was all talk and no action, although Sharon would make up stories to shock her. They raided her parents' drink store in the sideboard, took out the bottle of gin and had a glass each, making the dry, harsh shock of it more palatable with lemonade. They puffed Capstan cigarettes out of the window, so the smoke wouldn't linger in the living room, coughing and spluttering on the smoke, but pretending to enjoy it. They stayed up watching Christopher Lee with blood-tipped incisors, playing Count Dracula in the 'Hammer House of Horror'. Clutching each other on the sofa in mock terror at the frightening bits. Then the doorbell rang.

'Oh, bugger! That's them back! They must have forgotten their keys!' Sharon leapt off the sofa, rushing to put the gin bottle back in the sideboard, rushing to the kitchen to rinse the telltale odour from their glasses.

'You answer it, Jane.'

She went to the door apprehensively. Expecting to find Mr and Mrs Baker standing outside the glazed porch door, their faces stiff with false smiles and suspicion. 'Hope you've behaved yourselves, the two of you?' Mrs Baker would say.

But it hadn't been. Instead, two policemen in dark uniforms made darker by the night, their faces grim like undertakers.

'Is there a Jane Reynolds here?'

She had nodded, swallowed. 'Yes, that's me.'

Knowledge passed through her like a sword. *Something had happened. Something bad. Something that could never be put right again.*

'Are there any adults in the house?'

Sharon was edging up behind her now, her face pointed and curious, full of wonder at the sight of the policemen. She explained about her parents.

'Would you mind if we came in and waited for them, love?'

But just at that moment they were pulling up on to the driveway, were getting out of the car. Mr Baker's voice calling out in the dark.

'What on earth ... is everything all right, officers? What's happened ... ?'

Nothing had been said to her. She had been sent into the kitchen to wait with Sharon and one of the constables while the other one talked to Mr and Mrs Baker alone in the living room. She had felt pale and still with fear and shock. Would they smell the gin, the cigarette smoke? she thought to herself, stupidly, illogically, but at the same time knowing that they wouldn't care about that. They had come about something else. Something much more serious. Then Mrs Baker had come out and told Sharon she must go upstairs, she must go to bed. Her eyes looked alarmed and fearful. She was looking at Jane the way you look at a sick animal, a look of pity that twists the thing it pities out of shape.

Sharon had seen the look and just for once hadn't argued back. She had kissed Jane quickly on the cheek.

'See you tomorrow.'

But Jane had a premonition, as sharp and resolute as the sword, that she would never see Sharon again; she wouldn't be living here tomorrow, in the brown-roofed house down the lane. Sharon went upstairs to bed and Mrs Baker turned to her. Jane couldn't meet her eyes, she was slipping outside her skin . . . was standing there, a doppelgänger of herself, a soulless imitation . . .

'Jane, there's been an accident. Something has happened to your father. The police officers are taking you and Paul to your aunt and uncle's house in Stafford.'

She hadn't asked questions. Hadn't wanted to know where her mother was. Something inside her already knew. She hadn't protested or complained. She followed the constable towards the waiting car outside in the lane, climbed into the snug dark of the rear seat. Paul was already inside, sitting there waiting.

'Are you okay?' he whispered. She said, 'Yes.' Feeling safer now, slipping back into herself again. Then the car started up and moved off slowly down the lane and they said nothing else, just sat together in the darkness of the back seat, looking towards the tunnel of light made in the lane by the headlights. They passed the gap in the hedgerow, where a barred gate led into their front garden, but she kept her eyes fixed unflinchingly on the light carving its way into the darkness ahead. Paul sought out her fingers and held on to them. He hadn't done anything like that for years.

There's just the two of us now, she'd thought. Sitting there in silence, his warm hand clasping her fingers on the lea-therette upholstery of the rear seat. *Just the two of us against the world.* The sword of knowledge lay heavy and still in her flesh, yet still stripped bare of any facts. The facts would come later.

19

Her aunt had been waiting up for them when they arrived in Stafford, in her dressing-gown, her face blotched with tears, and her uncle too, standing around like a spare part with a glass of brandy in his hand for fortification. Few words were spoken. They were ushered upstairs and shown their bedrooms. She hadn't bothered to undress. She had slipped under the cool, clean sheets and lain there, staring dry-eyed into the darkness, thinking, *Something has happened to my father. What has happened?* Tomorrow she'd find out. The facts will cluster around the sword, bed themselves into it. She had lain there sleepless all night, waiting for morning.

Christmas hadn't happened either in her aunt and uncle's house, despite the fact that her aunt had been preparing for it for weeks, had done all the traditional things. A tree, a real one, stood loaded with baubles and lights in the lounge, but the lights weren't switched on that year. A cake, rich with rum and fruit under its pristine royal icing, stood untouched in the pantry.

Back in the house in the Fens, the unadorned tree would have been left standing there, bereft and barren, in the living room. Nothing in the house could be touched for weeks. Not until the Prosecution Service gave the okay. Later, her aunt and uncle had driven down to the house on their own. They had gone through the house, cleaning it from top to bottom, boxing up personal possessions – files and folders of papers, photo albums, her mother's record collections, stacks of her father's canvases. Loading the boxes containing Jane's and Paul's possessions into the boot of the car. Stacking the others in sentried rows under the eaves in the attic, where they would stay, undisclosed, for years.

The house was got ready for letting. A tenant was found. It was her mother's wish, Aunt Jean had told her, that the house was not sold, was rented out instead. Even when the prosecution proceedings found her mother guilty and sentenced her to fifteen years. Even after she had been moved down to Holloway to begin the harsh years of her sentence for real. Even after Paul had vanished. Even after her appeal had failed to reduce her sentence further. Even after all the years had passed during which Jane never saw her, never went to visit, turning her back on the past and pressing on with her life. Making up a new life, a new persona, that had no room in it for the twisted, deformed thing that was the past and what had happened that night in that stormy house only days before Christmas.

'I want to go back there to live, when this is over, when I've done my time,' her mother had apparently told Aunt Jean. 'Why should I sell it? It's the family home.' Jane hadn't understood, hadn't wanted to. *What family?* she had thought, the word bringing bitterness like bile to her mouth. What family life did they ever have, there in that house? *I'll never go back there. Never again.* And of course by then Paul had disappeared, and she was learning to shut him out of her thoughts, to push down the memories.

To pretend that he had died along with her father that night.

Over those first few weeks, the story about what had happened seeped into her consciousness. The facts bedding themselves into that sword of cold steel she carried in her flesh. She hadn't wanted to know, she hadn't asked any questions. She had learnt nothing from Paul; he didn't want to talk about it either, not at all, and she didn't want to ask him. It was as if they had some secret pact between them, not to talk about the events of that night. But fragments of her aunt's conversations with her uncle drifted into her ears as she loitered outside partially open doors. Then there had been intense conversations in later weeks between her aunt and uncle and various figures of authority – people connected with the legal system, with children's services. More and more facts, embedding into the sword that she carried inside her constantly, continually, buried so deeply into her flesh it had formed part of the fabric of her bone.

A row had taken place, she had learnt, a fight between her father and her mother. While she'd been at Sharon's. How it had started was inconsequential, didn't matter. And anyway, she could guess. The same old jealousies burning in his brain, fired by the drink. The same old accusations, the same ugly words. He had been goading her mother, apparently, about the piano. Trying to force her to play.

Even though he knew it was difficult for her, he knew

it was painful. She had never had her fingers set properly, never gone to the hospital. Didn't perhaps want the questions, the formal record on her medical notes. Two of her fingers had been broken, had healed but were slightly twisted, the knuckles enlarged. She had refused to play, had stood up to him, and he had hit her, she had told Aunt Jean. Hard, on the left side of the face. There was a deep mark on her cheek that had flowered into a purple bruise later. He had hit her again, and again, and then he'd fetched an axe from the shed and smashed up the piano. Just to hurt her, because – although she rarely played it now, and never when he was there – it was precious to her. Or perhaps because its silent presence in the living room reminded him of what he had done. The damaged, twisted thing that was their marriage.

She hadn't tried to stop him, there was no point. He was too far gone with drink now for that. She had watched him as he dragged the heavy chunks of desecrated wood, the ivory keyboard, the jangled strings, down the garden and put the first of the wood on the bonfire he had lit earlier to burn rubbish cleared from the garden.

The fight had started up again in the kitchen, afterwards. He was drinking, he wouldn't stop drinking. He hit her again, repeatedly, on her face, her shoulder. But this time, unlike all those countless other times in the past, something had snapped in her, like an elastic band stretched so tight it had no choice but to break. She had been standing at the sink and had reached out suddenly, desperately, towards the rack of knives on the wall, her hand closing on the dark ebony wood of a butcher's knife. They were always kept sharp. Her father had sharpened them himself only a few days before. Perhaps in preparation for the carving of the Christmas turkey, or perhaps just because they needed it. He did it regularly, like a ritual, sliding the long cool blades up and down, one at a time, on a large whetstone he kept in the scullery.

Something just snapped. I just wanted it to stop. Everything happened so quickly. I grabbed the knife from the rack, and the next thing I knew I had plunged it in his chest and he staggered backwards and fell to the floor. I stood there, with the knife still in my hand, the blade red with blood. I don't know how long I stood there. I was shocked, I was numb. He lay there, half on his side, he was wheezing. I saw blood coming from his chest. Then the wheezing stopped. I didn't feel his pulse, I couldn't bear to touch him. Paul was in his room; he hadn't been home long – five minutes perhaps. I could hear his footsteps on the stairs, in the hall. Then he opened the kitchen door and came in.

They hadn't taken long in coming. Apparently her voice on the phone had been clear and calm. *I've killed my husband. I've stabbed him with a knife. He's lying on the kitchen floor. Please come quickly.* She did nothing to hide the evidence. Left the knife lying on the draining board, with her finger-prints on its ebony handle. Left the body untouched on the slate tiles of the kitchen. When the police arrived she was sitting in the living room, waiting. Paul was next to her on the sofa, holding her hand. The police took down a statement from her straight away. No tears, no emotion. Then they radioed out for a second car, to take Paul and Jane away.

*

underwater

Jane could hear the small tides of Adam's breathing, not quite snoring but something approaching it, drifting through the stud wall that separated her room from his. He was asleep. She should be, but she couldn't sleep yet. Couldn't staunch the flow of this remembering. She tossed and turned on the small bed.

20

She only went once to see her mother in prison. Her aunt had been trying to persuade her to go for weeks, but she had refused. Turned a steely face away, shook her head in terror. 'No, I can't. I can't go.' But Paul had been the one to soften her resolve.

'Just this once, Jane,' he had said. 'Come just this once, while she's still in Peterborough. After the court case next week she might be sent down to Holloway, if they find her guilty. No one will make you go then, if you can't face it.'

And because Paul had said it, and because she could refuse her brother nothing, the edge of her will dissolved. She went with them, travelling to the prison on the bus. Sitting on the top of the double-decker and gazing down at all the people scurrying up and down the streets, shielded by umbrellas on the wet April day, and wondering if any of them had ever travelled to a destination as shameful as this one.

They were ushered into the visiting room at the allotted hour. The prisoners filed in, silent, subdued. Her mother joined them at the table where they sat waiting. She hadn't been able to look at her mother's face. Aunt Jean had done most of the talking.

Are you eating all right? Sleeping all right?

Have you seen your solicitor? What did he say?

You mustn't get too anxious about tomorrow. Of course you are, I know, but it'll be all right. The jury must listen to the plea of provocation. Surely they must.

Her mother had answered passively, as if she was resigned to her fate, as if she could do little to stem the tide that tomorrow would bring.

'You mustn't give up hope,' Aunt Jean said. She sounded vexed, almost angry. She wanted signs of a fight from her sister. Tears, rage: anything would have been preferable to this complicity.

'Don't you want to get out of here, Lillian? Don't you care what happens to the children?'

'Of course I do.'

Her mother was looking at Paul with concern Not at her. When did she ever look at her, except to see her as someone, as something, that was in the way? That took up space she wasn't entitled to. Paul was looking down at his plimsolled feet, then over towards the wardens who stood like statues against the wall. Over towards the visitors huddled at the table nearby . . . he looked distressed, on the edge of tears.

'Don't be a martyr, Lillian, that's all I'm saying. We all know what he was like, what he did to you. Just fight back. Tell them the truth. The children need you.'

'Perhaps I am to blame, Jean. I could have left him years ago, but I didn't. Perhaps I need to pay the price for that . . .'

'So you want to rot in here, let the children grow up without you . . .'

'They're hardly small children. They've got you and Bill . . .'

'But it's you they bloody want . . .'

Her aunt's face coloured with anger, her voice raised. One of the wardens glanced up sharply.

'The kids don't want to hear us argue,' her mother said.

Two spots of crimson in Paul's cheek. A slight tremor at the hinge of his jaw, shuddering like a tiny fish caught under his skin . . .

'Just work with your barrister. When they put you on that witness stand, tell them what he wants you to, that's all.' Aunt Jean's voice was calm now. She looked weary, pale with the strain.

'Of course, don't worry. It'll be all right,' her mother said. But she sounded like it wouldn't be. As if she knew it wouldn't be.

Her mother, looking at Paul still. *Did she look at me at all?* She couldn't remember. Paul had glanced up from the floor, briefly caught his mother's eye.

'We just want you to come home, Mum,' he said. Tears beneath his voice. But he was nearly seventeen then, nearly a man. He was fighting them back.

During those first awful weeks, months, waiting for the court proceedings, a conspiracy of silence reigned in her aunt's comfortable home. It had seized Jane's throat, taken her words from her, made her take refuge in her schoolwork upstairs in her room. Made her aunt dissolve into random tears she tried to hide, scald her hands carelessly on burning hot saucepans, clumsily drop things. Made her uncle pace the floor, sit staring vacuously at his hands.

She had been coerced to attend the trial against her will. (*The defence want you there, Jane, you might be called as a witness . . .*)

But she hadn't been. Although Paul had. Her mother's barrister was near retirement age, past his best. He spoke slowly, labouring the words, as if the mere fact of trying to uncover the truth wearied him.

'Had you ever witnessed your father hitting your mother?'

'Yes, often. He was always hitting her.'

He was asked to give examples of some of these occasions. He spoke about them mechanically, his voice expressionless, his eyes slightly downcast. Jane sat there in court, next to her aunt, and felt herself momentarily back in her bed in the Fenland home, the covers pulled over her head, her brother's slight body glued up behind her, his breath warm on her cheek. *Don't worry, Jane. It's all right. Go to sleep now.*

'Was there a general theme to these fights?'

'No, not really. He would drink too much. The drink made him crazy. If his dinner was too late, or too cold. If she hadn't ironed his shirt. He was jealous, sometimes, of other men. She never gave him a reason to be. He didn't need an excuse to hit her. He was crazy.'

'You said you went out to your friend's about three

o'clock that afternoon. Did you witness your father hitting your mother that afternoon, before you left?'

'No. He was in his shed down the garden, doing his painting. When I got home later that evening, just after ten o'clock, he was sitting slumped over his bottle of whisky in the kitchen. I didn't see my mother; maybe she was in the living room. I went straight upstairs. Then soon after I got in my room I heard him start shouting. I turned the music up loud. I hated it when they fought. Then I heard her scream and then suddenly everything was quiet. That's when I started to worry. I felt something had happened. I came downstairs and went into the kitchen and saw him lying on the floor . . .'

He paused, took a deep draught of air. The memory was painful to him, unbearable. The defence leant in, spoke gently.

'What was your mother doing?'

'She was holding the knife.'

'Would you say she was in a state of shock?'

'She looked as if she could hardly believe what she had done. She looked at me. "I have to phone the police," she said.'

The barrister for the prosecution was a small, weasel-faced man. Jane didn't want to listen to what he said. Didn't like the way her brother's face flinched under the barrage of questions. He seemed to want to put words in her brother's mouth, he seemed to doubt him. *How many times did you witness your father hitting your mother?' 'I don't know. There were many. Too many to count.' 'Did you ever go to your mother's defence?' 'No. Not really.' 'Why not?' 'I was frightened; he was a bully.' 'Tell me again what happened that night, what you saw when you entered the kitchen. Did your mother seem upset? Remorseful? Did she express any sorrow about what had happened?' 'She was quiet. I suppose you could say she was calm, but she wasn't, not really. Not underneath.' 'Why would your father want to burn her piano? Why would he try and force her to play?' 'I don't know. I've told you – he was crazy.'*

Sitting in the courtroom, Jane was making herself slip outside her body again. Making herself as thin and vapoured as air.

She didn't attend the day her mother had taken the stand. She had a headache, and perhaps she'd played it up a bit, made out it was worse than it was. Her aunt had been disappointed in her, but didn't push her. By then it was clear that the defence wouldn't call her to the witness stand. 'It would add nothing to the case,' they'd been told. When they came back from the court that day, her aunt and uncle and Paul, they had looked stunned and empty. She didn't even want to ask them what had happened. She knew, had always known, her mother would be found guilty, would be sentenced. The knowledge of this sealed itself into the sword inside her.

Her mother was sentenced to fifteen years. The judge had taken into consideration the plea of provocation. He was being lenient, he'd said, in the sentencing; she should count herself lucky. It was clear she had suffered abuse, but she had choices. She could have left him. Nothing could condone her actions that night . . .

After her mother had been sent down to Holloway, Jane's new life in Stafford resumed its ordinary day-to-day routine. She was working hard at school, coming top of the class regularly in French and history. And something else was changing in her now, hardening deep within her. A desire to turn her back on the past, to re-create herself, to be different. She felt less insubstantial now, less like a shadow. She was forcing herself to be more outgoing, was making a tight circle of new friends. Alison and Vanessa and Suzanne, who were kind girls, nice girls, from good homes, who all made a point of never speaking to her about her parents out of deference to her feelings.

Did you hear about Jane's parents? They died in a car crash last year. She's an orphan, how tragic, how sad!

At first she had been reluctant to invite her new friends home, fearing that something would slip out. About the trial, her mother's whereabouts, the dreadful events in the house that dark night before Christmas – her aunt or her uncle caught unawares, not realizing the importance to Jane of the secrets. But then as time passed, and the secret closed itself up inside each of them, she began to relax. Her friends would call round and she'd take them up to her room where they would sit and talk about clothes and boys. Whose mini-skirt was the shortest, who had the sharpest haircut. Whether Cliff was better than Elvis, which of the Beatles was the best. But this was the froth, the frivolous. The talk that mattered most was increasingly about school and exams, and their dreams for the future, which usually contained something called 'university' and 'getting away from here'. Not for them, the lives of their mothers. Early marriage and babies. They were bright girls, they saw the world as their oyster. They wanted more.

Perhaps it wasn't so easy for Paul. School wasn't quite the solace for him it was to her – she had always been the more academic of the two – but he seemed okay. Quiet at times, perhaps. A little moody. *He misses his mother*, her aunt and uncle would mutter sometimes, in those earlier weeks, when he'd spent long hours in his room. Playing those records that once belonged to their mother, those dark, depressing songs that made Jane cringe to hear them. *Let him be. He'll come around in his own time.*

And he did. Eventually he started getting out more, made new friends of his own. He discovered the local group that was affiliated to the Sea Scouts. Would often be away for the weekend, trekking on some mountain, kayaking on some Welsh river or Scottish loch. They were both moving on with their lives. Or so she thought.

Adam's deep tides of breathing had evolved into proper snoring now, low rumbles of sound rising and falling. She should try to get to sleep. Shut these thoughts out of her mind. She'd be too tired for the long drive home tomorrow ...

But something was disturbing her still. Making her feel

as if water was closing over her head; she was struggling to find her way up to the surface . . .

It had to do with the last time Paul had been to the prison. Travelling down to London on his own, on the train, to visit his mother in Holloway. She had a new solicitor by that time. An attractive young woman called Emma Johnson. She was newly qualified, and passionate about justice, passionate especially about justice for women. She had been helping to prepare the case for their mother's appeal hearing. She visited the house in Stafford, had long, intense talks with Aunt Jean behind closed doors. And then she asked to speak to Jane and Paul. Separately, on their own.

Jane told her the facts. She had been at Sharon's house that evening, keeping her company while her parents were out at the theatre. She had been planning to stay the night. Knew nothing about what had happened until the policemen had knocked on the door.

'Had your parents been arguing that day, or in the days leading up to it?'

'They were always arguing,' she had said coldly, dispassionately.

'But that night, before you left to go to your friend's, do you remember them arguing, fighting, about anything in particular?'

'No, not really. My mother was doing some sewing in the living room when I left. Darning socks, I think. My father was in his studio in the garden. I don't remember any arguments that day.'

'Before that night then, Jane. When was the last time you saw your father hit your mother?'

She paused. There was a cloud building in her head. She felt resentful. She didn't see why she should answer these questions. Why this pretty, young solicitor, who'd never known the terror of lying in bed under the covers whilst storms raged downstairs, should be dragging her back there.

'I don't remember.'

'Think back, to the days or weeks before. *Try* to remember.'

'I can't. I don't remember anything special. Things had been quiet before that. They'd been getting on quite well.'

Emma Johnson had given up then. She had looked disappointed, defeated. She left her to go and talk to Paul in his room upstairs.

What had happened between Paul and Emma Johnson – if anything had – she never found out. She didn't ask, and he didn't tell her. But he was withdrawn for days afterwards. A few days later he went down to Holloway on his own, to visit his mother. Then, shortly after that, he left home. The police had been called, but if an investigation took place, it was a half-hearted one. He turned eighteen two months later; he was an adult, free to roam where he chose. And young men often leave home. Especially young men with troubled backgrounds.

Naturally, her aunt and uncle had been deeply upset. They had placed a couple of notices in national papers, asking

Paul to contact them. Praying that he would read them, pick up the phone, but of course he never did. But there was Jane to focus on, to protect. In time, Paul and his whereabouts became another part of the silence. Another taboo.

Of course, her mother had been told, but Jane didn't really know how she had reacted. Didn't want to know. Suspicion was festering, fermenting inside her. Her mother had said something. *What had she said?* She was turning her back on her mother, refusing to go and visit her in prison. Her aunt would stand in the kitchen in her coat and headscarf and plead with her to accompany her on the train to London.

'She's your mother, Jane. She needs you. You're all she's got left.'

The phrase 'now that Paul's gone' hanging unspoken in the air between them. She was getting older, more confident. She would be lippy sometimes, bolshy. This new Jane, this hard, new persona. She'd take liberties with her aunt's soft-heartedness. Talk back in ways she'd never have dared to do, back in the Fenland house with her father. In the past she was making herself forget.

'I'm not going to that place. It's lousy in there. People stare at you in there like you're some muck the dog's brought in.'

Her aunt had looked at her, helpless with disappointment.

'You've only one mother, Jane. If you turn your back on her now, it may not be easy to undo later. She won't be in there for ever, you know ... you'll be surprised how quick the years will go by ... you'll need her one day.'

But she would shrug, walk away. Return upstairs to her

books, her schoolwork. Or fling on a jacket and slouch out of the house to go round to somebody else's. Meet friends in a coffee bar, where they'd talk earnestly about the future. *O-levels. A-levels. University.* A future that beckoned like a giant hand that would swoop down and pluck her out of here, put her down somewhere else.

Far away from her aunt's entreaties, the mother who languished in some unthinkable prison. Away from the past. The horror of the night her father had been stabbed to death with a knife that had pierced his heart.

21

She had done well in her exams. Passed seven O-levels and three A-levels. The giant hand of fate she had dreamt about reached down and plucked her away. Not to university in the end, but to something close enough. To art college.

She could have gone in a number of different directions – French, history, even maths – but had chosen art in the end. It wasn't necessarily the subject in which she'd been most talented, but it gave her a kind of freedom she'd never known before. A freedom to play, to experiment, to get her hands dirty. She'd kept her feelings, all her life, pushed down, boxed out of sight. Her art seemed to allow her to take her feelings out of the box in a wordless way that was safe.

Her early work was nearly always figurative. Female nudes painted boldly in thick, dark impasto. Hunched over usually, turned away from the viewer. Their backs and shoulders solid and impenetrable like boulders of stone, heads small and cowed, sometimes large hands up to their faces, as if they were hiding. Dark figures against even darker back-grounds, in which there was always a sense of something lurking in the darkness, waiting. Her clay work was figurative too. Female figures, kneeling, curled into foetal postions. Sometimes just busts of women's heads, with saucered eyes peeping over the top of giant, out-of-proportion hands.

Mr Peters was her Head of Year tutor at St Albans Art College. She liked him. He had a gentleness about him, a sincerity. He seemed to be drawn both to her and to her work, seemed to recognize her vulnerability. He would say encouraging things to raise her up, to increase her self-belief. She bathed for some time in his praise. Then one day he said too much. He was looking at another of her paintings, another figure hunched against a dark background, the head turned away.

'What do you think she's hiding from, Jane? What is it she can't face?'

She was nineteen. She was trying so hard to be someone else. Someone with this untainted, unspoilt past. She was attractive, with her pale, oval face framed by long, dark hair, large brown eyes half hidden by a thick, Mary Quant-type fringe, a slight, fragile figure. Boys were interested in her, although she gave them little encouragement. She rarely accepted the dates she was asked out on, although she secretly enjoyed the attention. Wouldn't have wanted to lose it.

She changed her style after that. Took up landscape painting. Safe pictures. Sunlight filtering through beech woods, silvered spires of village churches sitting amidst patchwork hills, windmills on marshes glimpsed through mist. Her grades went down. Mr Peters was disappointed.

'What's happened to you, Jane? You started out so promising. There had been real energy in your work.'

He held up one of her latest offerings. Two young girls

sitting on a beach, sunlight dappling their skin. A poor imitation of a Cézanne.

'This is pastiche, Jane. It's not real.'

'It's my best, sir. Some people like it.'

'People that care nothing for you,' he'd said.

She only just managed to scrape a 2:2 in the end. After that, a serious career as an artist was out of the question. Real art, serious art, would take her to places she didn't want to go to. She decided to do a teacher-training course in primary education. She would still specialize in art perhaps, but it would be safe art. Art for children, that copies and imitates. Bright, Kandinsky-inspired prints, paintings of sunflowers after van Gogh, Roman gods depicted in warm, earthy mosaics after a trip to the Baths at Welwyn.

Then she met Adam. He was different somehow from the other boys. Wouldn't push her, want to know more than she wanted to tell him, or try to make her other than she was. And perhaps she was ready, now, to take some risks. He was easy to be with, spontaneous, free from the weight of his past. He spilled out his secrets to her in bed at night, but she thought them tame and ordinary; they couldn't match hers. She kept hers hidden, pushed well out of sight. Made up a facile story to account for the missing members of her family.

My father and brother died in a car accident when I was thirteen . . .

My mother didn't recover from the shock, she disappeared out of my life.

I went to live with my aunt and uncle in Stafford. It was

all right, they were kind to me. I made friends, did well at school ... moved on with my life.

She had enlisted her aunt and uncle in her duplicity. *This is what I've told Adam ...* She taught them the details she had embellished around the story, just in case they were ever required to recount them:

Her father had taken Paul to the timber yard one Saturday, to buy some wood.

He was driving his Ford escort.

He didn't see the truck that pulled out suddenly in front of him ...

You must never tell him the truth, she'd said. They hadn't really approved of the lies, but they understood. How could they reveal the truth to this bright, happy young man Jane sometimes brought home for weekends. Who made them laugh. Made them forget Paul who was missing, Lillian in Holloway. How could they risk ruining Jane's happiness? Hadn't she lost enough?

Why had she chosen now to reveal the truth? *Why now, after all these years ... ?* Her hand moved up instinctively, to feel the knotted scar on her chest.

She pressed the button on the alarm clock on the bedside cabinet that illuminated its face. *Half past two.* She must get to sleep. Tomorrow she was driving back to Hertfordshire. Back to her life. Would a letter from Paul be waiting there for her on the doormat? *Is it safe now for him to return ... ?*

You need to go back further. Back to what happened just before that night. You need to remember ...

But she had remembered enough. She was weary with remembering. She shook her brother's voice out of her head. Sleep was slipping over her and she was sinking down into its darkness, into fragments of dreams in which she seemed to see Paul walking away from her, again and again. Her face was pressed mute and helpless against the window. *Turn around, Paul, come back.* ... But the words stayed locked in her head, couldn't find their way to her mouth. She tried to open the window to call out to him, but the catch was stuck; the window wouldn't open. She watched him walk away, turn the corner of the lane, watched until he was lost and out of sight. The words were finding their way into her mouth now, ringing in her ears, dragging her up from the deep water of her sleep into half-waking . . .

Turn around, Paul. Come back . . .

22

Driving home the following day, through the tight, cramped Cornish lanes, then up on to the A30, and finally the motorway that would lead her home, she was hoping, praying, that when she arrived home, turned the Yale key in the lock and pushed open her front door, she would see a letter from Paul sitting there on the mat, waiting for her return.

Please God, she said to herself, *let it be there.*

She imagined what Wendy would say, when she saw her again. *You didn't tell Adam about being ill, Jane! Why on earth not?* What would she reply? *Because he needs to be free. If I told him he would feel responsible for me.*

Wendy wouldn't understand. Why should she?

She thought of Dominic. The way his smiles still lit up the room, his spontaneous displays of affection. He had hugged her goodbye that morning. *Come back soon, Mummy*, he had said.

He's lovely, she thought.

He was not the son she'd wanted, no longer the son she'd once had. She used to watch him sometimes through the kitchen window, when he was a boy, practising his ball skills out in the back garden. She would delight in this, watching him, and knowing that he was not aware of her watching. He would control the ball by quick, subtle flicks of his heels, his toes, as if it were attached to his feet by an invisible cord. She remembered the fantasies she would play out in her mind. He'd go to university one day – yes certainly, he'd do that. He'd meet a girl from the right background, a perfect girl. They'd get married and she would go to the wedding holding Adam's arm, dressed in a fine linen suit with a broad-brimmed hat shielding her eyes from the sun. Before the grandchildren arrived Dominic and his wife would come to theirs for Christmas, then afterwards they would go to his. He'd have a perfect house in the suburbs filled with beautiful things, filled with beautiful children, and she'd never, *never* have to reveal the past to anyone. Those things that crouched inside her, dark with shame.

No, he wasn't that son. *But he's lovely still*. It was a revelation to her, the fact that she could think of him at last in this way. Not perfect, but still lovely.

Yet it seemed ironic that being on the verge of rediscovering him she was also losing him again. Anna had called that morning to wish Dominic a belated happy birthday. She had given him a present, a kite shaped like a bird, like a hawk. He had loved it

'If you like, Dominic, if the weather's fine, on Sunday we'll go to the beach and fly it.'

Jane had stood there in Adam's kitchen and looked at this slim, still-young Danish woman who was part of his life, the brave new life he was building in Cornwall. She saw the ease Anna had with her son, the ease she had with Adam. Anna had stood apart from Adam, had kept her distance, but Jane knew that this was because of her being there, was contrived for her benefit. She felt the connection between them, the chemistry, in spite of their pretence at distance.

It's over.

She wondered now how she felt about this. How she *would* feel about it, when it was out in the open. That they would need to get a divorce, and this new woman, this new love, would move into Adam and Dominic's life. She didn't know how she would feel.

Just let the letter be there, waiting, she thought. *Then I can cope.*

Bob had seen her car pull up on the drive, had perhaps even been watching out for it.

'You're just in time. I've got the kettle on.'

She wanted to make some excuse. Wanted to go straight indoors, to check whether the envelope was sitting on the doormat. But she couldn't. He looked pleased to see her; he looked like he was eager for company, for hearing her stories. He'd been looking after Josie while she'd been away. She would at least have to go into the house and collect the dog. Stay a while, have a cup of tea with him, give him what he wanted.

Josie was lying in her basket in Bob's kitchen. She stirred, her tail thumping a greeting. But didn't attempt to get up.

'Is she all right, Bob?' She felt alarmed. Usually Josie would get up, ramrod her with her heavy, writhing body, overjoyed she was home again.

'To tell you the truth, she hasn't been too well. I did try taking her for a walk yesterday, but I virtually had to pick her up and carry her back to the van. Her back legs just gave out on me.'

She knelt down by the basket. Josie laid a solemn head on her shoulder. A new fear was brewing in her now. One she'd been pushing away for weeks, for months even. That the old dog would not be around for much longer. She would leave her too.

'I expect she's just out of sorts for a while. She'll rally round,' Bob said. But she knew that he had read her thoughts, was feeling the same fear.

He made her a sandwich, a cup of tea. and they talked about her time in Cornwall – not the big things, the secrets she had told Adam, the revelation she'd had that it was over – but about Dominic. How well he was looking, how much he'd liked his present, how pleased he'd been to see her. She knew Bob was happy to hear these things. Knew he cared enough for her to stand and wave her goodbye, if she got back together with Adam and moved down to Cornwall, in spite of what it would cost him. His own loneliness closing in on him without her. She wasn't ready to spoil it for him yet.

Eventually she was able to make noises about going. She clipped the lead on to Josie's collar and between them they coaxed her up. Her legs were wobbly, unsteady still, but she was able to walk, small, shaking steps at her own pace. Jane guided her down Bob's drive and up her own. Taking it easy, not wanting to rush her.

Slipping the key into her front door, pushing it open. To see the white envelope waiting on the doormat.

But the flaring of excitement died in an instant. It was her own handwriting she was staring at, on the front of the envelope. The one she had asked to be returned to her if Paul wasn't there.

She took it into the kitchen. An *Inverness* postmark. While Josie settled wearily into her basket, Jane tore it open. Her hands were trembling. Perhaps there was a note inside it, a forwarding address. But no, of course not. Nothing. The sealed flap on the envelope had showed no signs of having been tampered with. *I should have put my phone number on the other letter, I should have told them more. I should have told them I'm looking for my brother. Stupid, stupid.*

Different options occurred to her, once she had got over the initial disappointment. She could phone Mr Mansfield, ask him to carry on searching. She could write again, to who ever lived there now at *6 Harbourside Cottages*. Ask if they had any information that would help. Yes, there were several things she could do; it wasn't all hopeless, it wasn't all lost.

Adam phoned her the next day.

'Just ringing to make sure you got back okay.'

'Fine, thank you. No problem.'

'Good. How are you? How's Josie?'

'I'm fine. Josie's finding walking a bit difficult. Her age catching up with her. But otherwise she's fine.'

She wanted to tell him the truth. She had started telling the truth, and she wanted to go on with it. Even small untruths – *I'm fine, Josie's fine* – seemed to be wrong. For a moment she had a sudden impulse to tell him about the address she'd been given in Scotland, her disappointment at finding out Paul didn't live there any more. She would have; she was on the verge of saying something, just needed a little more time to find a way into it ...

'Jane, look I don't want to upset you, if this is the wrong time for you, if you're not ready for this, but I've been thinking, it's been over two years now ... maybe it's time we thought about the next stage ...'

Divorce. He wants a divorce, she thought. She felt an edge of panic, a giddy rush of falling again. In her mind's eye she saw him with Anna. Tall, slim, blonde, beautiful Anna. Anna whom Dominic loves. Who can touch her son's face, kiss him, as if he belongs to her ...

'I see.'

Her words, the coolness of them, seemed to take him by surprise.

'It's got nothing to do with what you told me, Jane, about your mother ... nothing at all. You do believe that, don't you?'

'Yes, of course.'

'If it's a problem for you right now, we'll leave things as they are a little longer...'

'No, you're probably right, Adam. Maybe it's time to

think about formalizing it. After all, we're not going to live together again, are we?'

She was making herself sound neutral now, neither cold nor warm. As if it's okay, she's okay; it's time to move on. But another part of herself, the part that was still thirteen, was thinking, *He sees me as different now. He sees me as tainted.*

23

'Did you tell him then?'

The inevitable question. The one Jane knew that Wendy would ask.

'I couldn't.'

'Why not?'

'There's someone else. This Danish woman called Anna. She's a shiatsu therapist.'

'He told you that! I don't believe it.'

'Well, maybe not in so many words. She came over to see Dominic when I was there. There was something between them. I just felt it. She's nice. I don't blame him at all.'

'Are you sure?' Wendy was looking at her with a quiz-zical look in her eyes, as if she didn't quite believe her. And as if she felt sorry for her, pitied her.

'Don't look at me like that. I mean it.'

'What about Dominic?'

'She's good with Dominic too, this Anna. He thinks she's the best thing since sliced bread!'

'But he's your son, Jane, not hers!'

'I haven't exactly been a brilliant mother, have I? I've let him down.'

underwater

'Oh, Jane!'

Outside the window she could see Tara across the hospital lawn. She had her hands dug deeply in her jacket pockets and was walking slowly with her eyes cast down to the ground. As if she was searching the grass for something she had lost there. Something precious, something she wanted to find. It gave Jane a shock, seeing Tara again. She was supposed to be living in her half-way house, on the other side of the town, several miles away from where Ken had been moved out to.

'That's Tara, isn't it?'

'Yes. Haven't you heard? No, I suppose not – you've had a few days off. Ken's back. He's on Rivendale at the moment. I suppose Tara's just been to visit him.'

'The secure unit? What on earth for?'

She thought of the other patients in Rivendale ward. They had usually come through a legal system, having done something dreadful to someone at some time, although they could rarely be held accountable for it. They were usually in a full-blown psychosis at the time of the crime.

'I'm not sure. The story is he just couldn't cope. Only lasted a week. Got hold of a kitchen knife and threatened someone with it, apparently. The police had to be called.'

'Oh dear. That's awful.'

'It was probably intentional, in part. A cry for help. Ken's not ready to cope with life outside. There'll be plenty more episodes like that, when they've closed down this place.'

Jane watched Tara who was still walking slowly, aimlessly, staring hard at the ground. In her head she could see

Ken's painting. The hospital walls ripping apart and people flying through the air like misplaced missiles, mouths stretched in unbearable grimaces, eyes like saucers.

'Of course it'll be hard for us all. How long have we got? Not much more than a year now, I'd say. Have you started looking yet?'

'For what?' Jane said, feeling slightly flustered, as if she had been caught unawares.

'A new job, of course.'

'No. Not yet.'

This feeling of panic was returning. Everything was sliding away from her, closing down. What had she left? Even the hope that had sustained her over the last few weeks, that she might find Paul, had been shaken, fear and uncertainty put in its place. Tara was walking away now, a sense of direction and purpose back in her stride. As if she had suddenly found what she had been looking for. Or had given up searching.

'I would if I was you, Jane. Art therapy jobs aren't exactly thick on the ground.'

Josie had given up her need for walks. She would look at Jane with mild disdain when she dangled the lead.

'Come on, old girl. It'll do you good. It'll do us both good.'

Sometimes Josie would get up just to please her, walk a few steps, then sit down. Look at her, pleading in her eyes. *Don't make me.*

She took her to the vet's in the end, although she knew it was useless. Age wasn't an illness that could be cured.

underwater

'She's old now, Mrs Reynolds, very old for a Labrador. Perhaps you should be prepared for the worst.' The vet was young. Had a South African accent, precise, no-nonsense. He looked at her a little like she was wasting his time, in spite of the fact that she was paying for it anyway. She'd driven home in a panic, thinking, I'm not ready, I'm not ready to let her go yet...

She sat there that evening in the living room with Josie's head heavy on her feet, and tried to imagine what it would be like without her. Coming home from work to an empty house. No heavy body nudging against her legs, no thumping tail, or routine of walks. And when she sat alone as she did now, watching some rubbish on the television, thinking her thoughts, or trying not to, no solid, warm dog's body pushing up against her, to tell her she wasn't alone.

It had been Adam who had wanted the dog most. He'd pointed out the advert in the paper to her: *Pedigree yellow Labradors for sale.* Josie hadn't been a child substitute; she couldn't have been. Dominic had been there. A little boy of four, full of sweetness, always crawling into her lap and demanding hugs and kisses. No room for a child substitute.

'A home's not a home without a dog in it,' Adam had said. Remembering perhaps the dog he had longed for as a boy, but been refused. 'And boys need dogs.' And so one Saturday afternoon he brought home the squirming bundle of fur that came to be called Josie, after one of his aunts.

Dominic hadn't been too impressed. Preferring his toy cars and construction sets to this thing that chewed on knuckles and toes, got in the way of his play.

'Can we send it back?' he'd said to his father, vexed after the puppy had demolished his favourite car.

'She'll be fine when she's older. She needs to be trained, that's all.'

Jane heard the disappointment in Adam's voice, knowing he had bought the dog not for Dominic but for himself, for the boy that was still inside him. But in the end Josie became not Dominic's dog, not even Adam's, but hers.

The transference had been gradual, but was more or less in place by the time Dominic was seven. He had been making a transition of his own then, out of her lap and her arms into the rituals of male bonding with his father: fishing on Saturdays, football on Sundays. Maybe it left a gap, an absence. And then later, more than anyone, more than anything, during those terrible weeks after the accident, when she sat alone in the house numb with shock and refusing to be comforted, Josie had come close to her, had pushed a way through the barrier of her resistance. She'd felt the warm body against her leg, the pressure of the heavy head on her knee. When she could feel nothing else she had felt that. In the end she had no choice but to acknowledge her, to let her hand sink down on to the dog's soft head and stroke her. Smooth, slow strokes that seemed to be a way of stroking herself back to life, letting the blood flow to her heart again, the feeling return.

After that, the allegiance had switched completely. Josie was her dog now. She would shadow her, go nowhere without her, not even for a walk with Adam unless Jane came too. When Dominic had eventually come home to live, a different Dominic to the one who had fallen from the cliff that day –

his spinal cord severed, so that it was uncertain whether he'd ever have use of his legs again, a metal plate impressing his skull, the hair growing back in uneven, ugly patches – Josie seemed to recognize the danger she had of turning to stone again. Would watch her every move. Find a patch of skin somewhere, anywhere – on her knee, her hand – to lick with warm, moist strokes of her tongue. *I'm still here. I won't leave. Come back to life.*

24

She was supposed to be visiting her mother that weekend. A fortnight now since the last visit, that time she'd taken her mother out to Cley. But several days before the day she was going Mrs Clements phoned.

'Your mother's not been too well, Jane. She's got a chest infection. We're having a bit of an epidemic of things here right now. This warmer, wet weather bringing out the germs, I suppose . . .'

'Nothing serious, I hope . . .'

She was used to this game she played. The dutiful daughter, the concerned daughter.

'No, not at all. The doctor's prescribed some antibiotics, just to be sure. But it would be best to put off visiting for a week, perhaps.'

Putting down the phone, she felt relieved. She wasn't ready to visit her mother again. Remembered how she'd stared sullenly out of the window on that journey back. How she'd slouched off to her room, hadn't even said goodbye.

'Had a good time, Lillian?' Cheryl had asked her cheerily, as she'd passed her mother on the stairs. What had she overheard her mother say? 'I don't want to go out with that lady any more, dear. Tell her I don't want to.' Cheryl had shrugged helplessly at Jane. Mouthed, *She doesn't mean it, take no notice.*

But she had, of course she had.

She was angry with me. Because I spoke about you. Why shouldn't I? Why should I be silent any more?

The following Monday, during her lunch break, she went to visit Ken. She always hated going into Rivendale. There was a feeling of menace there, of things held back. Like an unexploded bomb had been left in the centre of the ward. You had to walk carefully, gingerly around it. You had to watch your step. It had a delicate, sensitive detonation device. Even your voice raised a little too loudly could set it off.

She rang the buzzer outside the locked security door. She recognized the nursing auxiliary who opened it. Jed. She sometimes saw him having lunch in the canteen.

She went in. This feeling like she was entering the lion's den. A need for eyes in the back of her head.

'Ken Richards? He was admitted last week?'

'He's still in bed. Hardly got up since he's been here. Not even for meals sometimes. Probably the drugs they've put him on. He was high as a kite when he first came in.'

Jed had that deadpan face and voice that the staff always acquired if they worked in Rivendale for long enough. Like they had stripped away their feelings, deadened them.

'I'll show you where he is.'

She followed him across the wide linoleum floor of the day room. He had a bunch of keys on a chain clipped to his trouser belt, like a jailer. They jangled when he walked. Patients were sitting on red plastic chairs that were bolted down to the floor, in front of a television mounted on a high bracket on the wall, that they weren't really watching. A few of them glancing up and glaring at her, as if they were seeing the enemy suddenly entering their territory, invading it. In the sleeping area beyond the day room, beds were cubicled off into sets of four. A wide-hipped cleaner with an even more shuttered face was rotating a polisher over waxed areas of floor.

Jed stopped. Mimed to her, pointed over to the far corner. She couldn't hear him over the drone of the polisher. She read his lips.

Over there. He's in the bed over there.

Ken was just a huddled shape under the horsehair blankets. She could only just make out his dark hair. She sat down on the wooden chair near the bed.

'Ken. It's Jane. Can you hear me?'

The polisher was swallowing up the sound of her voice. No point in talking. She reached down into the nest of his blankets, found his hand, locked his fingers in hers. She sat silently with him like this. Five minutes, ten. Finally the cleaning woman switched off the polisher. Jane heard footsteps, the sound of something heavy being dragged away, then in a little while the more muffled noise of the polisher starting up again somewhere further off.

'Ken. It's Jane here. Jane the art therapist. Can you hear me?'

underwater

The humped shape under the blankets stirred, the fingers tightening on hers.

'Can you hear me, Ken? How are you?'

Dark hair moved up the bed, two eyes peeping out. He was seeing, but not seeing. Here, but not here. She felt her heart lurch, bruise against her ribs at the sight of him. A sound that wasn't quite a human voice, but something close to it, stirred from beneath the blankets.

'Ken. How are you, dear?'

More grunts, then a little more audible.

'Not well, Jane.'

'I know, but you'll be better soon. You'll be back with me, painting in the art therapy room, soon, Ken.'

'No good, Jane.'

'What's no good?'

'It's falling.'

'What's falling, Ken?'

'The walls. The building. It's falling in, Jane. Can't get out any more.'

He turned, groaned again, the head of dark hair sinking back down under the blankets. The drone of the polisher was growing louder, moving closer again. She gave his fingers a small squeeze, but he didn't respond. She got up quietly and left him, hiding from the world in his bed, and walked down past the cubicles and across the day room again. Jed was sitting in one of the red plastic chairs, staring zombied up at the television with the rest of them. He stood up and walked towards her, jangling the keys again. He unlocked the door. A patient with a dark beard and penetrating eyes that burned into her back said, 'Fuck you, bitch!' out loud as she went out.

She had decided what to do. She would phone Mr Mansfield. Ask him if he could try and get some more information. Perhaps he could start by finding out the phone number of the people who lived at 6 Harbourside Cottages. They might have another address for Paul. Perhaps it would be that easy.

She phoned Mr Mansfield's office the following day, when she got home from work.

'Could I speak to Mr Mansfield? There's something I need to ask him . . .'

'I'm afraid he's gone on holiday for a week, Mrs Reynolds. Marbella. I'm here to handle routine enquiries. I've got an emergency number for him, if it's something urgent . . .'

She had to think for a moment. Was it urgent? Could it wait? What should she do?

'It's not really urgent. It's about the address he gave me. I've tried to follow it up, but nothing's come of it. I was going to ask if he could make some more enquiries.'

'Of course, Mrs Reynolds. I'll pass the message on to him, get him to ring you as soon as he gets back.'

'Thank you. I hope he has a nice holiday. Marbella. That's Spain, isn't it?'

'Yes. Mr Mansfield's got a holiday apartment that he usually rents out. It's vacant for this week, so he thought he'd use it. All right for some!'

She laughed, and Jane laughed with her. 'Yes, it is,' she said.

Never mind, she told herself, putting the phone down. It's only a week. He'll be able to help me. He'll find something else. Didn't he tell me, if anyone can be found then he's the man to find them?

But there was a fear cooling inside her. Whispers of doubt rustling in her heart.

What if he's wrong? What if Paul can't be found? Not ever. What then?

Almost immediately, she told herself to take a grip. Squashed the fear, the doubt down again. *I mustn't be stupid, I mustn't give up hope.* That evening she sat in the living room trying to read, but the print just blurred and swam in front of her eyes, not making sense. She put on the television, but the voices on every channel seemed too loud, jarred on her nerves. She turned it off. She stroked Josie, who was lying with her head on her slippered foot.

Somewhere in the corner of her mind, she was looking at a word that had been tucked away. The word a stranger had given her on the phone, late one night when she couldn't sleep. His name had been Simon. He had listened to her as if he really cared. How odd that someone could listen that way to someone they had never met, didn't know. She imagined him now, at the end of the phone somewhere, in a church hall, an empty room in a community centre, listening right now to someone else. The silence of his listening had banished the other silence that had pressed on her heart. But he would listen to everyone like that, she knew; she wasn't unique. The uniqueness belonged to him, not to her.

She imagined for a moment picking up the phone and dialling the number for the Samaritans. Would she get his voice again? No, not likely. It would be someone else. Perhaps someone who would listen in the same way, or perhaps not. But even if it was him, the moment had slipped away, the need, the desperation. Anyone could listen to her like that, as though she was the only person in the world that counted, and it would make no difference. The last few months had changed her. The months of the dreams and the memories leaking back. The radiotherapy that had both poisoned and perhaps healed her. And now this time of waiting . . .

It was as if these last months had taken her somewhere else. Away from that place where she could phone the Samaritans in the small, desperate hours of the night. Away to a high, dry place, where she looked down upon the world, the people in it, dispassionately, unmoved.

Doors were closing in her face. Adam was letting go, *had* let go. He had mentioned that word that neither of them could bring themselves to mention before. *Divorce.* She had let go, finally, of the perfect son she had loved, and found the room for the real one, but he didn't need her any more. Dominic would have Anna; Anna would take her place. He would be all right. She would have to be prepared for Josie passing away quite soon; she was old now, weary. Couldn't go on much longer.

The job at the hospital would go too, eventually. Maybe she'd have another year, maybe even more. But eventually she would have to move on, find another post. And Ken would have to move on too. Cope with the challenges of a new home, a home with perhaps less structure, less strictures. The tall, imposing Victorian edifices that had contained his life for years, tearing apart, ripping apart, making room for the new.

In the end, change was inevitable. It comes, no matter how much you try to resist it, she thought. You might as well let it. She still had that fear, that edge of panic, that Paul might not be found, would never come home to her. That the memories would complete their course – they would, she knew it, the tide was now unstoppable – and she would be left to cope on her own. As she had been on that day he'd left. Walking down the road away from her, not looking back.

She turned the word over in her mind again. It didn't frighten her. It made her feel strangely in control.

She tucked it away again, in the corner of her mind. Still there, but out of sight.

The following morning she was roused from her bed by the phone ringing. She wasn't working that day, was allowing herself the luxury of a lie-in. Yet it couldn't have been late, no more than eight-thirty. She answered the extension in the bedroom. Mrs Clements' voice again, but this time a little breathless, a little tremulous, sounding far away, telling her that her mother had died in the night.

Afterwards, forgetful of all the words that had been spoken, except the key words ... *your mother ... died ... in the night ...* she staggered downstairs, shaken, confused. She went into the kitchen to make herself some coffee, so she could wake up properly, could start to make sense of this sudden, shocking, unexpected news, and noticed Josie lying rigid and unmoving in her basket. Her heart lurched, knocked against her ribs. This was the greater shock, and yet she had been almost prepared for it. Had been expecting it to come soon. But never this soon.

She knelt down, placed her hand on the dog's chest. There was still a trace of warmth under her hand. But no flutter of movement, no heartbeat.

This was the greater shock. The one that sent her, slippered and still in her dressing-gown, sobbing and ranting incoherently to Bob Evans next door.

'She's died, Bob ... in the night ... a phone call from the home ... Josie ... she's not moving ... my mother ... she's gone, she's dead ...'

Bob Evans, who'd been her neighbour for years. Who watched out for her. Who took her in, made her sit down, mopped up her tears and thought mistakenly, she knew, that the tears she cried on his shoulder were mainly for her mother.

25

The following day she drove straight to the undertakers in Peterborough, before calling at the home to collect her mother's possessions. She'd been intending only to discuss the funeral arrangements. Where it should be, what time. What flowers she would like, what music, or reading. But now, sitting in the bland, comfortless office, with this thin man with pale, colourless skin – who had the manner of death about his person, moving, speaking, as if always under the weight of restraint – she knew she had to. This one last time.

He left her alone in the Chapel of Rest. She walked carefully over to the raised open coffin and stared at her mother, cushioned in peach satin. Her mother's hands, the skin white and dry like parchment, were folded carefully over her chest. She stared hard at them. Had never noticed her mother's hands as clearly as she did now. Noticed how long and fine and slender her fingers were – a piano player's hands. Noticed the two fingers on her right hand, still slightly twisted, from the time they had been broken.

I've never touched her, never been touched by her, with

affection. She reached out tentatively and touched her mother's right hand – the one with the broken fingers. She had always feared to touch her – feared the shock sensation that touching her mother's flesh might give her. The jumping-backwards feeling inside her, her own shrinking. But now nothing. The flesh felt strange beneath her fingers. Inanimate. She touched her mother's face, gaining courage. Pale and still, like wax. Nothing. There was nothing there. Whatever it was that had stirred her mother's flesh, gave life to it, had gone. As though a caged bird that had contained her mother's spirit had found its wings and flown. *Is that all death is*, she thought, *something as easy, as simple as that?*

There was nothing inside her, either. No sense of loss. Not even an emptiness, a void, that would give hope to something to fill it. She felt nothing. She turned and walked away.

Mrs Clements took her into the office, her voice solicitous and gentle, as if she was speaking to a child. She had paperwork to sign, the cheque for the balance of her mother's care to pay. It shouldn't have taken long, but Mrs Clements seemed to need to talk.

'I realize what a shock this must be for you, Jane.'

A shock? Was it? Yes, of course it was. She was thinking of poor Josie, how cold she felt, how rigid. Bob digging that deep hole in the ground . . .

'It's been a big shock for all of us. Especially for poor Cheryl. She was the one who found your mother, when she took up her breakfast on the tray. Of course, she'd been poorly, but we all thought she was getting better, seemed brighter. She was eating better, had eaten a light lunch, Cheryl told the doctor. None of us were expecting this . . .'

Jane let her run on. Tried to make her face look concerned, even sad. *The grieving daughter.* She felt nothing, wanted to go. She wasn't quite sure where she would go to. Nothing much to go home for. Josie was dead . . .

'The doctor said all indications are she had a coronary arrest in her sleep. He doubted it was related to the chest infection at all. It happens like this sometimes, with the elderly. The doctor said it would've been quick, she wouldn't have suffered . . .'

She put her cheque book away, stood up. She wanted to go.

'You'll want your mother's things, of course,' Mrs Clements said. 'Cheryl's put them somewhere – I'll go and ask her where she's put them.'

Yes, of course, her mother's things. Did she want them? She wasn't sure. But she might as well, no point in leaving them . . .

'Or perhaps you might like to ask her yourself. I think she's in the cloakroom, having her break. You might like to have a few words with her, Jane, being as she was the one who found your poor mother . . .'

Cheryl was sitting among the coats and lockers, having a cup of tea. She looked up, startled, seeing Jane suddenly appear in the doorway.

'Cheryl, do you mind. Can I have a word . . . ?'

'Yes, of course. No room in here to swing a cat, let's go to the dining room.'

The dining room was empty. Although one of the residents was hovering, getting ready to set the knives and forks on the tables for lunchtime. They sat down at one of the tables. She was suddenly feeling awkward, shy. What was she supposed to say? But Cheryl made it easier, by speaking first.

'I'm so sorry about Lillian, about your mother . . .'

'Thank you. Mrs Clements said you were the one who . . . you know . . . found her . . . That couldn't have been pleasant for you.'

'You get used to it, working here. It wasn't my first time . . .'

Cheryl stopped herself, a blush deepening on her cheeks, as if she was suddenly realizing what she was saying.

'I'm sorry . . . I didn't mean . . .'

'It's all right . . .' Jane smiled at her weakly. She felt like a fraud. Everyone speaking to her so gently, as if she was a child, as if she was ill.

'Have you decided when the funeral will be, Jane? I'd like to go, if I can. Some of the residents, too.'

Her mother had been close to Cheryl; they had liked each other. She could think this, and feel no sadness, not even a pang of jealousy. She felt nothing. Did it show? The dry eyes, the composed face she wore like a mask.

'Next Friday, at two. At the crematorium. It'll be a very simple service. The funeral director will act as Master of Ceremonies.'

'I see.'

Did she really 'see'? Or did it not seem right? To put her mother to rest with just a few words. No priests in long robes, no prayers, no hymns. She had a sudden thought – the undertaker had asked her about readings.

'There is one thing – they wanted to know if I had any special readings – poems, that sort of thing. Mrs Clements said she used to ask you to read poetry to her sometimes. I thought you might have some ideas...'

'Well, there's one I remember. Something about a piano. By D. H. Lawrence, I think.'

When she was very little, she and Paul warming their backs before the fire. Her mother playing the piano. Singing in a voice that belonged to someone else, to another time and place. *Plasir d'amour*. The hairs on the back of her neck, prickling.

'I know that one. *Softly in the dusk, a woman is singing to me; taking me back down the vistas of years...*'

'That's the one. Your mam liked that one particularly. Liked me to read it to her sometimes.'

'Would you mind reading it for her one last time? At the funeral. I'd really like you to. She would like it too, I'm sure.'

'But shouldn't you be doing that? Or what about your brother, Paul? Isn't he going to be there?'

'Paul? How do you know about Paul?'

The words snapped, like an accusation.

'I – I didn't m-mean ... she told me once, she had a son. She said his name was Paul.'

'She told you that? What else did she tell you?'

'Nothing. Just that she had a son.'

Her mother, talking about Paul to a stranger. Someone who could touch her, without shrinking. Help her in and out of the bath, cut her toenails. Read her poems on Sunday afternoons, when time would still and slow . . .

'I'm sorry, Cheryl. I didn't mean to snap at you.' She paused, breathed deeply. 'It's just that Paul is a difficult subject for me. He disappeared when I was fourteen. I haven't seen him since. It's all rather painful, you see.'

'Oh dear. I'm so sorry, Jane.'

She laughed, to displace the tension.

'Anyway, you see, Paul won't be there. He can't read it!'

'I'll read the poem, Jane, if you want me to. No problem.'

She was turning, about to go. Cheryl touched her arm, to stop her. Seemed suddenly to remember something.

'Just a minute, Jane.' She patted her pocket, as if to check something was still there. 'There's something else. I found this inside one of your mother's books yesterday . . .'

Cheryl slid an envelope out of her pocket, held it towards her. Just for an instant, she thought it was the letter she'd been expecting. On the front of the envelope, Paul's handwriting, the staccato jerkiness of her brother's writing. Then, understanding dropping like a stone . . .

Her hands, shaking as she opened the door of the car, as she turned the ignition. Shaking on the steering wheel, as she drove away. She felt sick, she felt nauseous. She had to stop. She didn't want to look inside the envelope, but she had to. She pulled up on a lay-by several hundred yards down the road.

A card inside. And two photographs. She slid them out of the ragged opening. Her hands still shaking. She looked at the photographs first. The first photo was of Paul, standing on a shingle beach. How old was he there? Perhaps sixteen. Perhaps taken that last summer they went to Cley for their holiday. A jetty behind them; it looked like Wells harbour. The man standing next to him was smiling, relaxed and happy; they both were. He wasn't her father. But she knew who he was. She had seen this photo before.

She looked at the other photograph. Paul again, but a different Paul. A Paul she had never known. A grown man now, in his mid-thirties or thereabouts. He was standing on a different beach now, a wide beach of white sand, leaning on the side of a boat, smiling. A young girl about eight or nine, wearing red shorts, blonde hair trailing across her face, standing next to him. *Who is she? His daughter?* She studied the girl's face, but found no trace of him there.

She turned to the card. The picture on the front was of a wide, white beach, like the one in the second photo. She turned it over. *The beach at low tide. Findhorn. Reproduced from a painting in oils.* The artist had a Scottish name. She opened up the card. Her heart was beating fast, tides of blood pulsing in her ears. The same spiky handwriting that had addressed the envelope: *Happy birthday, Mum. Love, Paul.*

A hot rage was filling her head, building in her chest. And that tidal wave again, rumbling and building in the distance. When she started the car again it was as if she had slipped outside her skin again. She wasn't sure where she was going.

PART FOUR

26

Bob stood outside in the garden and sniffed the air. He looked up at the sky. Dark clouds were building. It was going to rain later, it was going to pelt down. The grass was beginning to grow fast now; it had been untouched since the previous summer. Best do it now, he thought. He dragged the old electric mower out of the rubble in the shed. Plugged it in, clicked it into action. The whine of the electric motor filled his head. He guided the machine up and down the long lawn in smooth, straight lines, his hands vibrating gently on the long handles as if a tremor had set into them. At the far end, the bare patch of recently turned-over soil, where the old dog lay. He gave it a clean berth, didn't like to look at the place. Didn't like to think of Josie lying in the cold soil, missing this: the days lengthening rapidly now and the sense of things growing, coming back to life.

He felt uneasy. Partly because of the old dog, and the way Jane had looked that morning, standing in his porch pressing his doorbell, still in her dressing-gown and slippers. Raving about death and phone calls and her mother and Josie all in the same breath, so that it was hard for him to separate out her tears and her words. To decide which of the two she grieved for most – her mother or Josie. *Her mother, of course*, he had thought at first. But now, leaning on the mower, finishing off the last few rows, he knew he had been mistaken. He remembered the way she had shuddered with shock when she took him into the kitchen and showed him the dog. He'd knelt down by the basket, laid his hand against the stiffening flanks.

Goodbye, old girl. He said it under his breath. He felt the beginnings of a lump in his throat. He'd swallowed it down. Didn't want his upset to show, didn't want Jane to see it. He'd stood up and held her. Felt her weight leaning into his chest, her knees almost buckling against his trousered legs.

'She's gone, Jane. She's at peace now,' he said.

It was her idea to bury Josie in his garden. She wanted her close, but not too close. Didn't want to stand there with the earth under her feet, imagining its weight on the dog, crushing her bones in the dark soil. She hadn't said that. She hadn't needed to. But that was what she'd thought, he knew.

'Could we bury her in your garden, not mine? If you don't mind, Bob.'

He didn't mind. Not if it helped her, if it made it easier. She'd stood at his kitchen window gazing out, watching him as he dug the hole, panting with the exertion, throwing the soil over to one side so that it formed a soft, deep pile. The soil was easy to dig. There had been enough rain, but not too much so that it became cloying and sticky like clay. Just enough to soften it, to make the spade rip into it cleanly. The dog was heavy, heavier still now dead. He had to get on to his knees and push the awkward shape, parcelled in black bin liners, over to the edge of the hole, push it over the edge. It made him queasy, feeling the stiffened flesh of the animal under his hand. He imagined where the head was, the legs. Tried to make sure that when it slid into the hole it was the back end of the animal that landed first. He didn't want her landing on her face.

Jane stayed in his house until it was over. Every so often he glanced up and saw her at the kitchen window, her face behind the glass, a white flag of distress. She didn't come out until the hole was filled up, the surface smoothed off and pressed down neatly by the even stamping of his boots. She stood on the lawn with him, a few feet in front of the turned-over earth.

'I feel I should be saying something. A few words. Like a service. What do you think, Bob?'

'Up to you, Jane,' he'd said. 'You say what you want to, love. Or think it to yourself, if you prefer. Whatever feels best. The old dog won't mind.'

'Oh, Bob!' There was a break in her voice. They stood for a few moments in silence together. He was holding her hand. Felt the slight clench of her fingers on his. He didn't know what her words were, or if there were any words at all. She kept them to herself. She slid her hand out from his and turned to walk indoors.

'She was a great dog, Jane. The best,' he said, feeling it was safe now to let words out.

But putting the mower away, he glanced up at the thickening clouds again, feeling uneasy. He hadn't known that morning, when she'd left, about the storm that was coming, the gale-force winds that were predicted for later that evening. He'd heard about it on the radio. The worst of the storms would be in the north, the forecast had said. *That'll be all right then*, he thought. *They'll miss her. And anyway, she'll be back soon. She'll be back by fiveish.* He glanced at his watch. It was four.

After they had buried the old dog yesterday, and she'd let him make her some breakfast, hardly touching the toast, sipping the black coffee, she'd made some phone calls. She'd needed to call the care home, needed to arrange for an undertaker, she'd said. For a moment he'd been startled, not quite knowing what she meant.

Her mother's died, she's got her mother's death to deal with too, of course.

She was fingering the edges of the toast, pulling it to shreds.

'Don't go today, Jane. Go tomorrow, when you've had time to take this in. Let the shock settle down.'

She had listened to him. He felt like he was a father talking to a child. She was nearly twenty years younger than him; he could even be her dad, at a push. He often felt like that, around Jane. Something almost childlike about her, sometimes. A vacancy, a yielding. At times of stress she seemed to cave in, the spirit in her subsiding. Or maybe he imagined she did. Maybe he liked that feeling. Being fatherly, propping her up.

She phoned Orchard Park. Asked for a Mrs Clements. He'd listened to her voice suddenly switching into a different register, sounding calm, in control. *That's how she does it*, he thought. The childlike Jane suddenly taken over by this other persona. The rational Jane, the one who copes. Or seems to. He heard her discussing the funeral arrangements. Heard her say she'd call at the home tomorrow, settle the bill, collect her mother's things.

He was relieved. Didn't want her tearing off there straight away, the shock of two deaths in her eyes.

Afterwards, she'd gone home. She needed to be on her own, she'd said. He'd given her an hour, a couple of hours, then had gone knocking on her door.

'Let me take you out, Jane. Let's drive to the Downs. I'll treat you to lunch somewhere.'

She'd said yes, and he could tell from the look on her face that she needed to be out of the house now, away from the confining walls and the absence of the dog in the empty basket. Needed to be out under the open sky, the fresh air blowing through her thoughts; it was the right thing to do. She brightened up and took his arm. They walked for several miles, and she talked freely to him. He had expected her to reminisce about her mother, recall perhaps some childhood memories, but it was of Josie that she talked. She told him about the day Adam had brought the puppy home for the first time, carrying this dollop of fur and licking tongue into the house in his arms.

'Hey, look what I've got.'

He'd sounded like a kid at Christmas. He put the puppy down and the first thing it did was squat and do a puddle on the floor.

'I hope you're going to clean that up,' she'd told him. But laughing; she didn't mind.

They stopped at a high point on the hill and gazed down over the patchwork of fields far below. Below them a glider was being winch-launched into the air, its nose tilting forward, lifting into flight. It looked like a white prehistoric bird with a life of its own. One day, Bob thought, I'd like to try my hand at that, gliding. So many things he'd like to do, one day. Why was he waiting?

In the pub they ate tagliatelle in a creamy mushroom sauce, had a glass of dry white wine, and toasted Josie.

'And to your mum, Jane,' he said, and she'd clinked glasses again, half-heartedly. He felt embarrassed for a moment. Had he said the wrong thing?

'You weren't close, were you, Jane?' he said. His voice gentle, not wanting her to think he was judging.

Thinking about it, he realized he had always known – despite the regular trips in the last few years to visit her in Peterborough – that her mother was really an absence in her life. He didn't remember her ever coming to Jane's house to visit. Not even years ago, when Jane and Adam had first moved in. And all those years when the boy was growing up. Not even then.

That's when she told him everything. About her mother serving twelve years in prison for killing her father. About her brother who left home when she was fourteen, whom she had never seen again.

'Did you ever try to find him?' he asked.

He was shocked, trying to hide it. Finding it hard to take all this in. So much revelation, all of a sudden, all at once. He was thinking, *Why is she telling me, when she's never told me before?* She had the sky still in her eyes. Was there across the table, but not there. She had recoiled slightly at his words. Smiled, a smile like a grimace, like something was hurting.

'Not until a few weeks ago. I went to see a private investigator. He gave me an address. In Findhorn, Scotland. I sent him a letter but it was returned to me unopened.'

It pained him to see her look so dejected. He was thinking of the old dog in the ground, the mother who was more like an absence. He wanted to make things better, to bring the missing brother back for her.

'Do you know what I would do if I was you? I'd drive up there. Findhorn. That's a small place, isn't it? A fishing village. I'd call at the house you sent the letter to and ask whoever lives there directly. Someone might know something about him. If not at the address itself, then at the pub, the post office. It he lived there once, someone might know something.'

She'd looked at him then, hope dawning in her eyes.

'Maybe I'll do that, Bob.'

He suddenly wished he hadn't said anything. He had a vision of her driving miles and miles away, the sky and the shock of death in her eyes, and being lost to him.

At six o'clock he scraped the dinner he'd cooked her into the bin and phoned the residential home. He got the number from directory enquiries.

A woman with a brusque manner answered the phone. He asked to speak to Mrs Clements. Hadn't that been the name Jane had mentioned yesterday?

'Speaking.'

'I was wondering if a Jane Reynolds called there today? Her mother died yesterday morning.'

'Yes, she called here this afternoon. Who did you say you are?'

He hadn't.

'I'm a neighbour. I live next door to her. I was wondering what time she left? It's just that I'm a little worried about her. I was expecting her back by now.'

'Let me see now. It must have been about half two. She had a short conversation with a member of the staff about her mother's belongings.'

'Would it be possible to have a word with the member of staff?'

'No, I'm sorry. She's not on duty at present.'

The voice stiffened. He could sense her mistrust building. *Who is this? He says he's a friend, a neighbour. How do I know?*

'I'm sure she'll be back soon. Maybe she's dropped off somewhere to do some shopping.'

'Yes. Sorry to trouble you. Thanks for your time.'

He had tried her mobile, but knew he'd get no answer. Jane was one of these dinosaurs who rarely used technology. Didn't like it, didn't trust it. He had persuaded her to invest in a mobile – *For emergencies, Jane. In case the car breaks down.* But she rarely switched it on. He was diverted straight away to an answering service. He left a message: *Jane, this is Bob. Are you all right? Ring me when you pick up this message.* But he knew she wouldn't. He doubted if she even knew how to listen to the messages, what buttons to press.

The rain was coming down in sheets by the time he left for work. He imagined her – *Where? Somewhere, anywhere* – driving alone in the dark, in the heavy sheeted rain, grief loosening the memories. He had a feeling that something was unravelling in her, and it wasn't finished yet.

27

She stood on the shingle beach at Cley. On the ridged sand, left behind from high tide, and watched the waves roll in. They rolled in noisily, driven by the wind, and yet with the pull of the outgoing tide, each incoming wave seemed tired and spent, failing to reach the furthest lip of the water. She stood for a while, reclaiming her breath, looking out at the grey water that filled up the horizon, the grey of sea moving up into the grey of the banking cloud.

Memories were running clearly through her now.

She was remembering when she'd gone missing herself.

Several weeks after her aunt's funeral, seven years ago. She had dreaded going, not just because of the grief she'd felt, intensified because it coincided with that darkest time of the year that she'd always hated. But because she knew her mother would be there.

Uncle Bill had stood with her in the cold wind outside the crematorium, waiting for the first lot of mourners to come out. How close the services are, she'd thought. Each one following directly on another, as if death is everywhere, is all around us. Which of course it is, although in the

daylight clamour of the present it is possible to pretend
otherwise. She had held on to Uncle Bill's arm, and they
had walked in, each leaning against the other for support.
My mother isn't here, she hasn't come! she'd thought at first,
feeling a surge of relief. Then minutes later it was quelled
by a feeling that her mother was standing behind her, several rows back. She turned swiftly round to look, if only to
satisfy herself that she was mistaken. But she wasn't.

Her mother was dressed in black. She gazed directly
ahead, so that Jane, turning, caught her gaze, and what
passed between them – the past, all those years – shook her
to the core. Her mother didn't smile, gave instead a small,
discreet nod – *I know how you feel. I know, and I won't try
to change it.* Jane turned sharply away, tried to fix her mind
on the words that were being said.

There was only a handful of people there. A Methodist
minister said a few words about her aunt that her uncle had
prepared. *She had been a wonderful wife to her husband,
William, and a surrogate mother to her niece and nephew,
taking them in at a time of trouble in the family, giving them
love and stability.* That had been *her* imput; she had told
Uncle Bill she wanted that said.

'I'm not sure,' he had told her. 'Your mother – she
might be there. She won't like it, hearing that said out loud.'

'Put it in,' she'd told him. Insisted really. 'It's the truth.
Funerals are a time for saying the truth. I need it said.'

When it was read out she made herself turn and look
quickly at her mother's face – she wanted to catch the
expression there, however fleeting. But her mother's eyes
were closed; she saw nothing.

Her mother had no transport of her own, had travelled by train. It was natural that she should come with them in the car. Jane sat alone in the back. Stared at the back of her mother's head. *Did prison turn her hair that grey? What was it like, all those years?*

Back at the house, plates of egg and cucumber sandwiches and sponge cake were passed among them, prepared by kind Doreen from next door, who only had good things to say about her aunt, as indeed they all had: *Such a lovely lady, Bill. Never an unkind word to be said about any one. We'll all miss her.* Tears had glistened in Uncle Bill's eyes. He felt the years before him stretching as arid and unrelenting as a drought; he didn't know how he'd get through them.

For a while she could avoid her mother. Avoid standing too close to her, avoid catching her eye. But then people made excuses about needing to go, one by one taking their leave – *Let us know, Bill, if there's anything we can do, don't hesitate –* yet knowing he wouldn't; grief being like a disease requiring solitary confinement, something to get through alone. All of a sudden she found herself standing next to her mother and saying, 'Paul should be here; if only he was here.'

Why did she say it? The words seemed to come from her involuntarily, a reflex action. Or had they been lodged in her all the time, from the first moment of turning round and seeing the look in her mother's eyes? All the years piling in on her in that moment, the weight of the memories. And now grief making her open and vulnerable. She wanted her mother to hold her. She wanted to weep like a child on her mother's breast.

'How can he? He's much too far away for that. He can't come back.'

The words had drifted from her mother's mouth, as if she was saying them to herself, caught in a dream; they weren't meant for anyone to hear, to respond to. But Jane had heard them. And suddenly they took on all the significance of those wasted years, and the suspicion she had fermented in her mind all that time, hardly knowing it was there.

'You know where he is, don't you? You know.'

The question was hissed on her breath. Her mother turning from her now, alarmed. She reached out and grabbed her mother's arm.

'You know, don't you? Tell me where he is.'

'You're hurting me, Jane. I don't know what you're talking about. Let go of me.'

'*Tell* me where he is!'

But her fingers were slipping from her mother's arm, and the words were said with less vehemence, less hope of being answered. Her uncle was returning now from having seen a guest off at the door. Her mother walked towards him, leaving a trail of reproach behind her.

'I need to go now, Bill. Will you take me to the station? I need to catch a train home.'

'Did something happen between the two of you?' he asked when he returned. She was clearing up, stacking the plates in the dishwasher, the empty cups and glasses.

'Why? Did she say it had?'

'She said nothing to me, Jane. But she was upset. I could tell it.'

'I asked her about Paul, Uncle Bill. Something she said – it made me think she knew where he was – so I asked her.'

He sat down. The day had been too much for him. The funeral, and now this. The boy's name evoked like a ghost from the past.

'Heavens, Jane! Is this the day to bring all that up?'

She closed the dishwasher, straightened up. She turned to him.

'When has it ever been the right day for bringing Paul up? He's dead to us too, isn't he? He might as well be.'

He looked at her then. He was seeing her for a moment as she really was. Perhaps he had never seen her this way before. From the night she had landed on his doorstep, escorted by two policemen. A girl of thirteen, who wore her face like a mask.

'No, he's not, Jane. He's alive. I think you might be right. I think she might know where he is.'

It was something Aunt Jean had told him once. About a visit she'd made soon after Lillian had come out of prison, driving down on her own to the Fenland house that had been left like a mausoleum for years. Lillian was writing a letter when she'd arrived.

'Don't let me interrupt you. You finish your letter.'

'Don't be silly, Jean. I can finish it later.'

She had laid the letter to one side, placed it on the open lid of the bureau while they had talked. Jean told her about Jane's engagement to Adam. They had just announced it.

'That's nice. I hope she'll be happy,' Lillian had said. She went into the kitchen to put the kettle on then, to make another cup of tea. Jean had stood up to admire a picture hanging on the wall behind the bureau. It wasn't one she recognized. She didn't remember it being one of those she and Bill had stashed away in the attic. She hadn't meant to, it wasn't like she'd been prying or anything, but she'd caught herself glancing down, seeing the opening words of the letter Lillian been writing . . .

28

It had played on her mind incessantly. The thoughts of betrayal lacing the grief, making it harder to mourn. Her mother had betrayed her, by knowing where Paul was, writing to him even, and not telling her. And her aunt, hadn't she betrayed her too?

'Why didn't she tell me this?' she had asked Uncle Bill. He had tried to think back to the reasons, tried to justify the decision. Because a decision it had been. *Best not to tell Jane.* No need to upset her. She's getting on with her life. She's married now. She won't want to be reminded about all that stuff. And anyway, Adam doesn't know; she won't want to involve him in this. *Don't tell Adam the truth about what had really happened.* Isn't that what she had always said?

But a decision made for one time cannot be clearly understood when brought forward into another. His excuses sounded lame to her. Although she knew she couldn't hold him responsible for the silence; she knew she must shoulder some of the blame. The young woman she had been then, standing next to Adam in the registry office making her vows, would not have wanted her brother brought back to her. Could not have borne the affront in Adam's eyes. The questions, the accusations: *Why didn't you tell me the truth? Why did you lie?*

One deception meshed into a web of others. If Paul had been found then, if he had walked back into her life, everything would have crashed upon her head. Adam would've had to know everything. How much would she have told him, how much left out? Truth enmeshed with lies, worse perhaps than no truth at all. He would have looked at her differently. What would he have seen?

'But why didn't Aunt Jean confront her? Tell her she had seen the letter. Ask her where Paul was?'

Uncle Bill shook his head sadly. He had scattered his wife's ashes on the ground only hours earlier, on the rose bush planted in her name in the memorial garden. His heart was heavy. Hadn't he enough ghosts to lay to rest? And now Jane was bringing back this other one . . .

'She thought it best not to. Lillian hadn't long been out of prison, Jane. Who knows? Maybe writing letters was just her way of keeping Paul alive, keeping him with her. Maybe she never posted them. Maybe she didn't know anything. Your aunt thought it best forgotten. She thought *you* wanted to forget.'

But everything had changed by the time her aunt had died.

In the first night after Dominic's fall from the cliff, keeping vigil by his bedside, Adam had left her for a while to get some coffee to keep sleep at bay, to smoke a cigarette outside in the grey beginnings of dawn. She'd sat there alone, and gazed with despair at the tubes that fed in and out of her son's body, at his bandaged, misshapen head, and prayed that he wouldn't return to her unless he could return the way he had been. Perfect, unblemished.

When Adam returned, offering her black, bitter coffee in a polystyrene cup, she'd wanted to confess the prayer to him. But how could she tell him? He would have seen what she was capable of. The void she had in her heart.

God had punished her for that prayer. Given her son back to her, but damaged and broken. The Dominic she had loved had gone for ever. He would never make her proud now. Never go to university. Never marry, give her grandchildren. All of that wiped away, in the blink of an eye, in the upward, sudden flight of a bird on a cliff and a startled boy, who stood too near to the edge.

She had stood in the kitchen that Sunday, preparing the dinner for when they got back. Adam was out with Dominic, watching football on the Common. She wondered how he could do that. Take him in his wheelchair to watch other boys running around on beautiful, sturdy legs, like his used to be.

Tears from the onions filling her eyes, streaming down her face. She wanted Paul to come back again. Wanted him to walk down the street towards her, still carrying the rucksack on his back, his russet hair lit like flame in the sun, his face blurred with smiles. She would run to meet him. Would pretend that the world hadn't changed; bad things hadn't happened.

Her uncle's words churned in her mind; she couldn't

turn them off: 'Your aunt saw the letter that your mother was writing.' *Dear Paul, it was wonderful to hear from you . . .*

She had to know the truth. She threw down the paring knife. Left the onion lying on the chopping board, with its gleaming, translucent slices. Left the joint wrapped in foil, the saucepan of peeled vegetables. She grabbed her handbag. Her car keys and jacket from the hooks in the hallway. She couldn't remember if she had slammed the front door behind her or left it swinging open. She got into her car, reversed out on to the road. Her mind was fixed unwaveringly on where she was going.

She was driving to the house where she had lived as a child.

How long did it take her? Two hours, more? She drove all the way without stopping. What was she planning to do, or say? She didn't know. She had slipped outside her body; she wasn't there. Space in her eyes, and the countryside levelling to dark fields severed by straight lines of water. The sky opening up above her head, clouds massing like portents. This was remembered land. She felt afraid, she felt she was being set free. She wanted to turn back, she wanted to go on.

She reached the turning that led to the hamlet. Drove down the lane, passed Sharon Baker's house. She thought, for one crazy moment, about stopping and knocking on the door, to see if Sharon still lived there. But of course she didn't. What was she doing now? Was she married, did she have children? Grandchildren, even, coming to visit her this Sunday afternoon?

But perhaps Sharon's parents hadn't moved, were still there. She remembered Mrs Baker's alarmed face, the pity in her eyes. *There's been a terrible accident. Something has happened to your father.* Would she recognize her, if she knocked on the door now? Remember the subdued girl escorted away by two policemen to the waiting car in the lane . . . ?

She drove on by, twisting her head to see into the garden. Swings and a slide, small children clambering. A man with dark hair, in his thirties. The Bakers had gone. Moved on. The years had changed them all.

But for Jane, pulling up on the piece of waste land outside the gap in the hedgerow, nothing had changed. She walked across the front lawn, up the pathway that led along the side of the house to the garden at the back. Nothing had changed. She was a child, who moved as stealthily as a ghost. Fear crouched in her chest, in her stomach. She had eyes at the back of her head. She was watching out for a man who would suddenly lurk at windows, the light glancing off the glass he held in his hand. Who would paint pictures at the bottom of the garden while she and Paul played. His head, snapping up impatiently if they made too much noise: *Stop that bloody racket!*

Her father wasn't there. And the garden she remembered – the smooth lawn leading to the dark, turned earth, with its rows of cabbages, onions and swede; the beans springing up rampantly on stakes; the fruit trees, apple and pear and plum; the sprawling brambles of soft fruits down the far end, just before the rough ground where her father would burn leaves and rubbish in the autumn – all of that was gone. Nature had claimed it. Years of weeds and neglect turning it to wilderness. Although it was still winter and nothing was growing yet.

But a few neat flowerbeds outside the French windows remained. Her mother was there, kneeling on a rubber mat on the damp grass. Her back turned towards Jane, kneeling as if she was praying. Jane stood stock-still. The fear in her chest and belly was the same: *nothing had changed*. She made no sound, yet her mother turned and looked at her. Did she have eyes, too, in the back of her head?

'Oh, it's you. You've come then, at last.'

Her mother's voice flat, emotionless. Almost as if she had been expecting her. She climbed slowly to her feet. Stood there, looking at her daughter with empty, unreadable eyes.

'You'd better come in then. You'll want a cup of tea, I expect.'

She followed her mother into the house. Through the side door that led into the small utility room where coats and shoes were stored, through into the kitchen. Nothing had changed. Perhaps the walls had been painted a different colour. Cream now, instead of the mint green they had once been. But the same rough pine cupboards that her father had made himself, the same slate floors. Even the same weathered table and captain's chairs over by the wall. It was a little untidier perhaps, a little more cluttered, as if her mother didn't have the energy any more to keep things in order.

'You'd better sit down.'

She sat down at the table. Her mother turned on the taps, rinsed the black soil from her hands, dried them and filled the kettle. Then turned and looked at her.

'It's a long time since you were in this house, isn't it, Jane?'

Between the words, the things that were not said. *Why has it taken you so long? Why have you never been before?*

Jane didn't answer. Couldn't. It was easier to attack, to ask a question instead.

'Why are *you* still here? Why haven't you moved out to somewhere smaller? This house, this garden – it's all too much for you now.'

And between *her* words did her mother hear – *How can you stand to be here? Don't you hear him, when you lie in bed? Moving sullenly about downstairs. Or worse. Like now, when you're here in the kitchen. Don't you see him lying at your feet, in a pool of blood? How do you stand it?*

'Where else do I have to go? This is my home. I've nowhere else.'

Her mother reaching up to the glazed cupboard door, taking out white china cups, a teapot.

Her mother warming the teapot, spooning in loose, black-leafed tea from the caddy, pouring in the boiling water, placing a tea cosy on it. Doing it still the old-fashioned way. *Nothing has changed.* Her mother still made something in her shrink back. She could hardly look at her.

'Milk? Sugar?'

In a minute, Jane thought, she will ask me how the family is. How is Adam? How is Dominic? The son-in-law, the grandson she has never seen. I won't know how to

258

answer. I won't want to tell her my life isn't perfect. I won't want her to know.

Her mother turned to look at her again. Jane made herself look back. Her mother was leaning on the cupboard by the sink. The late afternoon sun slanting through the window cast shadows on her face. At her left, one of those fashionable wooden knife blocks. Something that *had* changed, something that was different. The kitchen knives had been kept before on a rack on the wall; they had dark ebony handles. The handles of these, sticking out from the deep slots in the wood, were smooth, stainless steel.

'Why are you here, Jane? What have you come to say?'

The past was coming back. Ghosts lurked with them in the kitchen, waiting for her words.

'I needed to talk to you. About what you said at the funeral. I mentioned Paul. I said how I wished he could be there. "How can he come? – he's much too far away for that," you said.'

'I don't remember saying that. If I did, it was a slip of the tongue. It meant nothing.'

There was coldness in her mother's voice, and distance. *She cares nothing for me, She never has.*

'Uncle Bill told me Aunt Jean saw a letter you were writing to him once. You've kept in touch with him. I want you to tell me where he is.'

'I don't know what you're talking about. I've never written . . .'

The ghosts were moving closer, were urging her on.

'I think you know where he is. I think you have always known.'

259

'How could I know? Don't be stupid, Jane.'

'I think you planned it with him. You told him to go.'

Her mother moved forward, her face sliding out from the shadows. She could see the tight set of her mother's mouth. Could see her brother's face moving out of the shadows, hear his voice: *Say it, Jane. Make her tell the truth.*

'That new solicitor you had for the appeal. She talked to Paul and me, as well. Separately, on our own. Did you know that?'

'She shouldn't have, she'd no right to . . .'

They could have been back there, on the night it had happened. She imagined her own fingers wrapping around the steel handles of the knives, wrenching them now from the slotted wood . . .

'Maybe Paul said something he shouldn't have. Let something slip, something you wouldn't have wanted him to say . . .'

'I don't know what you're talking about . . .'

'What did you tell him? Did you tell him to leave? Have you known where he is, all this time?'

'You're ranting, Jane. Just like your father.'

Her mother was moving towards her, her hands raised, reaching towards her. Jane stood up quickly. The chair clattered backwards on the tiled slate floor.

'Don't touch me! Don't come near me! Just tell me where my brother is. Just tell me the truth.'

Her mother laughed, strangely. There was something in the laugh that made Jane shudder.

'Why should you care so much?'

'He's my brother, I have a right to know.'

'Is he? *Is* he your brother?'

Something cold and ugly now, in her mother's voice. She didn't want to hear; water was closing over her head again . . .

'You said you want to know the truth? I'll tell you the truth. He's only your half-brother. That's all.'

'I don't believe you. You're lying. You've always been lying . . .'

'*Your* father wasn't *his* father. He thought the baby was his, but I always knew it wasn't. There was someone else. He was older than me, and married. But he was the one I loved. I never loved your father.'

She could hear a distant surging. That tidal wave she always imagined would rise up again and claim her . . .

'I only married him because it was a way of keeping the child. You were the mistake, not Paul. I never wanted you.'

She moved forward quickly. Grabbed the chair by the table, rammed it up against her mother's stomach.

'You're lying. You're a slag, a dirty whore.'

She was seeing the gleaming handles of the knives. She was thinking, *I could grab one now. I could stick it in her.*

But she didn't. She ran from the kitchen. Down the path at the side of the house, across the ragged front garden. She felt for a minute she had become her father. His words had climbed inside her mouth. His rage burning in her.

29

She hadn't driven back home afterwards. Instead, she had somehow found herself standing here, on the same shingle beach she was standing on now. Seven years later.

It had been a similar time of day, but a day in early February instead of April. Dusk was falling fast. She could hardly remember how she'd got there. Parking the car, stumbling on the footpath across the marshes. When she arrived, clambering over the ridge and down on to the beach, the tide was low, the waves sucking back. In the distance, down the long beach leading eastwards to Salthouse, she could see a man fishing. His body formed a bluish smudge in the dusk, the thin line of the rod extending from his arms barely visible.

She didn't know why she had driven to Cley that afternoon, what she had intended. Except that maybe her mother's taunting had brought back the need to be there. In this place that had once been happy for her – *almost perfect.*

She didn't know if she had it in her head all the time – what she would do when she got there. She just wanted the pain to go. The coldness of her mother's eyes and words, and this realization, like a knife in her own heart. *She's never loved me. Never.* More than that, memories, feelings, unbearable to look at. *Paul had a different father; your father was not his.* She couldn't bear it; she had to shut them out.

It wasn't a thought, a decision. Something carefully considered: *Do you ever think of suicide?* It was as if she had slipped outside her body again, was watching herself walking into the waves, gasping with the shock of the cold, but walking further and further. And even if she had wanted to turn back, she couldn't. Then all of a sudden she had slipped back into her body again, and the icy bite of the water was taking away her breath and filling her clothes, was dragging her down. She felt, in an instant, simultaneously, a longing to die, a terror of the water closing over her head.

She hadn't heard his voice, although later she realized he must have been shouting. All the way, running up the long beach towards her in the dusk. She didn't hear his voice, but she felt his arms around her, tugging her, like a fisherman tugs on a net. The sky suddenly opening over her head again and the light coming back. She was gasping on the air. Sucking on it, choking on it, not able to get enough.

He was locking her under his arm, moving her through the breaking waves towards the beach. Her feet were stumbling, trailing on the sea floor. She heard his voice – 'It's all right, you're safe, you're nearly there.' The sounds barely making sense, seeping into her through her deep weariness, but holding her up, sustaining her. For a moment she had wondered, *Is this real? Am I dreaming? Am I dead?*

She was thinking these thoughts again, seven years later, Standing here on the same shingle beach. This time there was no turmoil of emotions, churning, conflicting within her. She was calm. Estranged still on that high, dry plateau where little could reach her, touch her. She sat down on the shingle. She was remembering that time she had brought Adam here, several months after they had met. She'd wanted to show him, share with him, just a small part of her childhood. A part that wasn't completely tainted, that still held a grudging sense of magic. Ambivalent perhaps, but still there. The walks on the marshes with her father. Those times, the better times, when she could almost persuade herself that he loved her; that he wasn't so bad. He would point out the marsh birds to her. The ring-plover and teal, avocet and redshank. Once, a bittern. She remembered the chattering of the birds in the reed beds. The cottage where rules could be broken, where you could pretend that they were not there at all.

'It was one of my favourite places when I was a child,' she'd told him. She had stood there on that summer's evening, his arm around her, made herself shut out the ghosts that trembled softly in the dusk: Paul, his elbow hinged tensely, poised to skim pebbles over the water; her father walking ahead on his own, stopping to examine a shell, a stone, a piece of sea-worn glass; her mother standing apart, lost in her thoughts. There had been a small fishing ketch pulled up on the beach. Adam had led her gently behind it. He had made love to her, his body moving on hers and the stones moaning softly underneath her. The ghosts were quiet; she thought she had succeeded in making them disappear. Afterwards they went back to the guest house and he had proposed to her and she had said, *Yes. Yes, I will.*

'You're crying,' he'd said, stroking away a tear with the edge of his thumb. But she had never been so happy as she was then. The ghosts were quiet; she had even believed they had been vanquished for good.

But ghosts, she knew now, could not be vanquished. They could not be subdued by force. They might withdraw, lie quiet for years, as her ghosts had. But they had hovered at the edges of her world, leaked back, finally, into her dreams. Their voices whispering their secrets, clamouring for hers in return. She would have to go and meet them. She had no choice.

She took the photographs that Cheryl had given her out of her handbag again. She looked at them. The one of Paul on the beach with his father was hazy, as if the camera was pointed slightly into the sun. Despite the lack of clarity, she could see, anyone could see, the man's features were in the boy. The same jawline, deepset eyes, the same red hair. They were both smiling out at whoever was behind the camera. Her mother? Did she take it on the day when she had been walking alone with her father over the marshes to Blakeney Point? The day they'd seen a bittern for the first time. A mottled-golden, crouched shape in the reeds, its beak pointed sharply upwards, as if in terror, towards the sky.

His name was Michael. The man who had tugged her from the sea. He had hurried her across the beach, her feet dragging, slipping on the shingle, exhausted, and over to his car that was parked on the lane that led up to Salthouse, where he lived. In his cluttered terraced cottage, in his tiny bathroom, she'd stripped off her wet clothes and wrapped herself in a huge towelling robe that Michael had given her to wear. He put her clothes through a cycle in the washing machine to rinse out the stiffening salt, and she sat before a blazing open fire in his small front room, while they steamed on the clothes-horse behind her.

Over the three or four hours that she had sat there, he said little to her. A few facts about himself, to answer an enquiry from her perhaps. He used to work on the trawlers, off the east coast of Scotland. He had moved to Norfolk a few years back, taken a job laying gas pipes at Bacton. The fishing wasn't what it used to be, back home in Scotland, he'd said. His face was weatherbeaten; it was hard for her to tell his age. In his mid-thirties, somewhere, she thought.

He didn't interrogate her. Didn't ask her what she thought she had been doing, walking into the sea like that. Didn't ask her why. Didn't even ask her name, or where she was from. And she didn't tell him. He got up from his chair at the other side of the fire and went out into the scullery-kitchen from time to time. Brought out mugs of hot tea. A bowl of scalding tomato soup and rounds of cheese on toast. As the evening wore on he got up and felt her clothes, drying behind them.

'They'll take all night to dry,' he said, his voice cautious and even. 'You can stay till the morning. I've a spare room. You'll be safe.'

She slept well that night. It had surprised her, how well she slept. As if she was pulled into some deep place, her body healed, the exhaustion wiped away. She woke to the sun shining on her face, from the small curtainless window.

Her clothes were warm and dry. She took them and went back upstairs to dress. When she came back down, he had made her some breakfast, left her alone to eat it. She heard him washing up last night's plates and cups out in the scullery. Then he walked into the front room where she was sitting, finishing her coffee.

'I'll give you a lift to your car,' he said.

When they arrived at the car park back in Cley he got out of the car with her. She stood next to him awkwardly for a moment. What could she say, to this stranger, this man who had tugged her out of the sea and saved her? She shook his hand.

'Thank you,' she said. 'Thank you for everything.'

He smiled at her. Looked into her face, as if trying to read something in her eyes.

'You'll be all right now, won't you?' he said, gently.

'Yes,' she told him, and she turned to get into her car. She started the engine. She wound down the window.

'Goodbye, Michael,' she said. She started to move away. He said something. The words were half lost in the sound of the engine. *Remember, life is precious*, he said.

As she drove away, out of the car park, she glanced in her rear-view mirror and saw him still standing there, looking after her, his hand raised, waving. His hair, which she had thought was brown, golden brown, glinted with red lights in a sudden February sun.

*

She hadn't gone home straight away. She couldn't just drive home and tell Adam her story: *I went to see my mother. I was upset, something she said ... then I went to the beach at Cley and walked into the sea and a man who had been fishing nearby saw me, ran up, pulled me out of the waves. He took me back to his cottage and dried my clothes for me. I sat before his fire in his towelling dressing-gown. I stayed the night. Nothing happened.*

How could she tell him that?

She booked into a small hotel in Sheringham for two nights. In the day, she went for long walks. She walked on the other beaches of her childhood: Holkham, Hunstanton, Heacham and Cromer. She didn't go back to Cley. And then she went home. She had to, in the end. There was nowhere else to go.

Later, when things had settled down again; when Adam had forgiven her – or had seemed to – the ordinary routine of her life had taken over again. Going to work. Trying not to see, to *really* see, the beautiful children that surrounded her. Trying not to think, *remember*, how Dominic once had been. Coming home every night and trying not to see her son – to literally not see him – the damaged head, misshapen where the metal plate had been inserted, the withered legs as he stretched on the mat doing his exercises with Adam or the physio. Trying not to hear how his tongue searched to find the sounds for words. Shutting down, forcing herself through the same numbing routine, she would wonder, sometimes, if she had dreamt it. What had happened that Sunday afternoon. The terrible encounter with her mother, and the way she had driven blindly to Cley and had walked into the sea.

She stood up. The past was reaching into the present, was swallowing her up. Her memories running through her now, as clear, as perfect as rain. But she was calm, detached; she didn't care any more.

Last autumn she had feared that she would die. Even now, the cancer could be spreading and multiplying again in her flesh. She didn't care.

She made her way across the marshes, back to the car. Bob's words were in her head: *I know what I would do. I would go to Findhorn. I'd go to the house and ask directly. Someone might know . . .*

30

It had been a treacherous journey, getting this far. The wind buffeted the car all the way up the M1, the rain coming down in torrents so that she had to screw her eyes into the driving, could hardly make out the road. It was a relief to reach Stafford, to make her way into the familiar, comforting roads. She drove straight into the centre of town, where an old coaching inn had functioned as a small hotel in her teens. It still did. There was plenty of room. It was early April, still out of season.

'Don't you want to see the room first?'

The woman at the reception desk had a broad, implacable face. She looked like nothing had disturbed her much; she had never dreamt of getting away.

'I'll need your Visa card number, for security. How many nights did you say?'

'Only one.'

She took a record of the card number and handed it back.

'No luggage?'

'No. It's a rather spontaneous trip. I'm going to Scotland, to see my brother. Only decided several hours ago.'

underwater

'Ah, long way to Scotland. You'll not want to go any further, this late and in this dreadful weather. They say the storm is worse, up north. Gale-force winds are forecast.' She handed Jane the key attached to a solid wedge of wood.

'I'm afraid you're too late for the dining room. Dinner's been and gone.'

The room looked dated. Embossed wallpaper, a patterned Axminster in swirls of pink and cream. The double bed was covered with a cotton bedspread pricked out in Laura Ashley rosebuds. But it was clean and comfortable; it would do.

She went into the small, en suite bathroom. Splashed her face with warm water. Stripped off her clothes. She crawled beneath the covers of the bed, pulled the sheet up so it almost covered her face. Curled up her knees, like a child. *I must sleep. I must try to sleep.* She could hear the wind and rain buffeting the window. But it was useless, hopeless; she couldn't sleep. Memories were flooding her now.

Well done, Jane. You've remembered. You've remembered the truth, at last.

In some deep part of herself, hadn't she always known? That her father wasn't Paul's. Ever since that day, at least, when she had burst into his room without knocking and seen him looking at the photograph. *Strange how something like that could turn up again, suddenly come to light again, after all these years. Perhaps she hid it away carefully that night. Between the pages of a book perhaps, under the eaves in the attic . . .*

Paul hid it quickly, his hands behind his back.

'What do you want? You can bloody knock before you come in.'

'What were you looking at?'

'Nothing. None of your business, anyway.'

'It's a photograph. Why are you hiding it?'

'Go away, Jane. Fuck off.'

'I'll tell on you. I'll tell Dad you've been swearing.'

'Tell who you want. He isn't my dad, anyway.'

'What do you mean?'

'What I said. Fuck off, Jane. Go and play with your dolls or something.'

She ran at him and tried to wrench his arm out from behind his back. He pushed her away. He pushed too hard. She fell backwards, her head struck a chest of drawers. She got up, tried to force back the tears that burned in her eyes. He looked sorry then. Hadn't meant to hurt her.

'You all right?'

'It's bleeding.'

'No, it's not.'

He came up to her, peered at the crown of her head for signs of blood. Stroked the sore place with his thumb. His other hand, the one that was holding the photo, was hanging down at his side. She glanced at it, from the corner of her eye, couldn't see it clearly.

'There's a bump, but no blood. It'll be all right. You should knock, Jane, before you come in my room.'

'You never used to mind.'

'It's different now. I'm not a little kid.'

Between his words she heard – *but you are. You still are.*

'Why were you hiding that photograph?'

He flung it on to the bed.

'I wasn't. You can see it, if it means so much to you.'

She glanced over towards it again. Wouldn't pick it up, wouldn't show him she cared that much. She could make out two figures standing together. On a beach, somewhere. Paul standing next to a man with red hair.

'That your music teacher?'

'Yes.'

She touched her head again. The bump was swelling, it was sore.

'Why didn't you want me to see it?'

'I didn't want any trouble.'

The scar above his right eye was healed now, but still a raw shade of red, not yet faded.

'You know what he's like. What a jealous bastard he is.'

'Why did that man take your picture? If he's just your music teacher. Why would he take you out and have your picture taken with him.'

'He took us out one day, got Mum to take our picture. So what? Why shouldn't he?'

She shrugged. She was still rubbing her head, it was still hurting. Paul picked the photo up, slid it quickly into the top drawer of the desk.

'I'm sorry about your head, Jane. Don't tell Dad about the photo. You don't want him going nuts again, do you?'

She wasn't ready to let it go.

'Why did you say that?'

'What?'

'About my dad not being yours?'

Paul sat on the edge of the bed and started to pull on his plimsolls.

'I was being stupid. Sometimes I just wish he wasn't. He's a bastard, I hate him. Don't you sometimes wish that?'

You can know things, and not know them. I was a child then, barely thirteen. And children then, much more slow to grow up. Staying dangerously innocent – ignorant – perhaps for too long. But still I knew. Or at least I knew that you were lying; that she was. This man, with the red hair, whose smile and eyes resonated yours so clearly (I could see that; even from a distance, even though the photo was hazy) was not just your music teacher. I remembered my mother's face turning to him, laughing, the day I saw her get out of the car that day. No one had made her face light up like that. My father never had.

After that holiday in Cley, that time that had been spoiled by her father's jealous rage, her mother had carried on taking Paul to the music lessons. Usually on a Saturday, when her father was out of the way, in his studio painting, or fishing. He probably knew they went, yet he didn't try to stop them. She supposed he felt ashamed; he usually felt ashamed, when he was sober. She had to give him credit for that.

'Just taking Paul to his music lesson,' her mother would say. She would have put on a nice frock, painted her mouth with lipstick, brushed her hair so that it fell loose and gleaming on to her shoulders. Paul would be wearing his black school trousers. A clean shirt tucked into them. They would leave the house together to catch the bus to Wisbech, and when they got back there was something in the air between them. Her mother would smile at Paul in a certain way, and there was a coyness in Paul she'd hardly seen before. Just for a moment he wouldn't be her brother.

Paul was changing, growing away from her. He knew things she didn't understand. She still wore white ankle socks, read Enid Blyton. She would think of those nights when he would climb into her bed while storms raged downstairs, and hold her. How his body would harden and tremble against her, his breath warm on her ear.

'It's all right. Don't be scared.'

She wouldn't be. He took the fear away.

Nothing happened, those nights holding her in bed. But sometimes she wondered if she had wanted it to. If that Saturday afternoon, later in September, when she took the short cut across the fields on her way home from the bus, and saw him with Sharon Baker, lying in the long grass at the edge of Tanner's Wood, it was jealousy that burned inside her. Because he was doing things with Sharon Baker, and not with her.

No, I don't mean that. That wasn't it; that's shocking, it can't be true. But yet I was jealous. You were changing. You had this secret life, you were leaving me behind . . .

It was a hot afternoon, an Indian summer. Paul had seen her. He sat up. He looked hot and sweaty; something like fever in his eyes she didn't recognize. Sharon's hair was a

mess and her blouse was undone, hanging off her shoulder.
Paul looked embarrassed, but Sharon just smiled smugly
back at her.

'Oh, hello, Jane. Had a good time in Wisbech? What
did you buy? Another book?'

That smug smile. She was making fun of her. What did
she know? – always with her head in a book.

'Sharon Baker, you're a slut you are, you're a dirty little
slag!'

Her turn to shock them. Timid Jane, quiet Jane, speaking dirty like that. She ran on, crossed the field and out again
to the lane. Ran all the way home. Ran straight upstairs to
her room. Heard her mother call out, 'What on earth's got
in to you? Slamming the door like that!'

He didn't want to be close to her any more. Being close to
his sister, suddenly too dangerous now ... and she was
changing too. She'd started her periods back then, in that
summer. These moods would fall upon her, these sudden
thoughts enter her head. She'd crept into Paul's room one
day when he was out at Stuart's. She'd been looking for
something Sharon Baker said all boys of Paul's age kept
under their mattresses. She found them. Turned the pages
and looked at the women spreading their legs and pouting.
Their privates like raw wounds, like gashes. She took one
of the magazines back to her room – he had so many, one
wouldn't be missed. She would read the stories inside it,
over and over. Filthy stories, full of shocking words. Hot
shooting spasms shuddering through her body. When she
had masturbated, panting and writhing on her bedroom

floor, it was Paul and Sharon she was seeing again in her head.

She knew nothing really. The mechanics perhaps, from gossip at school. What the magazines taught her – the dirty words, the shocking images in her head. But nothing to match the experiences Paul was having. With Sharon Baker, or with other girls, whatever. Until that day her mother taught her something else. Something that wasn't in a book, a magazine.

Something that was real.

31

Her father was away that weekend. There was a training course for art teachers he had been enrolled in, paid for by the county. He didn't want to go. He was irritable, even more than usual, in the days leading up to it.

'Don't know why I'm bothering. Haven't I been teaching for long enough? Don't see what else I can learn that's worth learning.'

Her mother had smiled at him, encouragingly. 'It'll do you good. A new perspective, a chance to exchange ideas.'

'What do you bloody know about it?' he snapped at her. But her face didn't close off at him this time.

He did go, in the end. That morning on the Friday he put a small battered suitcase in the Ford Prefect.

'See you Sunday evening, then.'

He sounded grumpy still, recalcitrant. Like a child being made to go somewhere he didn't want to. They were sitting at the kitchen table, finishing breakfast. He stood behind them and twitched for a moment, as if he wasn't sure what to do, how he should say goodbye. Should he stoop and kiss their mother? But Jane had never seen him do anything like that before.

'Goodbye then, John. Have a nice weekend.'

Her mother got up and went to the sink, started clattering dishes about. As if she didn't want to give him a chance to kiss her. He grunted and went out through the utility door. Her mother moved around the kitchen, putting things away. A lightness, a sudden gaiety in her step. She turned towards them.

'What plans do you two have for the weekend?'

'Stuart and I are cycling tomorrow. The Ouse valley. See how far we can get in a day. I'll stay tonight at his house, if that's all right?'

'And you, Jane?'

'Nothing much.'

'You're not planning on seeing Sharon?'

'I'm going into town with her after school today. She's got some birthday money she wants to spend.'

My mother's face seemed to register something like surprise.

'You'll be late for your tea then, Jane?'

She didn't go into Wisbech with Sharon after school. She didn't come home late. In fact, she was early. A headache had started that morning in school. A screwed knot of pain behind her right eye, the beginnings of a migraine that usually heralded the beginning of her period. She had tried to ignore it at first. In the morning they'd had double English with Miss Turner and double maths with Mr Moldsworthy. *You remember him, Paul? Mouldy, we used to call him.* A bright red complexion, like a perpetual blush. Watery blue eyes. A stickler for discipline, for children being seen and not heard.

It didn't go away; it got worse. By lunchtime sharp lights prickled at the periphery of her vision. She wasn't hungry, but she made herself eat. Old Mouldy was on dinner duty that day. He didn't believe in children deciding for themselves whether they would eat or not. Wouldn't have let her leave the table without finishing. The beef stew had shiny globules of fat floating on the surface. It lay heavily in her stomach afterwards, made her feel sick. She put her hand up in French to ask to be excused: Miss Stanley had frowned impatiently, but let her go.

She puked up the beef stew, her head hanging wretchedly over the toilet bowl. Her stomach retching and retching until it hurt, bringing tears to her eyes.

They were still in her eyes when she eventually returned to class.

'You all right, Jane? You look very pale.'

'I've just been sick, Miss. And I've got a bad headache.'

The tears thickened in her throat.

'Oh dear,' Mrs Stanley said. 'Well, perhaps you'd better go home then, if you feel so poorly.'

So you see, Paul. All because of a headache, and eating greasy stew and puking it up. If that hadn't happened, if I had stayed at school all afternoon and then gone into Wisbech afterwards with Sharon, to the record department at Smith's to spend her birthday money, perhaps you would still be here, part of my life. Or am I being fanciful? Would it have happened anyway, something else provoking it? Was it waiting to happen, all the time? Predestined.

The car was parked outside on the lane. Sleek, dark, expensive. Perhaps she shouldn't have gone into the house, but she had to. She desperately needed the loo by the time she got home. The weather that day was icy; the sky that shuttered, iron grey that held in the cold, that threatened the possibility of snow. She couldn't just loiter outside. She was freezing cold, had nowhere to go.

Or was she still trying to twist the truth? She could have peed down the bottom of the garden. Hung about in her father's painting shed. He kept a paraffin heater in there; she could have put that on to stave off the cold. She didn't. She was curious. She wanted to see this man. Paul's music teacher.

She opened the front door as noiselessly as she could. No one around. But she could hear sounds coming from upstairs. Strange noises. Noises she didn't understand, but wanted to. She tiptoed up the stairs. Her parents' bedroom door was ajar. She stood outside it, on the landing. She couldn't see much, just their feet – her mother's slim feet, and someone else's, a man's – at the bottom of the bed. The noises made her tremble, with fear and excitement. Her mother, screaming, but not quite. She knew what the sound of her mother's screaming was like. This wasn't the same. More muffled, and with a pulse to it, a rhythm. She stood there. Couldn't move, was afraid to move. There were sharp, knife-like pains in her bladder, she was bursting. But if she moved they might hear the creaking floorboards, the squeak of the bathroom door. And anyway, this sound held her, fixed her to the spot. Underneath the sound that was like screams but wasn't, the creaking of the bedsprings, getting faster and more vigorous, and her mother's voice saying a name. *Shawn.*

Then it stopped. She could hear laughing now. Her mother's voice laughing, and a man's, and then her mother said something that she didn't hear, and the next moment the sound like someone getting out of bed, a scuffle of feet on the floor. The bedroom door flew wide open and her mother came out, still laughing, a dressing-gown half pulled over her naked shoulders. Her breasts were showing. The white slackness of her belly. The dark triangle of hair down there, shocking and shameful on the edge of Jane's vision. She couldn't look, couldn't move.

A fierce, hot shout of rage. The burning brand of her mother's fingers on her face.

'How dare you! What do you think you're doing!'

Her bladder opened then. She couldn't hold it any more. Hot scalding pee flooded her knickers, cascaded down her legs.

I know what you think. Yes, that's awful, Jane. Awful for you to catch them at it, awful for her to react the way she did. She shouldn't have done that; it wasn't your fault. But it was the shock that made her do it. It was just an unfortunate accident. If you hadn't been sick that day at school, been sent home early . . .

You see, you're thinking on the same lines that I am. Some inconsequential thing, like coming home from school early instead of late, setting into motion a chain of events. The course of lives – four lives – changed because of it. Okay, maybe you don't quite see that yet, but you will. When you hear the rest, you will.

She ran down the lane. She was crying, cold and wet with pee. She went into the shelter of some trees, near the field at the back of Sharon Baker's house. The same place where she'd caught Paul with Sharon, only several months earlier. She peeled off her knickers, which were wet and smelly. Screwed them up and put them in her satchel. She sat down behind some bushes. She wasn't sure how long she sat there. Fifteen minutes. Twenty. The ground beneath her was frozen, icy. Burned against her wet skin. *I hate her!* she shouted, between the fits of crying. *I wish she was dead!*

Then she went back home. She was thirteen years old. She was cold and hungry. Where else could she go?

The car was gone. The house was quiet when she got inside, but the sort of quiet you get after a storm. Like the quiet they used to hear when they were small. Lying upstairs, Paul holding her tightly in her narrow bed. Her mother was in the living room; maybe she had been waiting for Jane to come back. She must have heard the front door open. She came out into the hallway. Stood there, holding on to the doorjamb as if for support.

'I'm sorry, Jane . . .'

Jane glanced at her quickly. But long enough to notice the fear in her mother's eyes. It gave her a flash of satisfaction.

'Are you hungry? There's a quiche I could heat up. I could do some chips . . .'

She said nothing. Walked past, went upstairs to her room. Stayed there all evening, her stomach groaning. Later, after her mother had gone to bed, she crept downstairs and ate the quiche that was sitting untouched on a plate in the fridge.

In the morning, a quick tap on her door. Then her mother walked in. Jane sat up in bed.

'About last night . . . you won't say anything to your father, will you? You won't tell him who was here?'

What had she been expecting, hoping for?

'He mustn't know. You do realize that, don't you? He must never know.'

Her mother moved closer. Jane flinched instinctively.

'I shouldn't have hit you, Jane. But you shouldn't have been listening outside the door. Only peeping Toms do things like that. I'll forgive you, we'll forget about it, then. But it's got to be our secret. Do you understand?'

32

Maybe she would have got over it. Sort of, in a way. Starting looking at her mother, talking to her again. It would have slipped back, from time to time. What she had seen, *heard*, that afternoon. The slap on her face. But she would have let go of some of the resentment, eventually, perhaps.

If her mother hadn't said what she said the following Saturday.

Sharon had phoned that afternoon, just after lunch.

'You can come for tea. Mum says you can. And then you can stay all evening. They're going out, it's their wedding anniversary. They won't be back till late.'

Jane could hear the anticipation in her voice. *We can talk about boys. Sex. We can do things we shouldn't.* Like nick a drink from the stock of bottles in the sideboard. The last time it had been brandy. It had made them cough their guts up but Sharon had pretended to like it.

'I've got some cigarettes. My cousin gave me them. Capstan full strength. He's in the Navy.'

'I'll see you later, then. About four?'

*

She found her mother in the living room, darning socks.

'Sharon's parents have asked me for tea. They want me to stay the night, as well. They're going out for their anniversary.'

The fingers of her mother's left hand wormed down into the toe of her father's sock. She looked up at her, a flash of resentment in her face. *She's supposed to ask me. Not tell me . . .*

'Haven't you spent enough time around that girl's house this week?'

'They want me to keep her company. They're expecting me.'

'I'm not sure that Sharon Baker is good for you. She fills your head with dirty thoughts. I've seen some of the things you get up to together . . . the games you play . . .'

Her mother noticed the look on her face. Was surprised by it, shocked by it. *Timid Jane, quiet Jane. Who rarely had the nerve to answer back . . .* She ducked her head back down to the hole in the sock, spreading it with her fingers, the thick needle hooking on the ragged edge.

She's been snooping in my room, she's been reading my diary.

She'd been writing about things Sharon had told her about sex. Kept pictures folded up inside the diary. Drawings of things they imagined Mr Moldsworthy would like to do with Miss Stanley . . .

'I don't need her to teach me dirty things,' she said. Her father's rage, quavering for a moment inside her. *Not when I've got you.* She didn't dare say it. But her mother had heard the unspoken words.

'You watch your tone, my girl.' The needle was trembling slightly in her mother's hand. *My ammunition*, Jane thought. *She can't stop me going.* She moved towards the door.

'I'll tell her I can go, then. They've asked me for tea.'

As a parting rebuff, before she went out of the door. 'You just watch what you do with that little hussy, that's all,' her mother said.

Maybe if she hadn't said that. It had made Jane shake inside with rage and resentment. Made her remember the slap on her face. The humiliation of her bladder bursting, the sour scald of urine down her legs. *You dirty little...*

She went upstairs to wait till four o'clock, and to seethe with rage. She tore a page out of her English homework book and drew a picture of *her, doing it with him*. She drew them standing up, naked. His thing sticking out like a giant poker. A bubble of speech coming out of her mother's open mouth. *Oh, Shawn, oh, Shawn. Don't stop....* Then she picked up a red pen and scribbled violently all over it, all over his thing especially, obliterating it, tearing a ragged hole in the paper ... *I hate her, I wish she was dead.*

She heard Paul leaving the house. Calling out to his mother, 'See you later.' Her calling back, 'Goodbye, darling, don't be too late.' The front door closing. She was thinking of him. The man *she*'d done it with. The man with red hair. The man in the photo Paul had in his room. Perhaps there was something written on the back. Something that would tell her who he was. Although, somewhere deep in her bones, didn't she already know...?

She crept out of her room, across the landing and into Paul's. She remembered seeing him shove it into the drawer on his desk. She opened it, couldn't see it at first. Paul's diary was there. She took it out; the photo was underneath it. She picked it up, turned it over. Nothing. No, of course there wouldn't be. *She* wouldn't have let him write anything. *To Paul, love from Dad.* Something like that. *Don't write that, my husband might find it*, she would have said.

The diary. Perhaps there was something. A clue, an outright admission even. She put the photo down on the desk and opened the diary. Flicked through it. Every so often, on the Saturday dates. *Piano lesson. Piano lesson.* Nothing else. Then she heard footsteps suddenly on the stairs, the landing. Grabbed the photo and shoved it quickly under the waistband of her skirt . . .

Her mother opened the door. Her eyes narrowed, as if she was seeing something she disliked, something distasteful to her sight.

'What are you doing in Paul's room?'

Her mother's eyes swivelled down to the diary she had let fall on to the desk. She glared at Jane, icy with rage.

'Were you reading that? Were you reading your brother's diary?'

'No.'

Her mother's hand hard across her face, again. But this time, the slap hardly hurt her. She stood frozen, rigid, her face turned to stone.

'You're nothing but a liar, a snoop and a peeping Tom. Get out!'

underwater

She edged past. Her mother's hands were clenched at her sides. She went downstairs, out through the utility room door and down the path to the back garden. She didn't know what she was thinking, what she was planning to do. She had slipped out of her body, wasn't in control. . . . She watched herself walking down to her father's painting shed, where she knew he was working. She knocked on the door, then pushed it open. Her father was sitting at his easel, painting a scene of the marshes at Cley. A photograph, pinned up with a thumbtack at the corner of the canvas. The shed smelt of oil paint and turps, a cloying smell that made her catch her breath.

'What is it?' He glanced quickly at her, then back to his painting.

'He's been here,' she said, flatly.

'Who's been here?' He was concentrating on the right-hand corner of the painting. Painting highlights on dark green reeds with a slender brush.

She wasn't there. Someone else was there, speaking with her voice. Wearing her face. She was watching. This excitement and terror again, like that afternoon outside her mother's room. *She hates me, she always hates me . . .*

'That man they were with in Wells on holiday. We saw them getting out of his car. Paul's music teacher.'

Her father laid his brush down carefully on the table at his side. He was staring at her, a line of red deepening and spreading around the top of his shirt collar. *I hate her, I want him to hurt her . . .*

'He was here, last weekend. When you were away. I caught him with her.'

'What do you m-mean? You c-caught him with her . . .'
He was spluttering, choking on the words.

'I saw them in bed together.'

He blinked at her speechlessly. As if he couldn't believe what she was saying.

She took out the photo from under the waistband of her skirt. Smoothed down the crumpled edges. Put it down, face upwards, on the table next to the brush.

'I found this photograph in Paul's room. That's the man I saw.'

And then she left, running out of the shed. Coming back into herself, re-inhabiting her body again. Feeling the fear pumping blood into her running legs, her face smiling crazily. She saw her mother's face for an instant, bobbing up at a bedroom window. *That'll teach her, that'll teach her. . . .* She ran down the side of the house, across the front lawn, through the gap in the hedge and up the lane. She didn't stop until she got to Sharon's house.

So you see, Paul. That's what I did, that's why I'm to blame. But I wasn't thinking straight, wasn't really thinking at all. Something else, taking me over. If I wanted anything, it was just for him to hurt her, to slap her around a bit, like she did to me. What did he do, what happened next? Neither of us were there. We need to fill in the gaps . . .

Did her father get up from his stool in the studio, walk slowly towards the house, the rage a white heat in his belly? Did he get the whisky bottle out from the kitchen cupboard?

He'd been in a dry spell then. A rare one. He'd been in a good mood, for the last few days, until she'd gone and spoilt it. The teachers' course in Peterborough had gone well. He had just broken up for the Christmas holidays. A few evenings ago he had crawled up under the eaves in the attic and brought down the old artificial tree, stood it up in the living room by the side of the fireplace.

'I'll get down the decorations at the weekend and put them up,' he'd said. But that never happened.

Did he start drinking then, heavily, to make up for the abstinence of the last few weeks? Did the whisky go straight to his head, his belly, firing up his anger and his rage? Did he go into the living room where she was still darning the holes in his socks and confront her? What did he do? Did he try to make her get up and play the piano? *Go on. Play something. I want to hear you play. You haven't played anything for months. Don't tell me your fingers hurt, you can't play any more. Don't tell me that. You fucking whore, you fucking slut. You play for him, don't you? I bet you play for him!*

What did he do? Start to slap her around a bit, when she refused? When she sat there, as cold and frozen as ice. Refusing to answer him, refusing to perform for him. Did she feel the hard sting of his hand on her face, the brand of his fingers burning on *her* cheek? Did she start to scream, to cry, her hands going up to defend herself, the sock with the ragged hole like a wound, slipping off her lap to the floor?

Don't you know any tunes any more? Don't you play for him? Dance to his tune, sing to it, fuck him to it? Don't you?

When did he start to smash up the piano? Going back

down to the shed to fetch an axe. Heaving it in the air and letting it crack down on the beautiful oak wood, the strings bursting into a cacophony of discordant notes.

But we know what happened next, Paul, don't we? We don't have to imagine. We were both there.

33

They had been drinking. Her and Sharon. Gin, diluted with lemonade, from a bottle they found in the sideboard. They had been talking about boys and sex. Sharon's favourite subjects. Maybe it made her tongue run loose.

'It did happen, Jane. I know I said it didn't. But it did.'

'What do you mean?' But she knew what Sharon meant. Just didn't want to hear. She was seeing them again, sitting up suddenly in the long grass. The fever in Paul's face, Sharon's tits hanging out of the front of her blouse.

'I *did* do it with Paul. I told you I didn't because I didn't want you to stop being my friend. But I did. Not that afternoon, though. That time you saw us, we just snogged then, and I let him take off my bra. But later. In your dad's painting shed. Your dad wasn't there at the time. Of course.' She giggled.

She'd been angry, really angry. The gin going to her head, releasing the anger that normally she kept well hidden, pushed down out of sight. She called Sharon a dirty little slut, a tart. The words warmed her mouth. She enjoyed the sound of them. Enjoyed the feeling of power it gave her, using them. She wasn't sure now, who they were really meant for. Silly fourteen-year-old Sharon Baker, or her mother. She ran out of her house. Ran home. It was beginning to snow. Big, soft, powdery flakes snagging on her hair, brushing against her upturned face, cooling the anger. She thought, *It might be a white Christmas, it could be!* She was still kid enough to think that.

By the time she got home her anger had cooled to the extent that she was feeling regretful. She wished she had stayed. She shouldn't have called Sharon bad names. What was there at home for her to return to, anyway? She walked up the side of the house and went in quietly, through the utility room that led to the kitchen. She knew it would be open; it was rarely locked until everyone had gone to bed.

As soon as she stepped inside she had felt it. The sense of danger, like the quiet after the storm. But in this case, the quiet before a storm. A storm even worse than the one that had gone before. She stopped. Her face was up against her father's coat, the smell of turps and paint catching in her throat. The door was ajar. Through the gap she saw Paul come in from the door that led from the hallway. She saw the rage that he held tightly in his body; she felt it. A sickening clenching in her stomach.

'You bastard. Why did you smash up the piano?'

She heard her father laugh. That drunken, mocking laugh she had always hated. She saw his leg move out from where he was sitting, into her view.

'You calling *me* a bastard. You're the fucking bastard, you little shit.'

'What if I am? Better to be a bastard than have you for a father.'

Paul had touched the right nerve; he had hit the quick. She saw her father springing suddenly into the line of her vision. Lunging forward, shoving Paul backwards. Saw her brother fall against the kitchen cupboard, the thick padding of his parka coat insulating his back from injury. He stood up, his face bright red with a surge of righteous fury. *When did he learn not to be afraid – who taught him that?* Her father coming for him again, and her mother, flying in, latching on to her father's back, trying to pull him away.

Leave him alone! Leave him!

Her father's face, darkened now to purple with drink and rage. Foaming at the mouth, as if he had become something inhuman. Something blind and stumbling and incoherent. Moving his body in violent shakes, like a dog shaking after a bath, trying to dislodge her. She clung like a limpet. He turned, struck at her, his elbow, his fist, hitting the bone of her face. She didn't see her brother reaching over and grabbing the knife, pulling it from the rack on the wall. Only saw the flash of the blade moving forwards and then her father stumbling, falling. He made a little sound. A grunt, when the knife went in, a wheezing, as if struggling for breath. A soft, padded thud as he hit the floor.

Had she gasped out loud when her father fell? Had she moved slightly, a shock reflex jerking her body, her foot kicking against the bucket on the floor? Paul was standing stock-still, in the line of her vision, holding the bloodied knife. He looked up sharply towards the door of the utility room. Did he see her, through the crack in the door? Did he know she was there?

*

The time afterwards. When she must have gone quickly through the door and out again, into the soft fall of snow, and up by the side of the house. Moving quickly, running perhaps. Across the front garden and out through the gap in the hedge, up the lane to Sharon's house. This time was still lost to her. She could not recover it. It was as if she had slipped so far outside her body that she had become insubstantial. Like a shadow in the dark night, absorbed into the blackness. Frozen and stilled in the snow. She could only remember standing at Sharon's doorstep. Sharon's face poking sulkily around the door.

'Oh, it's you. You've come back then.'

'I'm sorry, Sharon. I'm sorry I called you names. I shouldn't have. I don't mind about you and my brother.'

'You don't mind?'

'No. You can do what you like. You don't have to tell me though. But I don't mind. I shouldn't have called you names. I won't do it again. I promise.'

The door opening to her, Sharon's body yielding, stepping aside. The light and warmth of the house behind, reaching out to her, drawing her in. In only minutes the row they had was forgotten. Everything was forgotten. Not just the journey back up the lane to Sharon's house, but the journey down too, and all that she had seen and heard in her parents' house that night. Even when the police had knocked later on the door. Forgotten, wiped out. Like the snowflakes that had melted almost the instant they had landed on the ground, so that later, sitting with Paul in the back of the car, the lane that led them narrowly away was at least free and clear from snow.

underwater

What happened afterwards, Paul? Did she hold you, comfort you? Tell you it wasn't your fault; you weren't to blame? She would have quickly, quietly, made up her mind what to do. Wiped your prints from the knife, replaced them firmly with her own. She would have told you what to say:

You came in from Stuart's. You went upstairs to your room for a few minutes. You heard your father shouting, swearing. You heard him hitting me. You heard me screaming. You came down to help. But by the time you got to the kitchen he was lying in a pool of blood on the floor. I was standing there, holding the knife. Soon afterwards – five minutes, no longer – I phoned the police. I wanted to. You made me a cup of tea. You stayed with me in the living room, waiting until they arrived. You knew nothing about the piano until later. How he had chopped it up with the axe, dragged it outside to burn on the fire. You don't know why he did it. Only that he used to try to make me play for him, and I didn't want to. Don't tell them about the time he broke my fingers, keep Shawn – your father – out of it if you can. Knowing about him would reveal too much. Tell them your dad would drink too much, get into violent rages for no good reason. It had happened many times before . . .

Her mother would have been frightened of course, that *she* would let something out. The police might ask her questions about the piano, and she would tell them about that first time in Cley when she had seen Paul and her mother get out of the car, the incident later in the cottage. The music lessons that weren't just music lessons. The music teacher that wasn't just a music teacher. Her mother would have prayed that the police wouldn't want to talk to her, that the solicitor wouldn't want her to take the stand.

She needn't have worried; I wouldn't have said a word.

It would have been too dangerous. It might have dragged out of her, from some deep, inaccessible place, the truth she was not able to face. That it had been Paul who had killed her father. But she had caused it; she was to blame.

The winds had died down; the rain had stopped. She lay in bed, longing for sleep. She longed to hear Paul's voice again in her head: *Well done, Jane. You've remembered everything. You've remembered the truth, at last.* Longed to feel the balm of his forgiveness slip over her. He was silent, he wasn't there.

What will I do if I don't find you, Paul? If you're nowhere to be found?

Eventually sleep came to claim her. She dreamt a familiar dream. But this time it felt different.

Paul, swimming alone in the river, again. She watches him from the shaded bank. He stops, treads water, waves at her. *Come in, Jane. The water's warm. It's safe.* She slides down from the bank and into the water, glides easily towards him. He wraps his arms around her, smiling. They slip together under the water, down into dark green depths. His face is up close to her. At first she thinks that he is smiling still, and then she sees that he is crying. She holds him tight. *Don't worry.* The words are formed soundlessly under the water. *I won't leave you. I'll stay.*

PART FIVE

PART FIVE

34

Sitting through the night in the brightly lit office, Bob had only half an ear on the story the charge nurse was telling him. His mind was adrift; he couldn't anchor it, keep it still. He was remembering the time when his wife had left him. He was remembering it because it felt significant. It had been the reason why it had started, his watching out for Jane.

He'd come home at six that evening, as was usual, turned the Yale in the lock and walked in. 'Hello, Margaret, I'm back.' Same thing he'd said for years. Same thing he thought he'd always say, until the day he retired.

No answer. The lights in the kitchen were on, his dinner in the microwave waiting to be heated. He walked upstairs. First into the room he shared with his wife. Then into the spares. Two spare rooms because they never had kids. They had problems in 'that department' – never found out whose fault it was. Margaret used the smaller as a sewing room. When they were first married she had made all her own dresses, and then when her sister's brood came along – three girls – she made little summer frocks for them, until they got to the tomboy stage and wouldn't wear girly things any more. In the last few years the sewing machine had been idle. It stood there, like something dead, under its plastic cover. He closed the door.

He went downstairs again. That's when he saw the note. It was scribbled on one of those spiral notebooks secretaries use, on the small table in the hall next to the phone.

Bob, I'm writing this note to let you know that I'm leaving you. I won't be back. I've been unhappy for some time and now I've met someone else. I've taken everything with me that I want. What's left, you can take to the Oxfam shop if you want to be rid of it. I will be seeing a solicitor about a divorce, when we've both had time to readjust to it all. We'll need to decide what to do about the house, of course.

Margaret

People would say, in the weeks and months afterwards, when he was trying to get back into the swim of things – *You must have known something, there must have been some signs.*

But he hadn't had a clue. The women would look at him with soft pity in their eyes. *Men can't see what's staring at them in the face. They never listen to what their wives are trying to tell them.* He'd feel, despite their pity, their sympathy had gone to Margaret, who had been made to live a life of such quiet desperation she had finally fled.

The only one who hadn't blamed him had been Jane. Before that time they'd hardly spoken. By a strange quirk of coincidence, Margaret was also one of Jane's colleagues;

she was a secretary at the school where Jane taught. They weren't exactly close, but they were friendly. Chatted over the garden fence, popped around each other's houses for coffee. When Dominic had been small Margaret had offered to babysit occasionally. If Adam and Jane had PTAs at the same time. Wedding anniversaries, birthday dinner treats. She liked the babysitting. Would come home and tell him what a lovely kid Dominic was, how good he'd been. Her eyes would shine, telling him about that little boy.

One thing he remembered. Maybe it was a sign, maybe he should have taken more notice at the time. He'd been out playing darts at the Three Crowns. An 'away' match. He'd got back a bit later than usual. When he got in the house was quiet, like she had gone to bed, but she hadn't. He found her sitting in the lounge on her own in the dark.

'That you, Margaret?'

This shadow in the chair by the fire. He turned on the light. She rubbed her eyes.

'Sorry.' He turned the dimmer down. She kept the back of her hands pressed against her eyes, as if she was shielding them from the light.

'Fancy a cuppa? Horlicks? Tea?'

'No, thanks.' Her voice sounded muffled.

'You all right?'

'How was the game?'

'We thrashed them.'

'Bob,' she said. Something in her voice made him listen. 'Why did we never do anything about it? Go to a clinic or something.'

'What d'you mean?' But he knew what she meant.

'Other people do, when they can't have kids. Why didn't we?'

'I don't know, love.' He spoke gently, as if he was speaking to a child. He was frightened. His heart was beating.

'Maybe we thought, if it happens it happens. Leave it to nature,' he said at last.

She said nothing back. She's been crying, he thought. He wondered if he should go and give her a hug. Would she want him to? But he went into the kitchen and put on the kettle instead. Maybe he was feeling guilty. Maybe he felt she was accusing him; it had been his pride that had stopped them going.

A year later she left.

He'd gone knocking next door, after finding the note. He needed to see someone, speak to someone, he was going out of his mind. He thought Jane might know something; he thought perhaps she might tell him where Margaret was.

She was on her own. Adam was out teaching pottery somewhere, Dominic in bed. He was garbling something, wasn't making sense. She took him into the living room, made him sit down, put a glass of whisky in his hand. He showed her the note. Then she dropped that bombshell.

'Bob, Margaret doesn't work at Highdown any more. She left last Friday. We even had a leaving do for her.'

When he'd recovered a little from the shock, the whisky softening the edge of it, he said it was like he'd never really known her. He hadn't seen this coming, hadn't a clue. His Margaret, who was menopausal, who would wake in the night sometimes, drenched with perspiration. Leaving him for another man.

'Did she say anything to you? Did you know she was seeing someone else?' He couldn't bring himself to say the word 'affair'. 'I won't blame you if you say you knew about it. I won't be angry. I just need to know.'

Jane was sitting next to him on the sofa. He had hardly ever talked to her about anything before, and now she was the only one he could talk to, the only one who seemed to understand. She'd placed her warm hand over his.

'I knew nothing, Bob. I promise.'

It was Jane who had helped him get through the early months. She'd call around occasionally, usually on Sundays. Knowing that was the day the whole world seemed to him to consist of couples going out enjoying themselves. This was the day he'd feel most alone, most out on a limb. She'd call sometimes in the week too, just to check on him.

'God's got a cruel sense of humour,' he told her. 'We were going to retire early. See a bit of the world before we die. I'll have to go on working now, till I drop.'

He'd to take out a second mortgage, use all his savings, to pay Margaret out on her share of the house.

Jane had pulled a face. 'You'd be bored, not working, Bob. Think of all the pretty nurses you'd miss.'

That was up to her too, the job at the hospital. He'd told her he was sick of plumbing. Sick of being bent double over pipes in cramped corners, working on his own while housewives chatted over coffee mornings in their designer kitchens.

'I'm too old these days for them to be panting after my body,' he'd said, and she laughed. But she'd picked up on the loneliness beneath the words, beneath his weak attempt at humour. She came round several evenings later with the advert cut out from one of the locals. *Auxiliaries wanted. Must be good with people.*

'You're good with people, Bob. Why don't you apply? They like older people, with more life experience. And men are always useful in a job like that.'

He was worried at first. He never would have thought of it when he was younger, him working in a place like that, being surrounded by so much misery. He'd never even have given it a thought. But it was good for him; he felt needed. Maybe other people's misery was a distraction. Wore away at his own.

He was thinking of these things, sitting in the charge nurse's office, that floated like a brightly lit oasis in the dark sea of the ward. The window he sat by looked over to the dormitory area beyond, where patients slept, or did not sleep, dreamt, or did not dream. Where some would toss restlessly on their beds and moan, the darkness and the night's still hours bringing the past back like a spectre to haunt them.

The ward at night was a different place. It required different rules, a different map of navigation. You could be stern when the patients played up in the day. You could set them boundaries, threaten them with withdrawals of privileges. Not quite so at night. At night, the panic could set in. The whispering of ghosts rustling like dry leaves down echoing corridors, across vaulted ceilings, growing too loud to contain. *Look what we've done. Look what's been done to us. Remember.* Hallucinations would spiral. The patients would see visions. Voices would shout back at them. They had to be cajoled, placated, reassured, like children waking from night terrors.

But tonight it seemed they were sleeping the sleep of the dead. Gloria, the charge nurse, was nodding asleep, her big head drooping down on to her ample chest. It was three o'clock, the dangerous time. He stood up, stretched, put on the kettle to make another cup of coffee. He wouldn't succumb; he would fight off sleep. He would allow the memories and the past to haunt him. He was trying to remember something. He was trying to catch it, to hold it in his thoughts. Something about Jane. What was it?

That time when she had gone missing. A few years after Margaret had left. The winter following the summer when Dominic had that dreadful accident. He'd seen the way she closed down, in the weeks and months afterwards, the shock settling on her face like stone.

His turn then to watch out for her. And he did.

He had seen her leaving the house that Sunday. She looked like she was in a hurry, her face fixed and steely, determined. And something in her eyes too. Space, lots of it, so that when she turned to get into her car, almost facing him as he stood at the front bay window of his house, his hand raised to wave to her, she had looked through him, seemed not to see him.

He remembered seeing the police call at the house. The sight of them in their uniforms alarming him, making him fear the worst. He was remembering how he'd felt over the next three days. Leaving for the night shift and coming home, driving through the dark winter streets up to the house, hoping so much to see her red Peugeot parked on her drive, to know that she was back, she was safe. Then several days later it was; his heart had lifted to see it.

He gave them both space for a few weeks. Whatever had been wrong would right itself. Whatever had emptied would fill up again. Not everyone leaves for good.

After a while, it was like things returned to something approaching normal. Jane had come back again. Not the old Jane, exactly. *That* couldn't happen. The clock couldn't be put back; Dominic couldn't be mended. But the stone softened on her face, her eyes began to contain something other than space. She began to talk to him again, to call round on Sundays. It was he who had helped to put the idea into her head about training as an art therapist, one Sunday morning when she had confided to him about feeling burnt out with the teaching, about needing a fresh challenge. How proud he had felt when she had come around to see him that day, over a year later, waving that piece of paper at him.

'I've passed, Bob! I've got a distinction!'

Like a father. Like a father would feel about a daughter.

*

Something had startled him. Perhaps he had been about to nod off too. All the memories and the thoughts in his head acquiring that fuzziness that precedes sleep, but now the real world, sharper and more distinct, breaking in, distracting him. Ken was tapping on the glass, pressing his blurry, distressed face against it, so that he looked grotesque. Gloria lifted her heavy head, her big eyes snapping open.

'You go and see to him, Bob.'

He went out of the office. Ken was bobbing about in front of him now, coming up too close, invading his body space, not even having a clue that he might have any. Ken's hands grabbing at his shirt, plucking at him like a small child plucks at its mother's clothing.

'Hey, calm down, mate. Calm down.'

Ken backed off then. Started hopping on one leg, putting his hands up to his head, as if he was trying to force some noise or vision out from his thoughts.

'What's the matter, mate? Can't sleep?'

'It's them, again, Bob. I've seen them. They're around my bed. Loads of 'em. They've come to get me, they won't leave me alone.'

He was pacing now, wearing the soles of his slippers away, twisting and turning his head between his big, rough hands. He was a man going on forty; he was a small boy. There was no need to ask what 'they' were. They took many guises; they were green or red or black; they were huge, or as small as insects; they spoke a constant stream of gibberish, or did not speak at all. They had claws and talons, or they held sharp knives in their hands, or popped at him with machine guns. It didn't matter what they were. They didn't belong to the real world, they didn't exist. It did no good to tell him that. Bob stood in front of Ken, blocking his pacing, letting him bump up against his chest. He took Ken's hands in his, moved them gently away from his head. He hugged the grown-man-little-boy, felt a tremor run through Ken's body, then die away.

'It's okay, mate. We'll make them go away.'

There is a certain time in the night when it is possible for demons to run amok. Ken's demons, or anyone's. His were his memories of Margaret, his guilt that he'd let her down in some way. By being a coward. Sparing her feelings, sparing his own. That night after the darts match, when he caught her in tears sitting alone in the dark. He should have walked over to her, taken her in his arms, held her. He should have said he was sorry. 'You're right,' he should have said. 'Yes, we should have gone to the clinic, we should have got help. We should have fought for what we wanted, not settled for less.'

He could hold Ken like that. A stranger. A man whose present was riddled with his past, was flooded by it. Sometimes it's easier to love a stranger, he thought. Someone you've not so invested in. Like Ken. Like Jane, even. Because she *wasn't* his daughter. He had no daughter. He had no one.

The light was coming up outside the tall windows in the day room. But an ethereal light, not quite belonging yet to the solid light of day. Ken had been sitting with them for the last two hours. Sometimes sitting calmly, sometimes trying to pace within the confines of the office until Gloria said, almost shouted, 'Stop that pacing, for God's sake, Ken!' Drinking the tea that Bob offered him, and telling them the sad details of his life, over and over again. As if the telling would make the memories run through him like water and be gone. It never did. He was sleepy now, the medication that Gloria had given him working its magic. His mouth had run out and his eyes were heavy, his head drooping down, then jerking awake again.

'Come on, mate, let's go back to bed,' Bob said. He lifted the man who was still a small boy up into his arms again, and guided him back through the dormitory of sleeping bodies back to his own bed. He tucked him up under the covers. Pulled a chair up close to the bed and stroked Ken's hair until he fell asleep. The demons had gone now, until another night.

'Don't leave me, Bob. Don't go,' Ken had muttered softly, just before the light in his head went out, and he slid into a darkness where Bob hoped no memories, no dreams, would trouble him for a while.

Going on forty, going on seven. What difference do the years make?

35

Adam reached up his arm – the one that wasn't caught under Anna's still-sleeping head – and angled the alarm clock so he could see the time. He screwed up his eyes to make it out; he could hardly see, in the dim light in the room, darkened by the blinds at the window. *Seven.* He lay there inertly for a moment. He was listening for the sound of his son coming from his bedroom downstairs. It was time for Dominic to get up, to start to get ready for school. He normally started to wake about this time. Adam would hear him talking to himself, singing out loud some latest pop song. Calling out to his father. *Dad. Time to get up, Dad . . .* There was nothing, he was probably still asleep. They had all had a late night. Anna had cooked a special supper and they had opened a bottle of wine. Or two. Even Dominic had had a glass. Adam didn't normally let him, because of the medication. But one, he decided, wouldn't hurt. And hadn't they been celebrating, in a fashion? What had they been celebrating? Anna's moving in?

The arm stuck behind her head was feeling dead, numb. He wanted to ease it out from underneath her, wanted to shake it back to life, let the blood flow easily again. But he kept it there. He didn't want to wake her. She looked lovely when she was sleeping. Her pale hair lay across her face like a curtain. He picked up a strand and eased it back behind her ear. He reached over and kissed her softly on the cheek. She stirred, and her eyelids flickered. But she didn't wake.

When had they decided? Or had they? It hadn't actually been talked about, in words. But in the last few weeks everything was falling so quickly, so naturally into place. Now he was thinking, it was a miracle it hadn't happened sooner. A miracle it had taken him so long. *You're not ready yet*, she had said to him. Then Jane had visited, and afterwards it was suddenly so clear. He had gone to see Anna the day after Jane had left, when Dominic was at school, and caught her at home – it was one of the days when she didn't work at the doctor's surgery. They had made love that afternoon, in her untidy bed, cluttered with throws and cushions. Slowly, lingeringly. As if both of them had waited a long time for this and now that he was ready, the time had come, they wanted it to take for ever.

Afterwards, she had lain there with her head nestled up under her chin and she had said, 'What happened, Adam? With Jane?'

He couldn't explain. He didn't know how to. And perhaps he didn't want to. It would seem disloyal to Jane, to the past.

'I don't know. I just suddenly realized I had been clinging to something that wasn't real. She wasn't the person I had loved any more.'

She never was. I had made her up. She had made herself up. I never really knew her. But he couldn't say that.

She had squeezed his hand, and turned and kissed him. She didn't need to ask any more. She didn't need to know. She had allowed him the privacy of his past. He was grateful to her for that.

Dominic was over the moon about it. Adam had worried that he wouldn't be, so soon after his mother had visited. He had been so pleased to see her, and the visit had gone well. That morning, the day she'd left, he had watched her saying goodbye to Dominic and had noticed her eyes shiny with tears. It was the first real sign she had given that she loved him. Not the old Dominic, but the 'after-the-accident' one. The one that wasn't 'perfect'. Like a new bond suddenly had risen between them. But it was odd, because Dominic didn't talk about his mum that often afterwards. Didn't ask when she was coming back, when he would see her again. But he would wear that watch on his wrist everywhere he went. Even in the hydrotherapy pool at school, his teacher said. *It's okay. It's waterproof, Mum said.* But he didn't really talk about her. As if the visit had sorted something out for him too. Some letting go of his own.

He should get up, it's time to get up, he thought. He was going through in his mind all the things he needed to do that day. After he'd seen Dominic off to school he would phone Nick Pierce. See if he could drop the window in at the vicarage that morning. It was finished. He had done the final work on it yesterday. Cut up and inserted the fine slivers of dark glass for the boat that pitched on the wave.

He would phone the number that Anna had given him when he got back . . .

A number for the Camphill Trust. There was a community, apparently, not too far away, in Devon. Anna had worked as a volunteer for them a few years ago. It was a place where adult people with learning disabilities lived alongside able-bodied carers. Building a community together, living creatively.

'Now you've got me, you want to move Dominic out of the way,' he'd said. Laughing, as if he was joking, to offset the accusation. She had looked at him quite sternly, not taken in by the pretence of humour.

'That isn't funny, Adam,' she had said. 'I can't believe you think that.'

'Of course I don't. I was joking.'

'What do you want for Dominic? To live here with you, propping you up? Giving you a reason for living. Or to be out there, living his own life?'

'Of course I want that, of course.'

His turn now to be hurt. But wasn't there a grain of truth in what she had said? Didn't he need Dominic just as much as Dominic needed him? Maybe more. What was it he needed? Atonement. Forgiveness. *I should have stopped him going. I should have been there that day on the cliff. I was to blame.*

Funny, he was thinking. Only a few weeks ago he had been feeling sorry for himself. He had been worrying about getting old. About not being able to cope with Dominic when he was old and on his own. And now? How surprising life was. The sudden turns it can take.

Unexpected graces. He moved his arm gently under Anna's head. She stirred again, but did not wake. When she wakes up, he thought, will she remember last night? Will she still feel the same about it? They had made love before going to sleep. He wasn't going to; he had suddenly remembered he had run out of condoms. She wasn't on the pill, or had a coil fitted, he knew. She didn't believe in them. They were too intrusive, upset the natural cycle of her body...

'Does it matter?' she had asked him.

'Not if it doesn't to you...'

I'll have to speak to Jane, again. About the divorce. A sinking feeling now, a slight heaviness in his belly, at the thought. She had sounded a bit down when he'd mentioned it to her on the phone the other week. He hadn't liked to push it. Was she moving on too? He hoped so.

The phone was ringing. He waited for a minute, just to check that he hadn't imagined it. Who would be ringing him at this time? It carried on. He moved his arm out from behind Anna's head. She opened her eyes. He kissed her before getting out of bed.

'The phone ... be back in a minute.'

He put on his dressing-gown and went downstairs. No sound yet from Dominic's room. He went into the sitting room, where the phone sat on a small table against the wall. He drew back the curtains to let in the light The room felt closed in, claustrophobic...

*

316

He wasn't expecting to hear Bob's voice. Had almost forgotten what Bob sounded like. As if he, too, belonged to the past. Something he had moved away from now.

'Bob Evans. Who used to live next door. When you lived in Redbourn.'

Bob. Yes, of course. He could see him now. A small, wiry frame that belied his natural strength. Thinning grey hair. His wife had left him. He had caved in a bit at the time.

'Bob, yes, of course I remember. How are you?'

'I'm fine, thanks, Adam. Sorry to disturb you, so early.'

'There's nothing wrong, is there, Bob? Is Jane all right?'

Why else would Bob phone him? And at just after seven in the morning. They were never that close.

'I don't want to alarm you, Adam. I know you have your own life to lead, now. But I am a bit worried about her. Her mother died on Monday. She went to the care home yesterday to collect her mother's belongings . . .'

'Yes?'

But now there were whispers starting up in him, like ghosts. Like a hand reaching out to clutch him, to spoil his feeling of happiness. Jane. Was she all right? What's happened?

'She never came back last night. I was expecting her. I had to go to work at half six – still do the night shifts – I was expecting to see her car in the drive when I got home, but she's still not back.'

'Have you tried knocking? Her car might be in for a service or something . . .'

'I'm in her house, Adam. I've got a spare key. No sign of her.'

'What are you thinking?'

'I'm concerned, Adam. She was upset before she left . . .'

'She would be, I suppose. If her mother had just died . . .'

'Not just her mother, Adam. They weren't really close. Never had been. She told me. You probably know that, anyway. It's Josie too. Josie passed away that same morning Jane got the phone call. Or in the night, anyway. We buried her in my garden.'

He felt his heart lurch and tears were in his eyes. *A dog. Only a dog.* And she had become Jane's dog, in the end. But she was lovely, that dog.

'Christ! I'm sorry. She'd take that badly.'

'Yes.'

More badly than her mother's death. He knew that to be true, and couldn't judge her for it. What he knew now, what she had gone through. It was a miracle, he thought, that she had pitched in there in the end. Sorting out that care home for the old woman, even visiting her regularly.

'There's something else.'

This feeling of dread growing. The hand, tightening now inside his belly . . .

'Did she ever tell you about her brother? He went missing when she was a kid. She hadn't seen him since . . .'

'Her brother Paul? She told me about him when she was here a few weeks back. She'd never told me the truth before.'

'She's been to see a private investigator. To see if he can

find out his whereabouts. He gave her this address. In Findhorn. Scotland.'

'I've heard of Findhorn A friend of mine down here, she's been there. Some kind of New Age community.'

'Maybe. I haven't heard about that. Anyway, Jane sent a letter to see if he still lived there, but it was returned. I said something about maybe she should drive up there. It's a small place. Maybe if she just asked around she might find out something.'

'Yes. That makes some sense.'

'I think she's gone there. I think she's driven straight up there after visiting the care home. She did go to the home, by the way. I've already phoned them.'

'Why are you worried, Bob? You must be, or you wouldn't have phoned me.'

That question there again. In the corner of his mind, at the tip of his tongue. *Do you have any reason to think she will do herself harm?* He couldn't bring himself to say it.

'There was a message from the private investigator on her phone, returning a call she'd made. I've just rung him. He didn't want to talk to me at all, at first. Client confidentiality. But I told him I was worried about her mental health. Because I am, Adam. I am worried.'

Like he had been that day. That time she went missing.

'He gave me the address, eventually. Where this brother of hers was living twenty or so years ago. I'm worried what she might do if she can't find him, the state of mind she's in at the moment, an' all. I'm thinking of going up there. I need to get some sleep first. I just thought you should know.

I'm not sure how things stand between you. Whether you might think it should be you that's going . . .'

'No, Bob. I couldn't, anyway. There's Dominic. And it's much too far from Cornwall. You go. If you think you can manage it. It's a bloody long drive. Let me know, if . . . when you catch up with her. I'll want to know she's safe.'

He could hear sounds now coming from Dominic's room. Odd mutterings. He peeked in on him. He was still lying in bed, but stirring now, beginning to wake. His big feet had kicked themselves free of the bedclothes, were sticking off the end of the bed. *Need to get him a bigger bed – he's outgrowing that one.* He was relieved to see the yellow hippo was nowhere in sight. *Time he gave that up.* He went back upstairs and into his bedroom. Anna had drifted back to sleep.

He thought about getting back into bed with her, for just a few more minutes. But it didn't feel right to now. He went downstairs again and put the kettle on for coffee. He sat at the kitchen table, stared at the marks in the wood. Dominic had made most of them, banging implements on it, not always able to control the jerking movements of his arms. He should be getting him up, getting him ready. But he couldn't quite face it yet. He was waiting for the kettle to boil, waiting to hear the hum of steam build to a climax. He was thinking of Jane. And Bob, prepared to drive all the way to Scotland on just a few hours' sleep. Should he be going instead, was it his place to?

Sometimes you have to make choices. Decide what to hang on to, what to let go of. Hadn't he made that choice?

But the weight of the years was upon him. He was remembering the way she looked in that little black dress, the beer he spilt, shining wetly on her cleavage. Remembering how she glowed with happiness in that hospital bed, when they'd put Dominic in her arms . . .

He closed his eyes, leant his head on his hands, and found – almost against his will – he was praying. He wasn't sure who, or what, he was praying to. Nick Pierce's Christian God, or Anna's angels. Those unseen beings of light that she says are everywhere, that are drawn to distress, bringing sudden blessings, surprising grace.

Help Bob to find Jane. Let her be safe.

36

It was dark by the time Jane reached Findhorn. She had wanted to get there while it was still light, but the journey had taken longer than she'd hoped. And she hadn't managed to get away as early as she'd wanted to. She'd slept in, past the alarm time in the end, after lying awake half the night.

The traffic on the stretch of the M6 that passed the junctions for Manchester and Preston had delayed her, and then it was impossible to drive for almost eight hours without a break. She stopped at a service station just north of Stirling and bought a takeaway burger and coffee to eat in the car. Then she'd tilted the seat back and shut her eyes, meaning to have a catnap, and had surprised herself, waking to find she had slept for longer than the twenty minutes she had allowed. But it had done her good, revived her.

What had she been expecting? She wasn't sure. A small town, a fishing community. Plain, no-nonsense cottages, white and spartan. She followed the road signposted to the harbour, passing along a broad, straight sweep of dunes. Streaks of pewter sparked softly in the distance, a hint of the sea beyond. She rounded the curve in the road and came to the harbour.

underwater

It was just as pretty as she'd imagined, perhaps more so. There were shadows of small boats pulled up close to the slipway. The lights from the overlooking pub revealed glistening striations of water amidst the dark estuary mud.

She parked the car in a small side street and went into the pub. It was busy. She edged her way to the bar. She would buy a drink. Find a corner, if she was able to, to sit and relax for a moment, gather her thoughts. The journey had tired her. The rest at lunchtime had helped, and the adrenalin firing had kept her going. Particularly as she had got closer to the destination, following the course of the Findhorn river, that sparkled like a silvered snake as she dropped down towards the Moray Firth plain. But now weariness descended upon her. Cloaking her limbs, numbing her feelings.

She stood in a jostle of bodies near the bar, waiting to be served. A hum of Scottish voices, like a foreign tongue on her ear. A couple of women behind her, holding half-pint glasses in their hands, laughed and talked in what sounded to her like American accents. Perhaps they're tourists, she thought. Although it seemed strange, tourists in early April. When the air still had that bite of ice in it, especially now, with the sun going down. Especially here, so far north . . .

Something was disturbing her. She seemed full of echoes. Crowded by impressions of things she thought she had seen, had known, before, The American woman closest to her, with her back towards her, had straight blonde hair hanging down past her shoulders. Why did she seem so familiar . . . ? Over in the far corner, in the shadows of an alcove, a man was sitting on his own, reading a newspaper. Glancing up every so often, looking over towards her. Why did she feel so afraid? *Don't let him get up*, she was thinking. *Don't let me see his face.*

'Yes, madam, can I help you?'

The man behind the bar was waiting for her order.

'Just a mineral water, please.'

'Sparkling or still?'

'Oh – still, please.'

'Ice and lemon?'

She had a strange feeling his words were a code for something. She must be careful what she said.

'Yes.'

'Both?'

'Yes. That's fine. Th-thank you.'

The other woman, the dark-haired one, was saying goodbye, moving away towards the door.

'That'll be seventy pence, please.'

She fumbled in her purse, slid the coins over the counter towards the barman. Picked up her glass, turned to move away. The man in the corner alcove was getting up, was moving out of the shadows. In a moment, in one terrible moment, she noticed his hair was red. She scanned his face frantically as it moved into the light. *Don't let it be him, let it be him.*

It wasn't. Her heart skipped a beat as relief, disappointment, flooded over her. He had a rough face, acne scars pitting his cheeks. He seemed to glare harshly at her as he passed by her and went out of the door.

She was suddenly drenched in water. She had collided

with the American woman, the one with long blonde hair, who had been turning, moving towards the bar to place her empty glass on the counter. Wetness seeped through the wool of her jumper on to her chest.

'Oh dear! I'm so sorry. You're soaked!'

'N-no. No, it was my fault. I wasn't looking.'

The woman, now dabbing at Jane's chest with her scarf. She was looking at her strangely. Did she recognize her too? Did she think she had seen her before?

'Are you all right?'

She wasn't.

'Yes, I'm fine.'

The water was cold on her chest. The glass in her hand half empty. She felt sick. She felt dizzy. *I must sit down.*

'Look, let me buy you another. You don't look well. There's a seat over there. You go and sit down. I'll bring it over to you.'

She didn't argue. She was too tired.

The woman returned to her in a few minutes carrying another glass of mineral water and another half-pint for herself. Jane had been sitting there, coming to, letting the pulse in her chest, in her head, quieten down. The sickness was ebbing away. *How stupid*, she was thinking. Of course it wouldn't have been him. Lots of men have red hair. Lots of Scotsmen have red hair. They can't all be Paul. *How stupid.*

'It *was* mineral water you wanted?'

'It's very kind of you. You shouldn't have . . .'

The woman placed the glass in front of her, sat down in the seat beside her.

'Are you feeling better now?'

'I was feeling a bit faint. I'm just tired, that's all. It's been a long drive, getting here . . .'

'How far have you come?'

'From Stafford.'

The woman looked puzzled, as if she didn't know where Stafford was.

'In the Midlands.'

'Oh. I've never been that far south. No, that isn't true. I went to London once. Years and years ago. With my parents, when I was a kid.'

Jane sipped the water. It was reviving her, making her head clear. Her heart was beating at a normal rhythm again. Her chest still felt damp and cold. She touched the wet wool of her jumper.

'You'll need to get changed into something dry.'

'It's all right for a minute. It's warm in here. It'll dry out soon.'

Change into what? she was thinking. She had brought nothing with her. Why was she here? What was she supposed to do now?

'By the way, the name's Sandra.'

'Jane.'

'Are you here on holiday, Jane?'

She didn't want to be here, sitting with this woman, this Sandra, making small talk. She wanted her to go away now. To leave her alone with her thoughts.

'No, not really.' She paused. 'I'm looking for someone.' Why not say it? Wasn't it true? Wasn't that the reason she was here?

'Perhaps I can help?'

'I don't think so. You don't live here, do you?'

'The American accent? I keep thinking I might lose it one day. End up talking like a Scot. I've been here for twenty-four years now, but it hasn't happened, so I don't think it ever will.'

'I'm sorry, I didn't mean . . .'

'Don't worry, it's okay. Actually, Findhorn is crowded with us, like a Yankee invasion. Because of the Foundation. You've heard of the Findhorn Foundation?'

'No. Perhaps. I'm not sure.'

Sandra was smiling at her. She had warm brown eyes that seemed out of keeping with her light blonde hair. An open face. Close up, her face looked much older than it did before. She was at least the same age as Jane; maybe older. She still seemed familiar. This feeling of *déjù vu* creeping back. Where had she seen a face like that before?

Something inside her was urging her on. This small flaring of excitement. *If she's been here that long, she might know something, she might.*

'You said you've been in Findhorn for twenty-four years?'

'Yes. Sounds like a life sentence, doesn't it? But I love it here. I couldn't imagine living anywhere else . . .'

She was fumbling now in her bag for the photograph. The one of Paul. The Paul she never knew. Standing on the beach next to the girl with blonde hair. Her hand was shaking slightly as she drew it out, held it towards the woman for her to see.

*

Sometimes the past slides effortlessly into the present, as if it had been there all the time. Like something shielded behind a veil. Anything can bring it back. The timbre of someone's voice. The fall of autumn leaves, unexpected snow. Bringing the past back, making it real again. In this case, a photograph. Sandra picked it up and looked at it carefully. Jane sat, poised, holding her breath, waiting to catch Sandra's words. She knew she would tell her something important. She knew by the blanching of colour in her cheeks, the sudden darkening in her eyes. It was as if she had felt herself the skip of Sandra's heart.

'Who did you say this man was?' Sandra spoke softly, in a low tone. Jane had to strain her ears to catch the words, against the background hum of voices.

'My brother. Paul. He went missing thirty-three years ago. I had an address where he once lived. 6 Harbourside Cottages. I sent a letter, with a note saying to return it to me if he wasn't known at this address. It was sent back to me. I thought if I came up here, asked around among the locals, someone might know of him.'

'Paul Saunders?'

'Yes. H-how did you know?'

She had dreamt this scene, hadn't she? Or something like it. The woman with blonde hair, an American accent. *I have someone I'd like you to meet. Someone who thinks he used to know you.* The man had stood up, had moved out of the shadows. *That's not my brother*, she'd said.

Sandra put the photo down. She looked at her. The past was in her face, her eyes. She couldn't put it away. Had no space yet for the present.

'He lived with me and my daughter. That's my daughter, the girl with him in the photograph. She's about eight there. I took the photo myself. God knows how you managed to get hold of it. '

'My mother, she had it. I think he must have sent it to her.'

'Oh, God. A mother and a sister. I didn't know about anything, he never talked to me about his past. But I always knew he had these secrets. He was very troubled about things, deep down. He would suffer from these terrible depressions. We met at the Findhorn Foundation. More or less anyone could live at the community back then, in the seventies. It's not the same now. You need money to live there now. But Paul, he was very useful to them back then. He was brilliant at gardening, could grow virtually anything. And talented. A very good artist. He learnt ceramics, more or less taught himself really. He set up a ceramic studio, taught lots of people how to make beautiful pots ... sold a lot too. We moved out after a few years. People need their own space, after a while. And it had all begun to change by then. We moved into Harbourside Cottages. My father left me some money when he died.'

The present was seeping back now, the past ebbing away. She was sitting in a pub at Findhorn. Her brother had sat here once, no doubt. Next to this Sandra, perhaps. Just like she was doing now.

'You've moved then? You don't live in the cottages any more?'

Sandra turned to look at her. *She's seeing him. There's the shadow of him in my mouth, in the high set of my cheekbones.*

329

'I'm sorry. It's been a shock for me.' Sandra picked up the photograph, then put it down again. 'It's like seeing a ghost, a bit. I'm sorry – what did you say?'

She felt alarmed now. She didn't want to say it again. She didn't want to hear the answer.

'You and Paul. You don't live at 6 Harbourside Cottages any more then?'

Her voice was like a whisper. Like it didn't belong to her. Like she was sitting at the neighbouring table, listening to herself. Thinking, *Who is this woman who sits, looking so pale and troubled at that table, talking to that woman with the blonde hair?*

'No. Oh dear. This is dreadful. I do, actually.'

'But the letter I sent. It was returned to me. As if the person who received it hadn't known him, didn't know where he was . . .'

'When did you say you sent the letter?'

'I'm not sure. About three weeks ago. Maybe a little more.'

It was just before she went to Cornwall. The daffodils were out, but not the bluebells. Dominic had been pleased to see her. Had called her *Mummy* . . .

'That was probably the time I was away. I went back to the States, to see my daughter, Claire. She's married, has a little girl of her own. My husband must have found it. He doesn't know much about Paul. It's a bit of an issue between us. I don't like to talk about it, and he doesn't want to know. I'm so sorry; he shouldn't have sent it back to you. He should at least have waited till I got back home.'

Jane was thinking, oddly, of Josie. Of her warm, tum-

330

bling body when she was a puppy. The way she would lick her hands, her face, if she could get to it. The wet urgency of the licking, the clamour for life. *I hope it's not too cold, too dark, for her now.* She didn't want to be here. With this woman, this stranger. She didn't want to hear any more. She wasn't even sure she wanted to find Paul now. *It's too late. Too late to put it right again.*

'We're not together now, I'm married now – to someone else. I'm so sorry – it's not fair for you to find out like this. I didn't know he had a sister. I knew nothing, really, about Paul's past. He would never tell me.'

Jane had turned her head away. Through the fluted glass of the pub window she could see lights glimmer from boats out in the dark water, crimson streaks of the setting sun . . .

'He drowned. Nearly nineteen years ago now . . . he used to go swimming every day in Findhorn Bay. Except in the winter, in the very coldest months. Although sometimes, even then. He was a very strong swimmer. He went out that day – to go swimming – but he never came back. I never saw him again. They found no evidence that he had drowned. No body. Not even his clothes found on the beach, although they did find his trainers. But I knew it, deep down, I always knew that's what had happened. You do, don't you? When you're close. You know things.'

37

It was a full moon that night. She was glad of the light it gave, glimmering hazily through a thin covering of cloud that cleared and gathered again. Without it, she thought, she would be sitting here in almost pitch darkness. Some light perhaps reflecting off the surface of the sea, but not much. She wouldn't be able to find her way back. To notice how close the water was to her feet. The tide was turning now, was on its way back in. She could just make out the shimmer of damp sand at the lip of the waves, where the water was licking back again.

This tiredness, this weariness. She remembered when they were children Paul would make a burrow in the beach at Holkham for her to lie in. He would dig out the soft, pale sand in fast flurries of his arms, and when it was deep enough she would lie in it, with only her head poking out. He would bury her, piling in the sand again to seal up her body. She would lie there for ages, tilting her head back towards the sky, letting the sun sit on her closed eyelids. Feeling safe, snug, concealed. She wished she had the strength now to carve a burrow to lie in.

She was cold. Her jacket felt thin, inadequate. She had

read somewhere that out of all the ways to die hypothermia is one of the least painful. It was like going to sleep, fading into oblivion. She lay down on the sand, curled herself up into a foetal ball, to try to retain her body heat. She was shivering, her teeth clattering in her head. She closed her eyes, listened to the slow lap of the ocean . . .

He drowned. Nearly nineteen years ago now. Nineteen years it'll be next September.

That would have been around the time she had found out she was pregnant. She could remember, as if it was only yesterday, standing in her slip on the cool bathroom tiles, holding the glass tube and waiting for the faint blue line to emerge, that would tell her life was changing, it would never be the same again. Nowhere, in the flaring of excitement, as she'd rushed, waving the tube in her hand to show to Adam, nor in the weeks that followed, when she had sensed this secret life inside her stirring and thickening, did she think of her brother. Drowning, fighting for air. Lying in his ocean grave.

She had made some excuses to Sandra. She had told her she was tired, hungry. She had a room booked somewhere nearby; she must go. She had shaken her hand, thanked her for the water.

'I'm so sorry. I feel so dreadful, breaking the news like that.'

'No, it's all right. Really. I needed to know. It's not your fault . . .'

'Look, you know where I am – 6 Harbourside Cottages. It's not far from here – anyone in Findhorn will tell you where it is. Come and see me tomorrow. I'll be at home all day, I work from home. My husband won't be there. Not that it would make that much difference if he was. But as I said, he doesn't really like to talk about Paul. He'll be out all day. We can talk. We need to talk.'

She said she would. She had promised. *Yes, I'll come round. I'll see you tomorrow. Yes, I'll stay for lunch, that'll be lovely . . .*

Lovely? What was lovely about it? What could be lovely about any of it?

'Till tomorrow then. You *will* come, won't you? There's something else, you see. Something I need to tell you . . .'

She would never know what it was. She wouldn't go; she didn't want to. She had heard enough. She didn't want to hear this Sandra tell her about a Paul she had never known, and never would know now. What point was there to it all, now?

He had gone out one morning to go swimming. He was a strong swimmer; he would swim every day.

That day he had never come back. What had he done? Had he walked, fully clothed, into the sea? Had he picked a quiet time, when there was no one on the beach likely to see him? No one to summon help, to try to wade in after him even, pull him from the waves. Had the cold taken his breath away? Had he sunk down under the water, the light from the sky shutting out? Had the strong currents swept him swiftly out to sea? She had passed a notice on her walk around to the beach from the harbour. It was just beyond the beach, on the path across the dunes, near where the lip of the Findhorn estuary curved into the broader, deeper bay of the Firth. She had hardly been able to make out the words in the darkness, but had run her fingers over the raised letters. *DANGER: Strong inshore currents.*

She was tired. She was almost beyond cold. Sleep was falling on her like a curtain. She could hear the sea lapping somewhere not too far from her feet, the tide returning. *I just need to sleep for a while* . . . She felt as if she was floating, out at sea somewhere, beyond the reach of the world . . .

Later, when she would think back to that night, she could never work out what had really happened. How long she had lain there, with this sensation of floating, beyond the cold, beyond all feeling. One moment, she was hearing the water lapping close by. The darkness was climbing into her head, dragging her under. She didn't care. It wasn't that bad. She wasn't cold, wasn't afraid any more.

Then the next thing she knew, she was struggling to sit up. Thinking, *What am I doing here? What am I thinking of?* The world seemed to rush at her then. The moon growing larger and brighter, the clouds that wisped across it more luminous and mysterious. The cold was making her shiver violently, burning on her cheeks and her lips. Salt crusted her face, the wind took her breath away. Everything was more real than it had ever seemed. The weariness slipped suddenly away from her. She felt alive. And the past seemed to be moving through her rapidly. She was a small child, nudging her hands through brambles. The fat berries were both tart and bitter in her mouth; juice trickled down her chin. She was playing down the lanes with Paul's friends.

Rough children, who would have laughed at her, teased her for her shyness, if Paul hadn't been there to stop them. She was in her early teens, caught in strong currents of feelings. She was seized by sudden moods, dark jealousies ... She was older now. Dreaming of a future, of getting away, in her aunt's house in Stafford. Stubborn, determined, the secrets shrivelled into hard kernels inside her. She was a student. She was popular; men found her attractive. She was never short of requests for dates, although she rarely accepted. She was falling in love. She was making love to Adam on the beach at Cley; the ghosts were fading into the dusk. She was full of possibility, pregnant with hope. She was holding her baby son in her arms. His newborn eyes were full of space, as blue as the ocean, as deep.

He was walking towards her up the beach. She knew it was him. He had the same gait he had as a boy. Holding his head erect, walking slightly on the outward edge of his feet. Yet she could scarcely make him out, except as this darkened shape of a man in the distance. Getting nearer, coming close. She could see that he had put on weight. He stopped, and sat down a few yards away from her.

'Aren't you cold, Paul?'

He was barefoot. Wearing only jeans and a T-shirt. She could see his tanned arms, flecked by sun-bleached hairs.

'No. But you are.'

She was hugging herself tightly. Shivers still shaking her body, rattling her words in her mouth. 'Yes, I am, I'm freezing.'

'What are you doing, Jane?'

'What do you mean?'

'Here. What are you doing here?'

'I've come to find you.'

'I've gone, Jane. I can't be found.'

'Yes, you can. You're here. Come back with me, Paul. Come home.'

'You know I can't, Jane. You must let me go.'

She could feel hot tears stabbing at her eyes. It was as if she had never cried for him. And now she wanted to. She felt that if she did her tears would never end, would fill up the ocean.

'Go home, Jane.'

She shook her head. 'I've nothing to go home to.'

'That's not true.'

'You don't understand. Everything is gone now. Everything is spoiled. Broken.'

'That's how it's meant to be. That's how it always is. It's how we live with the brokenness that counts.'

'*You* didn't. You couldn't live with it.'

'You were always stronger than me, Jane. I was the eldest. But you were always the strongest one.'

'You left me alone, Paul. You left me to cope on my own.'

The tears were streaming now, carving warm rivulets down her frozen cheeks. She wanted to hit him, she wanted her fists to rain upon him. She wanted him to feel her pain.

'I'm sorry, Jane. I'm so, so sorry. Go home. Live with the brokenness. Build something with it.'

He was standing up. He was walking away. He was fading into the darkness again. The last words he spoke

337

were snatched away in the wind. What did he say? *Life is precious*, he said.

The sea was lapping at her feet now, soaking through the seams of her shoes. She got up. She turned to face the shoreline, where she knew, beyond the dark, looming ridge of the dunes, she would find lights from houses, a road to take her away. The soft sand was pulling on her feet. She felt she was battling something, the tiredness returning. She kept on going, the effort now beginning to warm her. There was a light, she could see a light. Small, a pinprick of light. But growing stronger, moving closer, swinging in small arcs of movement. She could hear a voice now. A human voice, a real voice. Calling her name. Louder now, more distinct. 'Jane! Is that you, Jane?'

She fell against his sheepskin jacket. It smelt of dog and wood smoke. He wrapped his arms around her, like a good father would. She felt warm now, against his chest.

'It's all right, Jane. Everything's all right. You're safe now.'

38

She slept well that night; they both did.

Bob had had the foresight to book a couple of rooms in the small hotel, after calling at Harbourside Cottages. Sandra, apparently, had looked at him strangely.

'We met about a couple of hours ago, in the pub at the harbour. She was looking for her brother. I used to know him, you see.'

'Do you know where she is now?'

'She said she had to leave. She'd booked a room at the hotel, she said.'

He'd thought the woman had looked like she wanted to ask him in, like there was something she wanted to talk about. But she'd looked distracted too, kept glancing over her shoulder, as if she was wary about who might be listening. But he didn't want to stop, didn't have the time.

He asked after her as well, when he made the booking at the inn that functioned as a small hotel, the only one in Findhorn.

'We've nothing here in the name of Jane Reynolds,' the proprietor told him.

'Any other name? She might have used another name?'

339

'No sir, no one like that has made a booking.'

He didn't know what made him decide to drive straight to the beach car park. To clamber up the wooden walkway across the dunes, and down on to the beach. It was almost pitch dark, just the moonlight to guide him. And the torch that he'd found in the glove compartment. It was just an instinct, a hunch . . .

She wasn't going to. That previous evening, it had been the last thing she had wanted to do. But now, waking refreshed from sleep, she knew that what she had come for, the reason for being here, wouldn't be completed until she had.

'I have to go and see her, Bob. This Sandra. I have to talk to her about Paul. I have to put it to rest.'

'Are you sure?' he said. He was concerned, she knew, about her state of mind.

'I have to,' she said.

Sandra was an artist. Stacks of canvases everywhere leant against the walls. Mainly oils. Scenes of wide beaches and sea. Or flat, damp land, shrouded in mist, blurred with rain. If you looked hard enough, and she had done, it was possible to make out vague shadows emerging from the wetness and the mist, as if figures were lurking. It had disturbed her a little, seeing them. It had reminded her of the paintings she herself had once so obsessively created. *She still misses him. She's still waiting for him to come back.*

'I'll go for a walk,' Bob had said. 'Maybe stop at the pub and have a pint. I'll leave you two to talk.'

*

He was gone for nearly two hours. She stayed with this woman who had known Paul, a different Paul to the one she had known, for all that time. And after the first awkward silences, the talk flowed, along with the tears, and small stories about Paul that had made them both smile.

How much should I tell her? she had been asking herself, as she'd sat next to Bob in his car that morning. *Should I tell her the whole truth? Everything I remember?* But then the clear understanding passed through her, that her truth was hers alone; she did not have to share it. She only needed to tell Sandra as much as she felt she needed to know. She didn't need to burden her.

She told her the good things. How kind Paul was to animals. About the time, for instance, when they'd found a hedgehog in the woods. A young one, only a baby. Its small pink mouth opened wide in distress.

Paul had taken the creature home, and placed it carefully in a cardboard box, lined with rags and shreds of newspaper. Kept it overnight in the shed. But she didn't tell her how they'd found it frozen into a rigid ball the following morning, white maggots worming out of its eyes, out from its pink open mouth. How they'd rushed out in horror and Paul had retched over bushes outside.

It was her truth; no one else's. She could leave out the bad things.

She told her about the house in the Fens. The big garden they had to play in when they were small. How her mother grew vegetables, digging in the spring and autumn in the wet, dark earth. The lanes and fields and woods beyond the house, that they would lose themselves in, when the house

341

and the garden were no longer enough to contain them. How Paul had taught her to fish for roach and tench in the nearby rivers and dykes. How she would watch him swimming in the Ouse, how good a swimmer he was. How he had helped her overcome her fear of going underwater, coaxing her into the water every day for weeks.

'He didn't get on with his father, did he? He would never talk to me about it, but I always knew there was something there.'

'Our father was a damaged man. He would drink too much. He would get these jealous rages. He was violent to our mother. To Paul too sometimes.'

That scar above Paul's eye. It had stayed red and angry for weeks.

'And to you too...?' Sandra's face was wincing, as if she was feeling the pain of all those years...

'No, not really. I wouldn't go as far as to say he was nice to me. He ignored me, mostly. But he was different with me. I wasn't a threat to him, I suppose.'

When she was cruel to me, I edged over more towards his side.

'And his mother. Did he get on with her?'

'She adored him. I suppose he was her favourite.'

'He did talk a little about her. He said she was beautiful. Very musical too. She could play the piano very well. She used to take him for music lessons, but he said he never learnt to play as well as she did.'

'Did he tell you much about his music teacher?'

She wasn't going to mention him, but she had to. She couldn't help herself.

'He said he had a nice house. Full of interesting things. Paintings, bits of sculpture. Lots of books. He was a nice man, he said. He took an interest in him.' Sandra was looking thoughtful now, as if something was coming back to her. 'I remember him saying once that this man, the music teacher, was the kind of man he would have wanted for a father. That sometimes he wished he *had* been his father.'

'Yes, I expect he did.'

No, I won't say it. No need to burden her with things she didn't now need to know ...

And Sandra told her about the other Paul. The one Jane had never known. The man with a quiet voice and gentle hands, who would tend plants lovingly, who could, almost effortlessly, turn a lump of clay on the wheel into a bowl. Who had taught her to look at landscape, with eyes that were seeing it as if for the first time. Would appreciate the shifting changes of light and shadows, the interplay of the land and sea.

'There was something about him. This sense of mystery. As if he knew things that few of us do ... I don't know, maybe it was tied up with his secrets. The things he would never tell me. I used to try and make him open up, tell me about his past. He had been a drifter, it seemed, before he came to Findhorn. He would suddenly let slip something he had experienced, in Spain, in Greece, France. But really I knew so little about how he had lived his life, how he had survived before. Nothing about his childhood, except that it had been in England, in Cambridgeshire, although that meant little to me – I'd never been there. And that he had this beautiful mother who played the piano. That was about it . . .'

'Did you ever know . . . did you know if Paul was writing to his mother? Keeping in touch?'

Sandra looked at her, surprised. 'I didn't even know she was alive. That's why it was a shock to me, you see, when you told me his mother had just died. Because I thought she *had* died. Years ago, long before he met me. When he was about sixteen, he'd said. And I certainly didn't know he had a sister; I never knew about you.'

Sandra paused, as if she was letting the past seep through her. Paul was with her now, it seemed. Here in her cluttered, cosy kitchen. Sitting there, listening. Smiling sadly.

'I blamed myself, you know. That day he went missing. He had been very quiet for weeks, withdrawn. He always got a little down, in September. He couldn't bear knowing that summer was over. He dreaded the coming winter most, at that time. Once it had arrived, he found some way to cope with it, although he was never at his best in the winter months. He said he was going swimming – he usually went for a swim in the mornings. Just off the beach here, down past the marina. When he didn't come back, I phoned the police. The beach was trawled for signs of his clothes, anything like that, but nothing was found. His trainers had already turned up, on the dunes, behind some gorse.

'I asked everyone who I knew had a habit of walking on the beach if they had seen anything, but no one had. I even put an article out in the local paper, asking anyone who had seen a man swimming in the sea that day to get in touch.'

He was with them both, here in the kitchen. He had this look on his face, as if the words were causing him pain. *I'm sorry, I'm so sorry.*

'I spent weeks, months, looking for him. Every time I walked on the beach. Gazing out to sea, as if I was expecting to see him out there still, swimming slowly towards the shore.'

There were tears in her eyes. In his, as well.

'You see, Jane, I had another reason to want him to still be alive. To need him to come back to me.'

She got up from the table, walked over to a dresser. She picked up something that was lying there on the pale wood. A photograph. She placed it on the table. Jane looked down and saw her brother's face smiling up at her. The same greeny-brown eyes, the same soft smile, auburn hair. She touched it gently with her hand. The face seemed to melt softly into another. A face that echoed her brother but wasn't him.

'I was pregnant, you see. About two months pregnant. Paul didn't know. I hadn't told him. I wanted to wait until I was sure. I was meaning to tell him soon. . . . That's Paul's son. That's Shawn. I named him that because Paul told me once that Shawn was his favourite name. If he ever had a son, he'd said, he would like to call him Shawn. I met Richard when Shawn was only two, so he's grown up thinking of Richard as his father. His dad. Although he knows he isn't really, I've told him the truth. Richard's been very good to him. He loves him as if he was his real son. We were never able to have one of our own, so I guess it makes it harder for him like that. Knowing Shawn isn't really his. That's why it's a bit of an issue for him, why he doesn't like me to talk about Paul.'

'I'm so sorry,' Jane said. She wasn't sure who she was saying it for. Sandra, who had waited so long for Paul to return and knew deep down he never would. Shawn, who would never know his real father. Or the man who had been with them. Sitting quietly, tears of regret in his eyes. Who was now standing up and leaving them. Fading away.

39

A YEAR LATER

She stood back from the easel to get a better perspective on the painting. The huge wave seemed to lift itself right out of the canvas, to be coming straight towards her. It made her feel almost seasick, just to look at it. It was finished. It didn't quite satisfy her, but she knew that no amount of reworking would make any difference. All she painted these days was waves. Thick, chaotic swirls of paint. Violent surges of cobalt and aquamarine, shot with greens and turquoise, as the water thinned and lightened near the surface, where it unfurled just before the crest broke. Sometimes she even ground glass into a resin paste and mixed it into the paint, so that the light shivered and danced where the sun caught on the canvas. None of the paintings entirely satisfied her. She would go on painting them until they did. Or perhaps they never would. Another impossible search for perfection. It didn't matter.

It will have to do.

It would have to. Nick Pierce was due to view it in an hour.

'One of your wave paintings, Jane,' he'd said. 'It will be wonderful in our living room at the vicarage. Make Jenny and me realize every time we look at it the power the sea has. So we don't get above ourselves!'

She cleaned off the palette. Lifting the creamy clots of oil paint carefully with a knife, putting each colour into a separate small jar, screwing the lid tight to keep them from drying out. She took the palette knives and brushes to the small sink to clean them with turps and rags.

She looked out of the window on to the garden. The daffodils were out. Spring was on its way again.

She finished cleaning the paint off the palette knives and brushes. Put them away in the pot with the blue glaze. The one Sandra had given her that day, just before she had left with Bob, to start the first leg of the long drive home.

'Paul made this,' she had said. 'I'd like you to have it. Something to remember him by . . .'

It did make her think of him, every time she looked at it. But it didn't hurt her to think of him now. She could see the sea in the flecked-blue glaze, in the rippled circles down the glassy surface.

She locked the studio door and walked back up the garden to the house. Everything would start growing soon, she was thinking. She would have to pull up the weeds, clear the dry undergrowth, tidy it all up. Maybe dig up the area down by the studio, turn it into a vegetable patch. It would be good to grow her own vegetables, taste the freshness in them. Maybe she would plant a couple of fruit trees. *If I grew them from saplings, how long before they would fruit . . . ?*

She had the time. No need to rush. She had the rest of her life. It stretched before her now, with space, with time in it, for everything important. For paintings, and friendships. For getting the cottage and garden in order. Last year she had felt, among other things, the threat of the cancer. She hadn't known then if it would return, but since then she had been for two check-ups. The first with Mr Fazil in Hertfordshire, before she had moved. The second down in Cornwall. What was it that the consultant in Truro had said, when the result of the second test showed that she was still clear?

'I think we can presume, Mrs Reynolds, that you are as free from the threat of cancer as anyone. Statistically, you may still be at a slightly higher risk, but you should be living your life as if it is very much a thing of the past. As if you'll see a ripe old age . . .'

Would she? It didn't matter. *I've got now, I've got the present. What do any of us know about the future?*

She had told Bob everything. In broken, fragmented sentences, sitting in her living room at home in the evening, the day after they had arrived back from Scotland. He'd sat next to her on the sofa, held her hand. He didn't look at her with disgust when she told him what she had done. Didn't see her as tainted. Walk away.

'I couldn't face the truth, Bob. I think I hid it from

myself for all these years because I felt guilty, I felt I was to blame.'

'You were only a child, Jane. You weren't responsible for what your father or your mother did. Or Paul. No one made your father violent. No one made Paul stab him. You didn't make him do that.'

She felt like a child, sobbing against his chest. She felt like a child who had lost her father and found him, both at once.

She hadn't gone back to work. She'd gone sick. And she had been. For the first few weeks she lay in bed, this deep weariness aching in her bones, making her crave nothing but the darkness of sleep. Day after day, getting up usually only for a few hours. Usually when Bob got up from sleeping at three in the afternoon, when he would come round and cook them both a light meal, and stay and sit with her until she wanted to get back to bed. They would read, watch television. They would play cards or Scrabble. He would tell her humorous stories about work, make her laugh even.

Then slowly, slowly she found her strength returning. She would get out of bed, stay up for longer. Spring-clean the house for short spells, or work in the garden. She would recall sometimes, with a start of recognition, notes she had learnt in her art therapy course. *Suicidal feelings can occur when repressed traumatic memories start to emerge.* She would remember patients she had worked with who had alarmed her with this risk. *I've had a breakdown, she would think.*

Breakdown. Suicidal feelings. These were words she had always associated with the Kens and Taras of the world. Now she was one of them.

The letters had eventually been sent out, telling them the hospital was closing down. Negotiations were in place to sell the site to property developers. Much of the impressive Victorian facade would be retained, but inside it would be completely gutted. The echoing corridors. The vast wards with their dormitories and day rooms. The cell-like consultation rooms where patients would offload their despair. The cluttered art therapy room with its revealing paintings. All gone. Prestigious luxury flats would be put in their place. But would the memories be erased that easily, she'd wondered. All that misery, for years . . .

By the time the letter came through her door, none of it mattered; she didn't care. She had already decided what to do. She had already had her first oncology check-up, and the results that had brightened her, lifting the threat that the cancer had returned. She was getting better, coming back to life. The guilt she had felt – *it was my fault, I was to blame* – was softening. A shadow she could bear to look at now.

Sometimes she wondered if she should do something with this truth that she had recovered. Tell the police, perhaps. *It was Paul who killed my father. I was there, I saw it.* She told Bob about these thoughts – 'What good what it do?' he'd said. 'Your mother has served her time; the case is closed. All the people concerned are gone, are dead.'

Except her. And the voice, coming from inside her, that could be Paul's voice, that could be her own. *The past belongs to the past, leave it where it belongs . . .*

She went to Cornwall in the late summer to see Dominic off. He was leaving, to take up his place at the Camphill Community. Not the one in Devon, in the end. He had wanted to go further afield. He had chosen the community in Yorkshire. He had been on a number of trial weekends. They liked him; they thought he would fit in well.

'Pippa living there. She look like Emily. Blonde hair, very pretty, Mummy,' he had said. He was excited, full of plans for the future. Making his own friends, his own place in the world.

She had stood outside Adam's cottage when the car arrived. A member of the staff had come to collect him, to take him to Yorkshire to start his new life. She had stooped to kiss him goodbye, and he'd put his arms around her neck, held on to her tightly.

'Goodbye, Mummy,' he said. 'See you in holidays.'

That had decided her. Although she'd already more or less decided anyway, by then. She would sell up, move to Cornwall. She would be there, so that when Dominic came home for holidays – because he would do; wasn't that what sons did, when they left home – came home sometimes? To see parents. Touch base again. She would be there for him, when he came home again.

And then everything had fallen into place. As it does sometimes, when a decision has been made. Someone came and viewed the house and loved it, made an offer. And just after that Adam had phoned her up and told her about this cottage he had seen.

'As soon as I saw it I thought of you. It's even got a workshop thing in the garden. Needs a bit of clearing out, repairing, but it would make a perfect studio. You know you were talking about perhaps taking up painting again, when you were down last month.'

She had been. It was something that she had been letting herself think about for some time. Mr Peters, her old tutor from art school, she remembered, had once thought she had talent, real potential. She had wanted to run then from what the paintings were revealing. But now it was different. *She* was different. She loved the paintings she had seen in Cornwall. The ones of the sea, all light and blueness and endless space. Perhaps she could start painting again, see what happened. Who knows, she might even be able to make something of a living. Sell a few to tourists. Like her father had.

And to make things better, she had heard she was even going to receive a redundancy payout. She had been on sick leave for the last few months, but she was still a member of the hospital staff, entitled to a payout. It wouldn't be a fortune, of course; she had only worked there for six years. But it would help get the studio repaired. It would keep her going in paint and canvases for a good while.

A few days before she moved, she had gone to visit Ken. He was living now with a group of other ex-residents in an ordinary terrace in an ordinary street in Potter's Bar. He'd been over the moon to see her. He'd put on his best trousers and a clean shirt, because he'd known she was coming.

'I've been helping the staff to make a cake for you, Jane. I told them you were coming to tea today.'

He'd taken her up and shown her his room. It was clean and tidy. A small bookcase, a rack of CDs, a music centre. A dressing table covered with framed photographs. She recognized a few of the patients from the hospital, in the faces grinning out of them. One of him and Tara, holding hands and laughing. Tara, Ken told her, was still in his life. She visited him twice a week, catching the bus to see him. They had plans to share a flat together, one day when they were both well enough. Jane knew that day would never come. It didn't matter. The hope that it would was enough for Ken right now.

His single bed had a duvet cover in Man. United colours, footballers kicking balls all over it. *Like a boy's room*, she'd thought. *A room for a man who's still just a boy.* Thoughts of Dominic flashed through her mind.

And later, sitting with Ken and a few of the other residents, and Roger and Dawn who were on duty with them that day, looking around the warm, comfortable kitchen, she thought how much more like a home it was here than the hospital ward. How much more normal they seemed, too, in this environment. They had sorted out Ken's medication at last, got the dosages and intervals of treatment well balanced. There was still a feeling of space in his eyes, a sense that fear still lurked at the edges of his world. That if pushed to it, if stressed enough, he could be set off again. But right now, holding out the plate, so she could help herself to a slice of carrot cake, he seemed as sane as anyone, almost. As sane as she was.

'More tea, Jane?'

Another resident was smiling at her, holding the teapot, waiting for her answer. She had a feeling she had seen him before. Where had it been?

'Oh yes, please. Thank you, er ... I'm sorry, I've forgotten your name.'

'It's Colin. Colin's the name, Jane.'

He poured it out, careful not to spill any in her saucer.

'Milk, Jane? Two sugars, isn't it?'

The realization came to her with a shock. That patient, in Rivendale. He'd a beard back then, staring eyes. 'Fuck you, bitch,' he'd said as she'd walked out through the door.

Nick Pierce now, knocking on her door, giving a warm handshake when she opened it to him. Following her down the garden and stepping back to admire the painting. He said nothing for a while, then he turned to her, his eyes moist.

'It's wonderful, Jane! It's beautiful! I could look at it for hours, I could get lost in that wave.'

He had insisted on giving her the money there and then, peeling the notes out into her hand. Even though the paint wasn't dry, wouldn't be dry enough for him to take the painting away for at least another week. She had taken him back into the kitchen and made him tea, set out biscuits on a studio-made dish she had bought in Padstow, and they had talked briefly about Adam and Anna.

'He phoned me up the other evening and asked if I'd do a blessing for them. He's decided to make an honest woman of her at last.'

He was looking at her carefully. How did she feel about Adam getting married again?

She was remembering how she had held Adam and Anna's new baby in her arms. It was a girl; they had named her Noëlle because she had been born only days after Christmas. The baby had turned her head towards Jane's chest, pushed its small tight fist into its mouth. It looked like a very small, very young version of Anna. She had been relieved she could not see Dominic in the child's face.

Afterwards, when she was leaving, Adam had followed her down the path, stood out in the lane with her. He looked anxious, slightly embarrassed. She had wanted to make it easier for him.

'The baby's lovely, Adam. Anna's lovely too. Be happy. You deserve to be.'

He had looked at her hard. The years were between them now. Broken years that they hadn't been able to mend.

'You're all right now, aren't you, Jane? You're happy?'

She had touched his hand lightly.

'You mustn't worry about me any more. You've got your new wife, your baby to worry about. I'm all right.'

He had looked pained then. The years were holding him still. She wanted to make light of it, so they could both release each other, let each other go now.

'Of course I'm happy, Adam. Why shouldn't I be? I've a good life now. The cottage is lovely, I'm got my painting. And friends. Bob's threatening to descend on me in the summer, campervan and all . . .'

*

Bob had finally made the decision to retire. Her moving away, perhaps, deciding him. He was selling the house. He'd down-size, he told her, invest some of the surplus cash in a campervan. 'Time to do what I want to do, life's too short to waste,' he'd said.

He had decided not to buy another house quite yet. Didn't want to get tied down to bricks and mortar, not till he had a better idea where the bricks and mortar should be. He was going to put his furniture and stuff into storage. Would take to the road in the camper, become a gypsy for a while.

'I'll be invading your garden in the summer, if you're not careful,' he'd joked.

'You're welcome, Bob. Any time!'

He was. He always would be.

Was she happy? she wondered. Seeing Nick Pierce out, standing in the lane, watching him drive away. Yet happiness, she knew, wasn't something that could be searched for and found. It was a by-product, would steal up on her when she was simply living her life. Doing what was right, being herself.

Sometimes she would catch herself drifting back in her thoughts, worrying about questions that couldn't be answered. *Did Paul really drown, or is he still out there somewhere? Drifting, still running from the past. How long had he been writing to my mother? Had she always known where he was?* But then she'd stop herself.

No, let it go. Come back to the present . . .

She was happy. Or happy enough. As happy as most

people are, she thought. And excited sometimes. Fearful too, occasionally. Anxious and apprehensive, too. All sorts of feelings ran through her now, as clear and easily as water.

She was anxious later, on that Easter Saturday. Anxious, driving all the way on her own to Penzance, to meet her nephew, Shawn, who was coming to visit, for the first time ever. Parking her car in the station car park. Walking on to the platform. Anxious, standing there, waiting for the London train. And fearful now, as she saw the train approaching. Petrified, when the doors opened out and visitors, holiday-makers, tumbled on to the platform. Then fear turning to excitement, to happiness, seeing the young man alight from the train. Seeing him turn, recognize her, start walking towards her.

He was wearing blue jeans, a red T-shirt. A denim jacket was tossed casually over his shoulder. He held his head erect, walked slightly on the outward edge of his feet. He was smiling. His auburn hair flamed russet in the sunshine.

ACKNOWLEDGEMENTS

My sincere thanks to Lucy Childs of the Aaron Priest agency, New York, for all her wonderful support at the various draft stages of this novel. Also to Kate Walker and Arabella Stein at Abner Stein, London. To Maria Rejt, Anna Valdinger, Sophie Orme, Nicholas Blake and the rest of the lovely team at Picador. To Hugh for his unstinting support, and to Mary Jones, Keith Seabrook, and Neil and Angela Holmes for sharing their experiences.

And to Duggie, whose bravery and friendship has inspired me.

picador.com

blog
videos
interviews
extracts